THREE EYEWITNESS ACCOUNTS OF THE CRIMES IN VERDICT OF 13

"MARVELOUSLY WICKED, WITTY, AND WELL-TOLD!"
Stanley Ellin

"When the cream of the English mystery writers—which is saying a good deal—are given their heads to write a story about an interesting subject, and when the collection of these stories is edited and prefaced by the master, Julian Symons himself, there can be little surprise when VERDICT OF THIRTEEN lives up to its promises as one of the very best collections yet published."
Robert L. Fish

"IT'S A DELIGHT, BUT WHAT ELSE WOULD YOU EXPECT FROM THE DETECTION CLUB?"
Hillary Waugh

VERDICT OF 13
A DETECTION CLUB ANTHOLOGY

INTRODUCTION BY JULIAN SYMONS

BALLANTINE BOOKS • NEW YORK

Library of Congress Catalog Card Number: 78-69511

ISBN: 0-345-28901-3

This edition published by arrangement with Harper & Row, Publishers

Manufactured in the United States of America

First Ballantine Books Edition: June 1980

Contents

Introduction

The Detection Club was founded in 1932, with a Constitution and Rules adopted on 11 March of that year. It was, this document said, "instituted for the association of writers of detective-novels and for promoting and continuing a mutual interest and fellowship between them." Twenty-six members formed the original club, with Helen Simpson and Hugh Walpole as associate members who were perhaps thought to have written estimable books that were still not quite detective stories. The rules said firmly that members' work must be within the canon of the detective story, "it being understood that the term 'detective-novel' does not include adventure-stories or 'thrillers' or stories in which the detection is not a main interest."

Among the twenty-six who fulfilled these requirements were the best-known British writers of the day in the detective form: Agatha Christie and Baroness Orczy and Dorothy L. Sayers, E. C. Bentley, Anthony Berkeley, the collaborative Coles (G. D. H. and Margaret), Freeman Wills Crofts and R. Austin Freeman, Ronald Knox, A. E. W. Mason, Arthur Morrison and John Rhode. It is an impressive roll call that was made by the first president, G. K. Chesterton. And the years before the war added names equally illustrious: Gladys Mitchell, Margery Allingham, John Dickson Carr and Nicholas Blake among others. Carr was, I think, the only member ever elected who was not British. He had been living in England for some years, and for a while acted as secretary of the club.

The idea that rules could and should be laid down for the writing of detective stories was seriously regarded. An attempt had already been made by Ronald Knox to formulate the rules in his "Detective Decalogue," which specified that the criminal must be mentioned early on, that no undiscovered poisons might be used, "nor any appliance which will need a long scientific explanation at the end," that the detective must not commit the crime (although "a criminal may legitimately dress up as a detective and delude the other actors in the story with forged references"), that he must play fair with the reader by revealing his clues, and so on. There was an election ceremony for the club, said to have been devised by Chesterton and Dorothy L. Sayers, although Anthony Berkeley also may have had a hand in it, in which the about-to-be-elected member had to promise, with his hand placed upon Eric the Skull, that his detectives should well and truly detect, and that they would place no reliance on "Divine Revelation, Feminine Intuition, Mumbo-Jumbo, Jiggery-Pokery, Coincidence or the Act of God." He was asked to promise also that he would not "purloin nor disclose any plot or secret communicated . . . before publication by any Member, whether under the influence of drink or otherwise." The ceremony took place after a dinner at the Café Royal, but other, less formal functions were held during the year. In the period before the war, the club had rooms in central London where members could meet each other, or at other times sit and think about murder. After the war there was a room in Kingly Street, rented through Dorothy L. Sayers's influence with Church authorities, and meetings were held in this room. Christianna Brand, who had been elected immediately after the war, brought various delicacies in the way of food. There were no meetings in the war period, or at any rate no new members were elected. For a while after the war, however, the club flourished.

For a while. But the years of peace saw a dramatic decline in the detective story as the founders had conceived it, and this decline was mirrored in the club's fortunes. It had always depended on the intense enthusiasm of a few members, and now as these members died, or ceased writing, or lost interest, the numbers coming to meetings fell away. The Kingly Street room was given up, and although there was still a good attendance at the yearly election dinner, on other occasions there might be no more than half a dozen people present. This was true especially after the death of Sayers in 1957. She had been president for nine years, succeeding E. C. Bentley, who had occupied the position after Chesterton's death. Sayers was succeeded in turn by Agatha Christie, and because of Mrs. Christie's extreme shyness and her reluctance to make even the shortest speech, Lord Gorell was her co-president for five years, until his death in 1963. Thereafter Richard Hull, and later Michael Underwood, undertook most of the president's duties, although Agatha Christie played her part at dinners and in the election ceremony.

The dismal years were ended by two decisions. The first was to acknowledge that the old rules could no longer apply, and to broaden the membership to include the best writers in all forms of crime literature, including the spy story and the thriller. The other was the inspired suggestion that all dinners, except that at which new members were inaugurated, should be held in a club. This idea was an immediate success, and for several years now meetings have been held in the pleasant ambience of the Garrick Club, although the dinner for new members still takes place at the Café Royal.

The inaugural ceremony has been changed, and then changed again, to accommodate modern ideas and standards, but its form remains and so does Eric the Skull. Membership of the club is still by invitation, and although the names on the roll are different in kind from those early ones, they are equally distinguished. They include, apart from the contributors to this book, Eric Ambler, Josephine Bell, John Bingham, Edmund Crispin, Len Deighton, Macdonald Hastings, Geoffrey Household, John le Carré, Gavin Lyall, Anthony Price, Colin Watson—and the list could comfortably be lengthened without failing in quality. There seems every sign that the Detection Club has fitted itself wonderfully well to the changed climate of crime fiction.

The club has been responsible for two earlier publi-

cations, *The Floating Admiral,* which appeared in
1932, and *The Anatomy of Murder,* published four
years later. The first of these was a story told in turn by
several members of the club, and the second a collection in which famous real-life crimes, including the
cases of Landru, Adelaide Bartlett and Julia Wallace,
were critically reconsidered.

The present book has a distinctive approach. The
contributors were asked to write a story that should, in
some way or another, concern a jury: although it was
stressed that the jury need not be one sitting in a law
court, nor need it number twelve. It might be a "jury"
of soldiers or policemen, suburban housewives or
schoolboys, lawyers or old lags. Given this freedom,
with its small element of restriction, the contributors
have produced work that spans the whole field of crime
fiction. There is fantasy, exemplified by Peter Dickin-
son's quite literally way-out tale and Christianna
Brand's high-spirited romp among murders past, and
something like the club's old orthodoxy in the stories of
P. D. James and Michael Innes, both of which deal with
the verdicts of actual juries. There is H. R. F. Keating's
cunningly told Kiplingesque tale of India, and Michael
Underwood's jury of schoolboys. The jury may be tan-
talizingly small in numbers, as in Michael Gilbert's sub-
tle thriller and Ngaio Marsh's tale with its beautifully
evoked New Zealand setting. In Gwen Butler's story a
dog, and in Patricia Highsmith's a cat, play important
parts, and Dick Francis gives us a superb small puzzle
about horses and those who bet on them. There is Celia
Fremlin's apparently harmless romance about a possibly haunted cottage, and a tale which refers to Beatrix
Potter and blends the world of childhood with the world
of crime. They make up together what we hope readers
will regard as a lucky thirteen. The whole collection
shows the crime story, like the Detection Club, offering
talents as various as those of Cleopatra.

JULIAN SYMONS
President of the Detection Club

Great-Aunt Allie's Flypapers

P. D. JAMES

"You see, my dear Adam," explained the Canon gently as he walked with Chief Superintendent Dalgliesh under the vicarage elms, "useful as the legacy would be to us, I wouldn't feel happy in accepting it if Great-Aunt Allie came by her money in the first place by wrongful means."

What the Canon meant was that he and his wife wouldn't be happy to inherit Great-Aunt Allie's fifty thousand pounds or so if, sixty-seven years earlier, she had poisoned her elderly husband with arsenic in order to get it. As Great-Aunt Allie had been accused and acquitted of just that charge in a 1902 trial which, for her Hampshire neighbours, had rivalled the Coronation as a public spectacle, the Canon's scruples were not altogether irrelevant. Admittedly, thought Dalgliesh, most people, faced with the prospect of fifty thousand pounds, would be happy to subscribe to the commonly accepted convention that once an English court has pronounced its verdict, the final truth of the matter has been established once and for all. There may possibly be a higher judicature in the next world, but hardly in this. And so Hubert Boxdale might normally have been happy to believe. But faced with the prospect of an unexpected fortune, his scrupulous conscience was troubled. The gentle but obstinate voice went on:

"Apart from the moral principle of accepting tainted money, it wouldn't bring us happiness. I often think of the poor woman driven restlessly around Europe in her

1

search for peace, of that lonely life and unhappy death."

Dalgliesh recalled that Great-Aunt Allie had moved in a predictable progress with her retinue of servants, current lover and general hangers-on from one luxury Riviera hotel to the next, with stays in Paris or Rome as the mood suited her. He was not sure that this orderly program of comfort and entertainment could be described as being restlessly driven around Europe or that the old lady had been primarily in search of peace. She had died, he recalled, by falling overboard from a millionaire's yacht during a rather wild party given by him to celebrate her eighty-eighth birthday. It was perhaps not an edifying death by the Canon's standards, but he doubted whether she had, in fact, been unhappy at the time. Great-Aunt Allie (it was impossible to think of her by any other name), if she had been capalbe of coherent thought, would probably have pronounced it a very good way to go. But this was hardly a point of view he could put to his companion.

Canon Hubert Boxdale was Superintendent Adam Dalgliesh's godfather. Dalgliesh's father had been his Oxford contemporary and lifelong friend. He had been an admirable godfather, affectionate, uncensorious, genuinely concerned. In Dalgliesh's childhood he had been mindful of birthdays and imaginative about a small boy's preoccupations and desires. Dalgliesh was very fond of him and privately thought him one of the few really good men he had known. It was only surprising that the Canon had managed to live to seventy-one in a carnivorous world in which gentleness, humility and unworldliness are hardly conducive to survival, let alone success. But his goodness had in some sense protected him. Faced with such manifest innocence, even those who exploited him, and they were not a few, extended some of the protection and compassion they might show to the slightly subnormal.

"Poor old darling," his daily woman would say, pocketing pay for six hours when she had worked five and helping herself to a couple of eggs from his refrigerator. "He's really not fit to be let out alone." It had surprised the then young and slightly priggish Detective Constable Dalgliesh to realize that the Canon knew perfectly well about the hours and the eggs, but thought that Mrs. Copthorne with five children and an indolent husband needed both more than he did. He also knew that if he started paying for five hours, she would promptly work only four and extract another two eggs and that this small and only dishonesty was somehow necessary to her self-esteem. He was good. But he was not a fool.

He and his wife were, of course, poor. But they were not unhappy; indeed, it was a word impossible to associate with the Canon. The death of his two sons in the 1939 war had saddened but not destroyed him. But he had anxieties. His wife was suffering from disseminated sclerosis and was finding it increasingly hard to manage. There were comforts and appliances which she would need. He was now, belatedly, about to retire and his pension would be small. The legacy would enable them both to live in comfort for the rest of their lives and would also, Dalgliesh had no doubt, give them the pleasure of doing more for their various lame dogs. Really, he thought, the Canon was an almost embarrassingly deserving candidate for a modest fortune. Why couldn't the dear silly old noodle take the cash and stop worrying? He said cunningly:

"She was found not guilty, you know, by an English jury, and it all happened nearly seventy years ago. Couldn't you bring yourself to accept their verdict?"

But the Canon's scrupulous mind was impervious to such sly innuendos. Dalgliesh told himself that he should have remembered what, as a small boy, he had discovered about Uncle Hubert's conscience; that it operated as a warning bell and that, unlike most people, he never pretended that it hadn't sounded or that he hadn't heard it or that, having heard it, something must be wrong with the mechanism.

"Oh, I did accept it while she was alive. We never met, you know. I didn't wish to force myself on her.

After all, she was a wealthy woman. Our ways of life were very different. But I usually wrote briefly at Christmas and she sent a card in reply. I wanted to keep some contact in case, one day, she might want someone to turn to and would remember that I am a priest."

And why should she want a priest? thought Dalgliesh. To clear her conscience? Was that what the dear old boy had in mind? So he must have had doubts from the beginning. But of course he had! Dalgliesh knew something of the story, and the general feeling of the family and friends was that Great-Aunt Allie had been extremely lucky to escape the gallows. His own father's view, expressed with reticence, reluctance and compassion, had not in essentials differed from that given by a local reporter at the time:

"How on earth did she expect to get away with it? Damn lucky to escape topping, if you ask me."

"The news of the legacy came as a complete surprise?" asked Dalgliesh.

"Indeed, yes. We never met except at that first and only Christmas six weeks after her marriage, when my grandfather died. We always talk of her as Great-Aunt Allie, but in fact, as you know, she married my grandfather. But it seemed impossible to think of her as a step-grandmother. There was the usual family gathering at Colebrook Croft at the time and I was there with my parents and my twin sisters. I was only four and the twins were barely eight months old. I can remember nothing of my grandfather or of his wife. After the murder—if one has to use that dreadful word—my mother returned home with us children, leaving my father to cope with the police, the solicitors and the newsmen. It was a terrible time for him. I don't think I was even told that Grandfather was dead until about a year later. My old nurse, who had been given Christmas as a holiday to visit her own family, told me that soon after my return home, I asked her if grandfather was now young and beautiful for always. She, poor woman, took it as a sign of infant prognostication and piety. Poor Nellie was sadly superstitious and sentimental, I'm afraid. But I knew nothing of Grandfather's death at the time and certainly can recall nothing of the visit or of my new step-grandmother. Mercifully, I was little more than a baby when the murder was done."

"She was a music hall artiste, wasn't she?" asked Dalgliesh.

"Yes, and a very talented one. My grandfather met her when she was working with a partner in a hall in Cannes. He had gone to the south of France with a manservant for his health. I understand that she extracted a gold watch from his chain and when he claimed it, told him that he was English, had recently suffered from a stomach ailment, had two sons and a daughter and was about to have a wonderful surprise. It was all correct except that his only daughter had died in childbirth, leaving him a granddaughter, Marguerite Goddard."

"And all easily guessable from his voice and appearance," said Dalgliesh. "I suppose the surprise was the marriage?"

"It was certainly a surprise, and a most unpleasant one, for the family. It is easy to deplore the snobbishness and the conventions of another age, and indeed there was much in Edwardian England to deplore. But it was not a propitious marriage. I think of the difference in background, education and way of life, the lack of common interest. And there was this great disparity of age. My grandfather had married a girl just three months younger than his own granddaughter. I cannot wonder that the family were concerned; that they felt that the union could not in the end contribute to the contentment or happiness of either party."

And that was putting it charitably, thought Dalgliesh. The marriage certainly hadn't contributed to their happiness. From the point of view of the family, it had been a disaster. He recalled hearing of an incident when the local vicar and his wife, a couple who had actually dined at Colebrook Croft on the night of the murder, first called on the bride. Apparently old Augustus Boxdale had introduced her by saying:

"Meet the prettiest little variety artiste in the business. Took a gold watch and note case off me without any trouble. Would have had the elastic out of my pants if I hadn't watched out. Anyway, she stole my heart, didn't you, sweetheart?" All this accompanied by a hearty slap on the rump and a squeal of delight from the lady, who had promptly demonstrated her skill by extracting the Reverend Venables's bunch of keys from his left ear.

Dalgliesh thought it tactful not to remind the Canon of this story.

"What do you wish me to do, sir?" he inquired.

"It's asking a great deal, I know, when you're so busy at the Yard. But if I had your assurance that you believed in Aunt Allie's innocence, I should feel happy about accepting the bequest. I wondered if it would be possible for you to see the records of the trial. Perhaps it would give you a clue. You're so clever at this sort of thing."

He spoke with no intention to flatter but with an innocent wonder at the peculiar avocations of men. Dalgliesh was, indeed, very clever at this sort of thing. A dozen or so men at present occupying security wings in Her Majesty's prisons could testify to Chief Superintendent Dalgliesh's cleverness, as indeed could a handful of others walking free whose defending counsel had been in their way as clever as Chief Superintendent Dalgliesh. But to reexamine a case over sixty years old seemed to require clairvoyance rather than cleverness. The trial judge and both learned counsel had been dead for over fifty years. Two world wars had taken their toll. Four reigns had passed. It was probable that of those who had slept under the roof of Colebrook Croft on that fateful Boxing Day night of 1901, only the Canon still survived.

But the old man was troubled and had sought his help. And Dalgliesh, with nearly a week's leave due to him, had the time to give it.

"I'll see what I can do," he promised.

The transcript of a trial which had taken place sixty-

seven years ago took time and trouble to obtain even
for a chief superintendent of the Metropolitan Police. It
provided little potential comfort for the Canon. Mr.
Justice Medlock had summed up with that avuncular
simplicity with which he was wont to address juries, regarding them, apparently, as a panel of well-intentioned
but cretinous children. But the salient facts could have
been comprehended by any intelligent child. Part of the
summing up set them out with admirable lucidity:

And so, gentlemen of the jury, we come to the evening of 26 December. Mr. Augustus Boxdale, who
had perhaps indulged a little unwisely on Christmas
Day and at luncheon, had retired to rest in his dressing room at three o'clock, suffering from a slight re-
currence of the digestive trouble which had afflicted
him for most of his life. You have heard that he had
taken luncheon with members of his family and ate
nothing which they, too, did not eat. You may feel
that you can acquit that luncheon of anything worse
than overrichness. Mr. Boxdale, as was his habit, did
not take afternoon tea.
Dinner was served at 8 P.M. promptly, as was the
custom at Colebrook Croft. Members of the jury, you
must be very clear who was present at that meal.
There was the accused, Mrs. Augustus Boxdale;
there was her husband's elder son, Captain Maurice
Boxdale, with his wife: the younger son, the Reverend Edward Boxdale, with his wife; the deceased's
granddaughter, Miss Marguerite Goddard, and there
were two neighbours, the Reverend and Mrs. Henry
Venables.
You have heard how the accused took only the
first course at dinner, which was ragout of beef, and
then left the dining room, saying that she wished to
sit with her husband. That was about eight-twenty.
Shortly after nine o'clock, she rang for the parlourmaid, Mary Huddy, and ordered a basin of gruel to
be brought up to Mr Boxdale. You have heard that
the deceased was fond of gruel, and indeed, as pre-

pared by Mrs. Muncie, the cook, it sounds a most nourishing and comforting dish for an elderly gentleman of weak digestion.

You have heard Mrs. Muncie describe how she prepared the gruel, according to Mrs. Beeton's admirable recipe, in the presence of Mary Huddy, in case, as she said, "The master should take a fancy to it when I'm not at hand and you have to make it." After the gruel had been prepared, Mrs. Muncie tasted it with a spoon and Mary Huddy carried it upstairs to the main bedroom, together with a small jug of water in case it should be too strong. As she reached the door, Mrs. Boxdale came out, her hands full of stockings and underclothes. She has told you that she was on her way to the bathroom to wash them through. She asked the girl to put the basin of gruel on the washstand to cool and Mary Huddy did so in her presence. Miss Huddy has told you that, at the time, she noticed the bowl of flypapers soaking in water and she knew that this solution was one used by Mrs. Boxdale as a cosmetic wash. Indeed, all the women who spent that evening in the house, with the exception of Mrs. Venables, have told you that they knew that it was Mrs. Boxdale's practice to prepare this solution of flypapers.

Mary Huddy and the accused left the bedroom together and you have heard the evidence of Mrs. Muncie that Miss Huddy returned to the kitchen after an absence of only a few minutes. Shortly after nine o'clock, the ladies left the dining room and entered the drawing room to take coffee. At nine-fifteen, Miss Goddard excused herself to the company and said that she would go to see if her grandfather needed anything. The time is established precisely because the clock struck the quarter hour as she left and Mrs. Venables commented on the sweetness of its chime. You have also heard Mrs. Venables's evidence and the evidence of Mrs. Maurice Boxdale and Mrs. Edward Boxdale that none of the ladies left the drawing room during the evening, and

Mr. Venables has testified that the three gentlemen remained together until Miss Goddard appeared about three quarters of an hour later to inform them that her grandfather had become very ill and to request that the doctor be sent for immediately.

Miss Goddard has told you that when she entered her grandfather's room, he was just beginning his gruel and was grumbling about its taste. She got the impression that this was merely a protest at being deprived of his dinner rather than that he genuinely considered that there was something wrong with the gruel. At any rate, he finished most of it and appeared to enjoy it despite his grumbles.

You have heard Miss Goddard describe how, after her grandfather had had as much as he wanted of the gruel, she took the bowl next door and left it on the washstand. She then returned to her grandfather's bedroom and Mr. Boxdale, his wife and his granddaughter played three-handed whist for about three quarters of an hour.

At ten o'clock, Mr. Augustus Boxdale complained of feeling very ill. He suffered from griping pains in the stomach, from sickness and from looseness of the bowel. As soon as the symptoms began, Miss Goddard went downstairs to let her uncles know that her grandfather was worse and to ask that Dr. Eversley should be sent for urgently. Dr. Eversley has given you his evidence. He arrived at Colebrook Croft at 10:30 P.M., when he found his patient very distressed and weak. He treated the symptoms and gave what relief he could, but Mr. Augustus Boxdale died shortly before midnight.

Gentlemen of the jury, you have heard Marguerite Goddard describe how, as her grandfather's paroxysms increased in intensity, she remembered the gruel and wondered whether it could have disagreed with him in some way. She mentioned this possibility to her elder uncle, Captain Maurice Boxdale. Captain Boxdale has told you how he at once handed the bowl with its residue of gruel to Dr. Eversley with the request that the doctor should lock it in a cupboard in the library, seal the lock and himself keep the key. You have heard how the contents of the bowl were later analyzed and with what result.

An extraordinary precaution for the gallant captain to have taken, thought Dalgliesh, and a most perspicacious young woman. Was it by chance or by design that the bowl hadn't been taken down to be washed as soon as the old man had finished with it? Why was it, he wondered, that Marguerite Goddard hadn't rung for the parlourmaid and requested her to remove it? Miss Goddard appeared the only other suspect. He wished that he knew more about her.

But except for the main protagonists, the characters in the drama did not emerge very clearly from the trial report. Why, indeed, should they? The accusatorial legal system is designed to answer one question. Is the accused guilty beyond reasonable doubt of the crime charged? Exploration of the nuances of personality, interesting speculation and common gossip have no place in the witness box. Was it really possible after nearly seventy years that these dry bones could live?

The two Boxdale brothers came out as very dull fellows indeed. They and their estimable and respectable sloping-bosomed wives had sat at dinner in full view of each other from eight until nearly nine o'clock (a substantial meal, that dinner) and had said so in the witness box in more or less identical words. The bosoms of the ladies might have been heaving with far from estimable emotions of dislike, envy, embarrassment or resentment of the interloper. If so, they didn't choose to tell the court. But the two brothers and their wives were clearly innocent, even if it had been possible to conceive of the guilt of gentlefolk so respected, so eminently respectable. Even their impeccable alibis for the period after dinner had a nice touch of social and sexual distinction. The Reverend Henry Venables had vouched for the gentlemen; his good wife for the ladies.

Besides, what motive had they? They could no longer

gain financially by the old man's death. If anything, it was in their interests to keep him alive in the hope that disillusionment with his marriage or a return to relative sanity might occur to cause him to change his will.

And the rest of the witnesses gave no help. Dalgliesh read all their testimony carefully. The pathologist's evidence. The doctor's evidence. The evidence of Allegra Boxdale's visit to the village store, where, from among the clutter of pots and pans, ointments and liniments, it had been possible to find a dozen flypapers for a customer even in the depth of an English winter. The evidence of the cook. The evidence of the parlourmaid. The remarkably lucid and confident evidence of the granddaughter. There was nothing in any of it which could cause him to give the Canon the assurance for which he hoped.

It was then that he remembered Aubrey Glatt. Glatt was a wealthy amateur criminologist who had made a study of all the notable Victorian and Edwardian poison cases. He was not interested in anything earlier or later, being as obsessively wedded to his period as any serious historian, which indeed he had some claim to call himself. He lived in a Georgian house in Winchester—his affection for the Victorian and Edwardian age did not extend to its architecture—and was only three miles from Colebrook Croft. A visit to the London Library disclosed that he hadn't written a book on the case, but it was improbable that he had totally neglected a crime so close at hand and so in period. Dalgliesh had occasionally helped him with technical details of police procedure. Glatt, in response to a telephone call, was happy to return the favour with the offer of afternoon tea and information.

Tea was served in his elegant drawing room by a parlourmaid in goffered cap with streamers. Dalgliesh wondered what wage Glatt paid her to persuade her to wear it. She looked as if she could have played a role in any of his favourite Victorian dramas, and Dalgliesh had an uncomfortable thought that arsenic might be dispensed with the cucumber sandwiches.

Glatt nibbled away and was expansive.

"It's interesting that you should have taken this sudden and, if I may say so, somewhat inexplicable interest in the Boxdale murder. I got out my notebook on the case only yesterday. Colebrook Croft is being demolished to make way for a new housing estate and I thought I might visit it for the last time. The family, of course, hasn't lived there since the 1914–18 war. Architecturally it's completely undistinguished, but one hates to see it go. We might motor over after tea if you are agreeable.

"I never completed my book on the case, you know. I planned a work entitled *The Colebrook Croft Mystery, or Who Killed Augustus Boxdale?* But alas, the answer was all too obvious."

"No real mystery?" suggested Dalgliesh.

"Who else could it have been but the bride? She was born Allegra Porter, incidentally. Allegra. An extraordinary name. Do you suppose her mother could have been thinking of Byron? I imagine not. There's a picture of Allie on page two of the notebook, by the way, taken in Cannes on her wedding day. I call it 'Beauty and the Beast.' "

The photograph had scarcely faded and Great-Aunt Allie smiled plainly at Dalgliesh across nearly seventy years. Her broad face with its wide mouth and rather snub nose was framed by two wings of dark hair swept high and topped, in the fashion of the day, by an immense flowered hat. The features were too coarse for real beauty, but the eyes were magnificent, deep-set and well-spaced; the chin was round and determined. Beside this vital young Amazon poor Augustus Boxdale, smiling fatuously at the camera and clutching his bride's arm as if for support, was but a frail and pathetic beast. Their pose was unfortunate. She looked as if she were about to fling him over her shoulder.

Glatt shrugged. "The face of a murderess? I've known less likely ones. Her counsel suggested, of course, that the old man had poisoned his own gruel during the short time she left it on the washstand to cool while she visited the bathroom. But why should he? All the evidence suggests that he was in a state of postnuptial euphoria, poor senile old booby. Our Augustus was in no hurry to leave this world, particularly by such an agonizing means. Besides, I doubt whether he even knew the gruel was there. He was in bed next door in his dressing room, remember."

Dalgliesh asked, "What about Marguerite Goddard? There's no evidence about the exact time when she entered the bedroom."

"I thought you'd get on to that. She could have arrived while her step-grandmother was in the bathroom, posioned the gruel, hidden herself either in the main bedroom or elsewhere until it had been taken in to Augustus, then joined her grandfather and his bride as if she had just come upstairs. It's possible, I admit. But is it likely? She was less inconvenienced than any of the family by her grandfather's second marriage. Her mother was Augustus Boxdale's eldest child and married, very young, a wealthy patent medicine manufacturer. She died in childbirth and the husband only survived her by a year. Marguerite Goddard was an heiress. She was also most advantageously engaged to Captain the Honourable John Brize-Lacey. It was quite a catch for a Boxdale—or a Goddard. Marguerite Goddard, young, beautiful, secure in the possession of the Goddard fortune, not to mention the Goddard emeralds and the eldest son of a lord, was hardly a serious suspect. In my view defence counsel—that was Roland Gort Lloyd—was wise to leave her strictly alone."

"It was a memorable defence, I believe."

"Magnificent. There's no doubt Allegra Boxdale owed her life to Gort Lloyd. I know that concluding speech by heart:

" 'Gentlemen of the jury, I beseech you in the sacred name of justice to consider what you are at. It is your responsibility and yours alone to decide the fate of this young woman. She stands before you now, young, vibrant, glowing with health, the years stretching before her with their promise and their hopes. It is in your power to cut off all this as you might top a nettle with one swish of your cane. To condemn her to the slow torture of those last waiting weeks; to that last dreadful walk; to heap calumny on her name; to desecrate those few happy weeks of marriage with the man who loved her so greatly; to cast her into the final darkness of an ignominious grave.'

"Pause for dramtic effect. Then the crescendo in that magnificent voice. 'And on what evidence, gentlemen? I ask you.' Another pause. Then the thunder. 'On what evidence?' "

"A powerful defence," said Dalgliesh. "But I wonder how it would go down with a modern judge and jury."

"Well, it went down very effectively with that 1902 jury. Of course, the abolition of capital punishment has rather cramped the more histrionic style. I'm not sure that the reference to topping nettles was in the best of taste. But the jury got the message. They decided that, on the whole, they preferred not to have the responsibility of sending the accused to the gallows. They were out six hours reaching their verdict and it was greeted with some applause. If any of those worthy citizens had been asked to wager five pounds of their own good money on her innocence, I suspect that it would have been a different matter. Allegra Boxdale had helped him, of course. The Criminal Evidence Act, passed three years earlier, enabled him to put her in the witness box. She wasn't an actress of a kind for nothing. Somehow she managed to persuade the jury that she had genuinely loved the old man."

"Perhaps she had," suggested Dalgliesh. "I don't suppose there had been much kindness in her life. And he was kind."

"No doubt. No doubt. But love!" Glatt was impatient. "My dear Dalgliesh? He was a singularly ugly old man of sixty-nine. She was an attractive girl of twenty-one!"

Dalgliesh doubted whether love, that iconoclastic passion, was susceptible to this kind of simple arithmetic, but he didn't argue. Glatt went on:

"And the prosecution couldn't suggest any other romantic attachment. The police got in touch with her previous partner, of course. He was discovered to be a bald, undersized little man, sharp as a weasel, with a buxom uxorious wife and five children. He had moved down the coast after the partnership broke up and was now working with a new girl. He said regretfully that she was coming along nicely, thank you, gentlemen, but would never be a patch on Allie, and that if Allie got her neck out of the noose and ever wanted a job, she knew where to come. It was obvious even to the most suspicious policeman that his interest was purely professional. As he said, what was a grain or two of arsenic between friends?

"The Boxdales had no luck after the trial. Captain Maurice Boxdale was killed in 1916, leaving no children, and the Reverend Edward lost his wife and their twin daughters in the 1918 influenza epidemic. He survived until 1932. The boy Hubert may still be alive, but I doubt it. That family were a sickly lot.

"My greatest achievement, incidentally, was in tracing Marguerite Goddard. I hadn't realized that she was still alive. She never married Brize-Lacey or, indeed, anyone else. He distinguished himself in the 1914–18 war, came successfully through, and eventually married an eminently suitable young woman, the sister of a brother officer. He inherited the title in 1925 and died in 1953. But Marguerite Goddard may be alive now, for all I know. She may even be living in the same modest Bournemouth hotel where I found her. Not that my efforts in tracing her were rewarded. She absolutely refused to see me. That's the note that she sent out to me, by the way."

It was meticulously pasted into the notebook in its chronological order and carefully annotated. Aubrey Glatt was a natural researcher; Dalgliesh couldn't help wondering whether this passion for accuracy might not have been more rewardingly spent than in the careful documentation of murder.

The note was written in an elegant upright hand, the strokes black and very thin but unwavering.

Miss Goddard presents her compliments to Mr. Aubrey Glatt. She did not murder her grandfather and has neither the time nor the inclination to gratify his curiosity by discussing the person who did.

Aubrey Glatt said, "After that extremely disobliging note I felt there was really no point in going on with the book."

Glatt's passion for Edwardian England extended to more than its murders and they drove to Colebrook Croft, high above the green Hampshire lanes, in an elegant 1910 Daimler. Aubrey wore a thin tweed coat and deerstalker hat and looked, Dalgliesh thought, rather like a Sherlock Holmes, with himself as attendant Watson.

"We are only just in time, my dear Dalgliesh," he said when they arrived. "The engines of destruction are assembled. That ball on a chain looks like the eyeball of God, ready to strike. Let us make our number with the attendant artisans. You as a guardian of the law will have no wish to trespass."

The work of demolition had not yet begun, but the inside of the house had been stripped and plundered. The great rooms echoed to their footsteps like gaunt and deserted barracks after the final retreat. They moved from room to room, Glatt mourning the forgotten glories of an age he had been born thirty years too late to enjoy, Dalgliesh with his mind on more immediate and practical concerns.

The design of the house was simple and formalized. The second floor, on which were most of the main bedrooms, had a long corridor running the whole length of the façade. The master bedroom was at the southern end, with two large windows giving a distant view of Winchester Cathedral tower. A communicating door led to a small dressing room.

The main corridor had a row of four identical large

windows. The curtain rods and rings had been removed, but the ornate carved pelmets were still in place. Here must have hung pairs of heavy curtains giving cover to anyone who wished to slip out of view. And Dalgliesh noted with interest that one of the windows was exactly opposite the door of the main bedroom. By the time they had left Colebrook Croft and Glatt had dropped him at Winchester station, Dalgliesh was beginning to formulate a theory.

His next move was to trace Marguerite Goddard if she was still alive. It took him nearly a week of weary searching, a frustrating trail along the south coast from hotel to hotel. Almost everywhere his inquiries were met with defensive hostility. It was the usual story of a very old lady who had become more demanding, arrogant and eccentric as her health and fortune had waned; an unwelcome embarrassment to manager and fellow guests alike. The hotels were all modest, a few almost sordid. What, he wondered, had become of the Goddard fortune? From the last landlady he learned that Miss Goddard had become ill, really very sick indeed, and had been removed six months previously to the local district general hospital. And it was there that he found her.

The ward sister was surprisingly young, a petite, dark-haired girl with a tired face and challenging eyes.

"Miss Goddard is very ill. We've put her in one of the side wards. Are you a relative? If so, you're the first one who has bothered to call and your're lucky to be in time. When she is delirious she seems to expect a Captain Brize-Lacey to call. You're not he, by any chance?"

"Captain Brize-Lacey will not be calling. No, I'm not a relative. She doesn't even know me. But I would like to visit her if she's well enough and is willing to see me. Could you please give her this note?"

He couldn't force himself on a defenceless and dying woman. She still had the right to say no. He was afraid she would refuse him. And if she did, he might never learn the truth. He thought for a second and then wrote four words on the back page of his diary, signed them, tore out the page, folded it and handed it to the sister.

She was back very shortly.

"She'll see you. She's weak, of course, and very old, but she's perfectly lucid now. Only please don't tire her."

"I'll try not to stay too long."

The girl laughed. "Don't worry. She'll throw you out soon enough if she gets bored. The chaplain and the Red Cross librarian have a terrible time with her. Third door on the left. There's a stool to sit on under the bed. We ring a bell at the end of visiting time."

She bustled off, leaving him to find his own way. The corridor was very quiet. At the far end he could glimpse through the open door of the main ward the regimented rows of beds, each with its pale-blue coverlet; the bright glow of flowers on the over-bed tables; and the laden visitors making their way in pairs to each bedside. There was a faint buzz of welcome, the hum of conversation. But no one was visiting the side wards. Here in the silence of the aseptic corridor Dalgliesh could smell death.

The woman propped high against the pillows in the third room on the left no longer looked human. She lay rigidly, her long arms disposed like sticks on the coverlet. This was a skeleton clothed with a thin membrane of flesh, beneath whose yellow transparency the tendons and veins were plainly visible as if in an anatomist's model. She was nearly bald, and the high-domed skull under its spare down of hair was as brittle and vulnerable as a child's. Only the eyes still held life, burning in their deep sockets with an animal vitality. And when she spoke her voice was distinctive and unwavering, evoking as her appearance never could the memory of imperious youth.

She took up his note and read aloud four words:

" 'It was the child.' You are right, of course. The four-year-old Hubert Boxdale killed his grandfather. You sign this note 'Adam Dalgliesh.' There was no Dalgliesh connected with the case."

"I am a detective of the Metropolitan Police. But I'm not here in any official capacity. I have known about this case for a number of years from a dear friend. I have a natural curiosity to learn the truth. And I have formed a theory."

"And now, like that Aubrey Glatt, you want to write a book?"

"No. I shall tell no one. You have my promise."

Her voice was ironic. "Thank you. I am a dying woman, Mr. Dalgliesh. I tell you that not to invite your sympathy, which it would be an impertinence for you to offer and which I neither want nor require, but to explain why it no longer matters to me what you say or do. But I, too, have a natural curiosity. Your note, cleverly, was intended to provoke it. I should like to know how you discovered the truth."

Dalgliesh drew the visitor's stool from under the bed and sat down beside her. She did not look at him. The skeleton hands, still holding his note, did not move.

"Everyone in Colebrook Croft who could have killed Augustus Boxdale was accounted for, except the one person whom nobody considered, the small boy. He was an intelligent, articulate and lonely child. He was almost certainly left to his own devices. His nurse did not accompany the family to Colebrook Croft and the servants who were there had the extra work of Christmas and the care of the delicate twin girls. The boy spent much time with his grandfather and the new bride. She, too, was lonely and disregarded. He could have trotted around with her as she went about her various activities. He could have watched her making her arsenical face wash and when he asked, as a child will, what it was for, could have been told: 'To make me young and beautiful.' He loved his grandfather, but he must have known that the old man was neither young nor beautiful. Suppose he woke up on that Boxing Day night overfed and excited after the Christmas festivities. Suppose he went to Allegra Boxdale's room in search of comfort and companionship and saw there the basin of gruel and the arsenical mixture together on the washstand. Suppose he decided that here was something he could do for his grandfather."

The voice from the bed said quietly:

"And suppose someone stood unnoticed in the doorway and watched him."

"So you were behind the window curtains on the landing, looking through the open door?"

"Of course. He knelt on the chair, two chubby hands clasping the bowl of poison, pouring it with infinite care into his grandfather's gruel. I watched while he replaced the linen cloth over the basin, got down from his chair, replaced it with careful art against the wall and trotted out into the corridor back to the nursery. About three seconds later Allegra came out of the bathroom and I watched while she carried the gruel in to my grandfather. A second later I went into the main bedroom. The bowl of poison had been a little heavy for Hubert's small hands to manage and I saw that a small pool had been spilt on the polished top of the washstand. I mopped it up with my handkerchief. Then I poured some of the water from the jug into the poison bowl to bring up the level. It only took a couple of seconds and I was ready to join Allegra and my grandfather in the bedroom and sit with him while he ate his gruel.

"I watched him die without pity and without remorse. I think I hated them both equally. The grandfather who had adored, petted and indulged me all through my childhood had deteriorated into this disgusting old lecher, unable to keep his hands off his woman even when I was in the room. He had rejected his family, jeopardized my engagement, made our name a laughingstock in the county, and for a woman my grandmother wouldn't have employed as a kitchen maid. I wanted them both dead. And they were both going to die. But it would be by other hands than mine. I could deceive myself that it wasn't my doing."

Dalgliesh asked, "When did she find out?"

"She guessed that evening. When my grandfather's agony began, she went outside for the jug of water. She wanted a cool cloth for his head. It was then that she noticed that the level of water in the jug had fallen and that a small pool of liquid on the washstand had been mopped up. I should have realized that she would have seen that pool. She had been trained to register every detail; it was almost subconscious with her. She thought at the time that Mary Huddy had spilt some of the water when she set down the tray and the gruel. But who but I could have mopped it up? And why?"

"And when did she face you with the truth?"

"Not until after the trial. Allegra had magnificent courage. She knew what was at stake. But she also knew what she stood to gain. She gambled with her life for a fortune."

And then Dalgliesh understood what had happened to the Goddard inheritance.

"So she made you pay."

"Of course. Every penny. The Goddard fortune, the Goddard emeralds. She lived in luxury for sixty-seven years on my money. She ate and dressed on my money. When she moved with her lovers from hotel to hotel, it was on my money. She paid them with my money. And if she has left anything, which I doubt, it is my money. My grandfather left very little. He had been senile for years. Money ran through his fingers like sand."

"And your engagement?"

"It was broken, you could say, by mutual consent. A marriage, Mr. Dalgliesh, is like any other legal contract. It is most successful when both parties are convinced they have a bargain. Captain Brize-Lacey was sufficiently discouraged by the scandal of a murder in the family. He was a proud and highly conventional man. But that alone might have been accepted with the Goddard fortune and the Goddard emeralds to deodorize the bad smell. But the marriage couldn't have succeeded if he had discovered that he had married socially beneath him, into a family with a major scandal and no compensating fortune."

Dalgliesh said, "Once you had begun to pay, you had no choice but to go on. I see that. But why did you pay?

She could hardly have told her story. It would have meant involving the child."

"Oh, no! That wasn't her plan at all. She never meant to involve the child. She was a sentimental woman and she was fond of Hubert. She intended to accuse me of murder outright. Then, if I decided to tell the truth, how would it help me? How could I admit that I had watched Hubert, actually watched a child barely four years old preparing an agonizing death for his grandfather without speaking a word to stop him? I could hardly claim that I hadn't understood the implication of what I had seen. After all, I wiped up the spilt liquid, I topped up the bowl. She had nothing to lose, remember, neither life nor reputation. They couldn't try her twice. That's why she waited until after the trial. It made her secure forever. But what of me? In the circles in which I moved, reputation was everything. She needed only to breathe the story in the ears of a few servants and I was finished. The truth can be remarkably tenacious. But it wasn't only reputation. I paid because I was in dread of the gallows."

Dalgliesh asked, "But could she ever prove it?"

Suddenly she looked at him and gave an eerie screech of laughter. It tore at her throat until he thought the taut tendons would snap.

"Of course she could! You fool! Don't you understand? She took my handkerchief, the one I used to mop up the arsenic mixture. That was her profession, remember. Sometime during that evening, perhaps when we were all crowding around the bed, two soft plump fingers insinuated themselves between the satin of my evening dress and my flesh and extracted that stained and damning piece of linen."

She stretched out feebly toward the bedside locker. Dalgliesh saw what she wanted and pulled open the drawer. There on the top was a small square of very fine linen with a border of hand-stitched lace. He took it up. In the corner was her monogram, delicately embroidered. And half of the handkerchief was still stiff and stained with brown.

She said, "She left instructions with her solicitors that this was to be returned to me after her death. She always knew where I was. She made it her business to know. You see, it could be said that she had a life interest in me. But now she's dead. And I shall soon follow. You may have the handkerchief, Mr. Dalgliesh. It can be of no further use to either of us now."

Dalgliesh put it in his pocket without speaking. As soon as possible he would see that it was burned. But there was something else he had to say. "Is there anything you would wish me to do? Is there anyone you want told, or to tell? Would you care to see a priest?"

Again there was that uncanny screech of laughter, but it was softer now.

"There's nothing I can say to a priest. I only regret what I did because it wasn't successful. That is hardly the proper frame of mind for a good confession. But I bear her no ill will. No envy, malice or uncharitableness. She won; I lost. One should be a good loser. But I don't want any priest telling me about penance. I've paid, Mr. Dalgliesh. For sixty-seven years I've paid. Great-Aunt Allie and her flypapers! She had me caught by the wings all the rest of my life."

She lay back as if suddenly exhausted. There was silence for a moment. Then she said with sudden vigour:

"I believe your visit has done me good. I would be obliged if you would make it convenient to return each afternoon for the next three days. I shan't trouble you after that."

Dalgliesh extended his leave with some difficulty and stayed at a local inn. He saw her each afternoon. They never spoke again of the murder. And when he came punctually at 2 P.M. on the fourth day, it was to be told that Miss Goddard had died peacefully in the night, with apparently no trouble to anyone. She was, as she had said, a good loser.

A week later, Dalgliesh reported to the Canon.

"I was able to see a man who has made a detailed study of the case. He had already done most of the work for me. I have read the transcript of the trial and visited Colebrook Croft. And I have seen one other person closely connected with the case but who is now dead. I know you will want me to respect confidences and to say no more than I need."

It sounded pompous and minatory, but he couldn't help that. The Canon murmured his quiet assurance. Thank God he wasn't a man to question. Where he trusted, he trusted absolutely. If Dalgliesh gave his word, there would be no more questioning. But he was anxious. Suspense hung around them. Dalgliesh went on quickly:

"As a result, I can give you my word that the verdict was a just verdict and that not one penny of your grandfather's fortune is coming to you through anyone's wrongdoing."

He turned his face away and gazed out the vicarage window at the sweet green coolness of the summer's day so that he did not have to watch the Canon's happiness and relief. There was a silence. The old man was probably giving thanks in his own way. Then he was aware that his godfather was speaking. Something was being said about gratitude, about the time he had given up to the investigation.

"Please don't misunderstand me, Adam. But when the formalities have been completed, I should like to donate something to a charity named by you, one close to your heart."

Dalgliesh smiled. His contributions to charity were impersonal; a quarterly obligation discharged by banker's order. The Canon obviously regarded charities as so many old clothes; all were friends, but some fitted better and were more affectionately regarded than others.

Then inspiration came.

"It's good of you to suggest it, sir. I rather liked what I learned about Great-Aunt Allie. It would be pleasant to give something in her name. Isn't there a society for the assistance of retired and indigent vaudeville artistes, conjurers and so on?"

The Canon, predictably, knew that there was and could name it.

Dalgliesh said, "Then I think, Canon, that Great-Aunt Allie would agree that a donation to them would be entirely appropriate."

The Rogue's Twist

GWENDOLINE BUTLER

Coffin fell in love with the Admiral's lady when he'd really decided he was past all that sort of thing. But there were two very good reasons for it: first, she was charmingly pretty and flirtatious in an old-fashioned, Edwardian kind of way; and second, she helped illuminate a dark corner in his life. A dog, some dog's hair on a dead body, and a twist of rope: these three fused together to make a cone of light.

She was a well-bred Pekingese with bright big eyes and a face like a pansy. In the Dog Training Circle, where Coffin was known as Womble Coffin's master, she was the Admiral's lady and the Admiral was called Silver Moonlight's dad. Both men answered well to their titles, but except for a Jack Russell terrier, their dogs were far and away the most recalcitrant animals in the class. The Airedale and the boxer and the Alsatian were all moderate animals and modestly obedient to their masters' commands, sometimes stupid but never deliberately unheeding. These were the big dogs. The small ones, like Coffin's Yorkshire terrier and the Pekingese, lay bright-eyed and comprehending, but obstinately still.

"He does *know*, you know," said Coffin, sweating, as Womble ignored repeated requests to "stand." "He understands, but he won't."

"Oh, yes; Moonlight's just the same," said the Admiral proudly. "Knows every word I say, but won't do it."

Bright-eyed Womble and Moonlight ignored their owners and growled at each other.

The Jack Russell terrier, called Nancy Sykes, taking advantage of the fact that her master was staring at Coffin's face, dragged herself the full length of the piece of rope she wore around her neck and bit Womble's tail. From the resulting tumult their nearest neighbours, an Afghan and a Great Dane, drew back in anxious silence. Calm eventually returned through the fierce efforts of Coffin, the Admiral, and the Jack Russell's owner, aided by commanding shouts from the organizer of the Dog Training Circle, Miss Champion, an ex-Wren. She was a sturdy lady with a profound grasp of the politics of power, as a result of which the group met in an unused shed attached to the old Rope Walk in Chatham Dockyard, with the kind agreement of the dockyard police and the polite permission of the present Admiral in command of the dockyard, who was a cat lover. The old Rope Walk was a long, dark building in regular daily use for the making of rope. Once men had trudged the whole length of the walk, pulling the rope after them; now machines rattled and bowled along. It was in an outbuilding at the side that the training class met.

The Circle met weekly on Wednesday evening to practise their rites and drills amidst the vegetable smells and dustiness of the old rope manufactory. Twelve good dogs and true.

"Nice to see you in these parts again, my dear chap. I thought I recognized your face, but it took a bit of time for it to click," said the Admiral to John Coffin. They had known each other a decade or two ago. "Live here now, do you?"

"Yes."

"Retired, eh?"

"Mmm." For it was more or less true: policemen did retire early. He'd retired from life once, and had been obliged to join up again.

"Good plan to come to Kent. I love the Medway myself. Served in Dockyard twice. Once in the twenties, and then again in the forties."

"That's right," said Coffin. "That's when we met."

"What a different world."

"I know," said Coffin. "Nineteen forty-seven."

"I'd just retired; the dockyard was full of ships. It had been full in the twenties, of course, but then they were laid up because we couldn't afford the fuel to send them to sea. Even now I think things are better than that, but changed times, changed times. But it's always suited me hereabouts. I'm a Kentish man, you know, and that's why I've come back here to live. I've got a very decent cottage about three miles out of town. Very small and no garden to speak of, but my wife's dead now, and the place suits me. And what about you? What brings you back?"

"Memories, I suppose." One memory, anyway.

"Ah, like me, then. We all do it."

Coffin hoped the Admiral's memories were not the same as his.

"And what are you doing now you've retired?"

"Oh, security work," Coffin said vaguely. "A private firm."

"Ah, you're still at it, then, really," said the Admiral. "Policemen never retire, do they? Remember when we met before?"

"Certainly. When Josephine Beaumont disappeared."

"Yes. Thirty years, and I miss her as much now as I missed her then."

"So do I," said Coffin.

"Yes, you were sweet on her a bit, weren't you? I always thought so. But you only knew her a few weeks, and I'd seen her grow up. And she was that sort of girl. Unforgettable."

"And unforgotten," said Coffin. "By the police, anyway."

The Admiral gave him a sharp look. "Ah, I've always wondered. Never closed the file, I suppose?"

Coffin shook his head. "It couldn't be. No solid fact to close it with."

"You were just a lad."

"Yes. I was a baby policeman," said Coffin with a serious face. "It was just before I transferred to London. Superintendent Duffy was in charge. He's long dead, of course. He was probably a dying man even then. So are Macgowan and Beadle; they were the inspector and sergeant. One went in a car crash—that was Beadle. I don't know what got Macgowan, but he looked like a man with something eating him. Slowly, you know, but sufficiently. No, I'm about the only one left with personal memories."

In that peaceful summer of 1947, Josephine Beaumont had left the Wrens and set about making preparations to go to Somerville College, Oxford, in October, where she had a place to read Geography under a special arrangement for ex-service women. It was a place she was not destined to occupy. In July she had packed her bags for a short holiday, and left them at Chatham railway station with the blithe comment that she would be back soon to collect them. She never came back; she was never seen again. She was wearing an old blue linen suit (clothes were still rationed), a new silk shirt, and a scarf borrowed from a friend.

"It was because she was such a *good* person. I'd watched her become an adult. She was my goddaughter, and you've got to remember she was growing up in a time when it looked as though she might never live through it. I remember thinking: Thank goodness a girl like you survived the war. It's people like you that are going to make something of the peace. We were hopeful then, remember? And then she was gone. . . . I suppose she *didn't* survive, did she?"

"No." Coffin shook his head.

"I couldn't help wondering. It's been the question I've carried inside me all these years. Whether she might not have just . . . gone off. For her own reasons."

Miss Champion broke into their conversation; she hated to see anything except full attention to the dogs. "You two aren't attending to the instructions properly.

And you as well." She shook her finger sternly at the Jack Russell's owner. *"Walk* your dogs round the grand circle." And, as the Admiral and Coffin showed signs of pairing off, "No, not together; ten paces in between."

When they next got a chance, the Admiral said, "Are you sure, about her not surviving?"

"Quite sure."

"I see." Then he added heavily, "I suppose I always knew it. But while there was doubt . . . Still, thirty years is a long time. And now you know?"

"Yes. We've got her back."

The body lay curled up, almost as if, all those years ago, she had fallen asleep. The workmen who had disturbed her resting place in the foundations of a building once bombed, then restored, now being demolished, looked down and saw dust covering a blue suit, head covered with a scarf, knees drawn up, and one skeletal hand protruding. A yellowed piece of newspaper just visible under the body had the date 19 July, 1947, on it. "Must be murder," said the young workman, half pleasurably excited, half appalled. "No one takes theirself off to sleep in the foundations of a house." But even without that thought, the police knew they had a murder victim because of the piece of rope still in position round the skeletal neck. And they knew her name: she had her ration book with her.

Miss Champion said loudly, "Now tell your dogs to *wait,* and go outside the door. I'll tell you when to come back." And any dog that moves will bring shame on its owner's head, she implied.

Outside the door, the Admiral and Coffin were reunited.

"I know Moonlight will move," said the Admiral to Coffin. "She's probably scratching at the door this minute. And if she's sitting still, then she's probably very upset, and I shall have trouble afterwards. She doesn't understand treatment like this." And, as they waited: "Tell me about Josephine."

"You remember the row of little cottages outside the dockyard gates? They were bombed, then rebuilt in

1947. Now they're coming down because a new block of flats is going up. Her body was there."

"I see. So she was so close, all this time."

Silently they obeyed the summons to go back into the room, where Womble Coffin and Moonlight and the Jack Russell were mouthing each other in noisy combat, amidst a circle of well-behaved, silent large dogs. Nancy Sykes emerged triumphantly from the fight, trailing a sodden piece of rope round her neck. "Chews up all her leads," said her owner proudly. He was a burly man in careful tweeds. His hands bore ancient scars and callouses, as if they had once known hard labour. But he was very gentle with Nancy Sykes.

"You really must keep better control of Womble," said Miss Champion sternly, "and not let him get the upper hand. How long have you had him?"

"Just a few days," said Coffin humbly.

A week passed before the next meeting, but there was a full attendance of all twelve dogs, together with their handlers and one or two hangers-on, such as a small boy and an even smaller girl (who nevertheless could control the Airedale with a word) and the wife of the owner of the Jack Russell.

"She's twice the man he is with the dog," confided the Admiral to Coffin. "He's made a packet out of the construction business since he left the navy, but she's got him nicely under control. You remember her father was in the dockyard police here? Killed in 1942, when his house got a direct hit. She's an ex-Wren like our charming ringmaster," and he cast a baleful look at Miss Champion. "She thinks I'm weak with Moonlight, and of course I am. It's *people* who get trained at this class, not dogs." He stroked Moonlight's soft head. "How have you been getting on with your little brute?"

"Badly."

"So have I, so have I," said the Admiral joyfully. "Hello, Bob." This was to Nancy Sykes's owner. He introduced them. "This is Ann and Bob Tweedie and this is an old friend of mine called Coffin."

Nancy Sykes strained at the end of her usual piece of

rope, but since she was held firmly by Ann Tweedie, she was relatively docile.

"Bob's always had a dog as long as I've known him," said Ann in her deep, soft voice. "But he can never discipline them and never will. I always have to take a hand." She was as casually dressed, but as expensively, as her husband.

Afghan, Airedale, boxer bitch and Labrador, black mongrel, fox terrier, poodle, Alsatian and Old English sheep dog, and Pekingese, Yorkshire terrier and Jack Russell, stood, sat or lay in a more or less patient circle, with their handlers (it seemed the safest title) erect behind.

"I saw in the papers," said the Admiral (his manner was more formal today), "that you got the cause of death: Josie was strangled."

"With a piece of rope." Coffin nodded.

"Shorten your leads and walk your dogs clockwise round the room. Keep your dogs at heel," commanded Miss Champion, who never wasted time in preamble or greetings. She looked tired, and her own Alsatian, which she always brought with her, seemed more subservient than usual. Her class more or less obeyed, some with more good will than others. The Labrador performed well, and so did the Airedale: walking at heel was a specialty of his, executed with precision. "Stop. Let the lead drop and tell your dog to sit."

The Afghan sank gracefully on one side, hardly sitting, especially considering his size, but it was allowed to pass; the Labrador sat, the poodle sank onto her stomach and was hauled up by her neck; the fox terrier rose up and was pushed down again; while the boxer bitch stood unyielding and her owner, a nervous woman, said to Miss Champion that she'd just leave it this time. The Jack Russell did sit, but spoilt the picture by dragging her makeshift lead under her chin and chewing it in bright-eyed disarray.

"Do stop her," said Ann Tweedie irritably to her husband. "You've got no control over her at all."

Miss Champion moved across. "Raise your voice, Bob. It won't hurt to shout at her. Ann does."

"Thank you," said Ann. "If it *was* praise you were giving me; I couldn't be sure from your voice. And you could raise more than your voice, Bob. Slap her."

"Couldn't do that," murmured Bob.

"Oh, you're too gentle with her. I wouldn't be," and she turned away to stare at the wall.

"Saw about Josie Beaumont in the papers," murmured Miss Champion. She was looking at Bob and Ann; but perhaps the Admiral was included in what she said. "Funny, isn't it, after all these years? I've never forgotten her, have you? You couldn't say she brought us together, because I knew you and Ann before we all knew *her;* and after all, you married the boy next door, didn't you, Ann? But she was a link, wasn't she? The more so after she'd gone. For a bit, anyway. It's worn off now."

"It's a bad business," said Bob Tweedie. "She was a lovely girl."

"She'd be as old as we are now," said Ann, with a sigh. "Perhaps she was the lucky one."

"Oh, no, that's silly talk," said Miss Champion vigorously. "Life must be best, whatever it does to you. And it hasn't treated you so badly, Ann. I'd say you'd got what you wanted."

"More than you, you mean?" asked Ann Tweedie.

"Perhaps. But the dogs make up for a lot. They're better than humans, often. Not so intelligent, I don't say that, but less bloody trouble." Her listener raised an elegant shoulder in a shrug. "I suppose they'll never get to the bottom of what happened to Josie, now."

The Admiral's kind old face looked troubled. "Strange what a lot of us here knew Josie. Funny thing, that. She wasn't a dog lover, either. I don't believe really good people are: it's only the weak ones that need propping up by dogs. Still, there's quite a group of her old friends here tonight. That is odd."

"Think so?" said Coffin.

"I *did* think so," said the Admiral. "How long have

you had your Yorkie?" He cast a look at the animal. "Looks a young dog, but not a puppy."

"Just a matter of weeks," said Coffin.

"And that's another funny thing," said the Admiral. "By Jove, it is."

Coffin kept silent, but he smiled slightly.

"Someone killed Josie Beaumont: we know that now, we don't just fear and suspect it. And it must have been someone close to her, not a casual act of violence. Four of the people who were closest to her are in this room now. That's what you joined for, isn't it? Revenge."

"Knowledge," said Coffin. "I just want to know."

"After all these years, how can you ever know? For sure?"

Coffin was silent for a while. "I think so."

What remained of Josephine Beaumont sill lay on its slab, unburied, mostly bones and hair.

On another table, in another room, were the clothes she had worn and the rope which had been drawn round her neck. A technician pointed to the dusty blue jacket. "There were dog hairs on the jacket. I've kept some specimens for you in that box." He held out the box, in which were some short ginger and white hairs, carefully protected by a sheet of transparent plastic. "From a terrier of some sort."

"You can't name the breed?" It was said half jokingly.

"No, I doubt it. Does it matter?"

"Probably not." The policeman picked up the piece of rope. "And the rope? Anything to say here?"

"As you can see, I have opened it up and cut up a section." He pointed a pencil. "See the coloured strands twisted in: yellow. You can still see the colour, although the rope is quite discoloured."

"What's the rope made of?"

"The best-quality Manila."

The two men looked at each other, assessing the information.

Miss Champion called out, "Direct obedience training now, please. One after the other into the middle of the room and call up your dog. The rest of you: we'll have some silence, please."

While the Airedale was being summoned by the minute girl who controlled him with a word: "Bruce, here!" Miss Champion walked quietly round to Coffin. "While they're getting on with that, we can talk. I've recognized you now: you used to be a policeman. Perhaps you still are. It's been years."

"Don't dogs bring people together?"

Ella Champion was wary of irony. "They're better than humans, most days. Most days, most dogs, not saying always or all dogs—I've known some brutes. And you do get rogues. Same as with people. Funny thing: you can never tell by the looks."

"No," said Coffin. "But it shows up in the end, don't you think?"

"Oh, yes; circumstances bring it out," she said, with the confidence of one who knew of the shortness of dog generations. Afterwards she thought that Coffin hadn't meant quite what she meant. She turned towards the ring of faces and barked, "Foxy Wood: go and do your business in the yard and not in the reaching ring." The fox terrier lowered his leg self-consciously and moved towards the door; he looked like a villain from a Dickens novel, indescribably furtive. "Mrs. Wood, what were you thinking of? You ought to keep an eye on your animal and not stand there gossiping."

It was only too true: this week the class showed a tendency to stand in corners and talk. They had something to talk about in the finding of Josephine Beaumont. Mrs. Wood detached herself from a group and took her dog out, urging her friends not to go on with what they were talking about. "Wait till I get back; I want to tell you what I know about that house where they found the body. I remember the night it was bombed."

Miss Champion swore under her breath. To Coffin, she said, "I knew Josie Beaumont pretty well. She borrowed my scarf, just before she disappeared. She was a good person, just like the Admiral said. I heard him, and it was true. But after all, she had her faults. She liked men and she always had plenty around. She attracted them. And she was very romantic. I always think those two things together can be dangerous. There might have been jealousy. In fact, I know there was. In those days there were one or two men I thought she might marry. All happily married men now, I daresay, and have been for years, whereas Josie . . ." And she shrugged.

"Yes," said Coffin. "Well, that's what we want to rectify."

"What do you mean?"

"All that happiness so unfairly distributed," explained Coffin. "Even things up a little."

She looked at him uncertainly. "It's right what the Admiral said about you. Revenge is what you want. Were you in love with her yourself? What was Josie to you?"

"The pleasure principle," said Coffin.

"That sounds dirty talk," she said. "I don't like you any more."

The room seemed to have become very noisy. "Your class has broken up while we've been talking," pointed out Coffin.

It was true. The tight, neat circle had disintegrated. One or two heavy smokers had gratefully lit up (something Miss Champion abhorred). The children were sitting on the floor. With the exception of the Jack Russell, the dogs looked bored. Nancy Sykes was not bored, because she had discovered the attractions of Womble Coffin. Moonlight growled possessively.

"Right. Now, form two lines," yelled Miss Champion. But the effort was almost too much for her. She was no longer in control of the class. The dogs knew it at once. Always contemptuous of their owners, they had hitherto held Miss Champion in awe because of her loud voice and strong right arm. Now they sensed that she was losing her grip. Snaps, snarls and quiet growls began to be heard. Mrs. Wood, who had good reason to fear her sharp-toothed and malicious dog, moved nervously.

The Admiral looked at Coffin. "You are a devil, you know. It's you that's done this."

"No, it's not coming from me. They can sense fear, that's all. Twelve dogs, and they're passing judgment."

"Some jury," said the Admiral sceptically. "Look at them—very nearly at each other's throats."

"But juries often are," said Coffin. "That's fear, too."

Nancy Sykes screamed as Moonlight bit her. The Airedale stared at the boxer, awaiting the signal for battle, and the fox terrier at once turned to his neighbour, a quiet mongrel, and bit him. Leashes, collars and bits of old rope were seized and animals dragged apart.

"Why don't we do the obedience routine again?" suggested the Admiral peaceably (Moonlight had come out of her fight well). "And then you can hand out sweets. You know they love that."

"Right." Miss Champion clapped her hands. "Obedience tests, and choc drops for the lucky boys and girls."

Quietness descended again.

"Please keep your dog back," said Ann Tweedie frigidly to the Admiral. "She's bothering my dog again."

"Aggressive little bitch, isn't she?" said the Admiral fondly. "I'm afraid she's had a bit of your dog's leash. Got it in her mouth."

"So I see."

"I'll get it off her. Here, girl." Moonlight gave a hoarse growl. "I'll try later," said the Admiral, drawing back. "Bad girl."

"You don't like me and my husband. I'm well aware of that. So it's only natural your dog should pick it up."

"It's not true." His old face was indignant.

"Not good enough for your precious Josie."

"Hush, you stupid woman; they're all listening."

And it was quite true. A hush had fallen over the obedience tests and the subsequent handing out of chocolate drops, as if everyone was concentrating on something else.

There had been a happy custom, after the class dismissed, of lingering for coffee, brewed by Miss Champion with an old kettle, or beer. Usually only the hard core addicts remained (and there were addicts—one dog had been training for six years), but on this evening the whole class of twelve and handlers pushed into the little room.

"This is a good building," said Coffin. "I suppose they've been making rope here for centuries." He looked hopefully at the Admiral, knowing his enthusiasm.

He obliged at once. "I'm fond of the old Rope Walk. It's quiet now, but you should come here when it's at work. Dark and full of noise and movement. Marvellous. Like an illustration by Gustave Doré. I like to think Dickens went round looking at it when he was a lad. *Hard Times* and all that, you know. His father worked just across the road."

"The techniques of making rope have changed since Dickens's time," observed Bob Tweedie.

"Ah, you're right there. And the materials, too. Lots of synthetics now. As well as Manila and sisal. But you can't beat the natural materials," said the Admiral.

"Oddly enough, you're right," said Bob.

"And I suppose over the years some of the rope went missing from time to time?" Coffin looked at the Admiral.

"We did lose some. But there were checks. And then, we knew our own rope. There was a big scandal about rope disappearing in the twenties, and that brought things to a head, and the police told the dockyard to mark the rope. We built a special colour into the rope so that it could always be identified: the Rogue's Twist, we called it. Every dockyard had its own colour (and Devonport and Portsmouth made ropes then). Chatham was yellow."

"Was?" He was quick. "Not now?"

"Not after 1945," said the Admiral. "Devonport was bombed out in 1942. At the end of the war Portsmouth stopped making rope. So only Chatham was left."

"So you didn't need a yellow strand to distinguish a rope from Chatham from one from Portsmouth or Devonport?"

"Not after 1945," said the Admiral. "They started to mark Manila with a red strand and sisal with yellow, didn't they Bob? I'd retired by then."

"Yes," said Bob Tweedie.

"I suppose you use a lot of rope in your business?"

"Not more than you'd expect." He was cool.

"You had a bit to do with the Rope Walk when you served in the dockyard, Bob," said the Admiral.

"It came my way, yes. With a good many others. Even you, Ella."

Ella Champion smiled bleakly. "I made rope in the Rope Walk. It was my war work. Then I joined the Wrens. It was easier on the hands."

"Did Josephine work there then?"

"No, never. I only met her when we were together in the Wrens. She was officer material, so they said, but she wouldn't change."

"You were a close little group of friends in those days?"

Bob Tweedie tried to interrupt, but Ella wouldn't let him. "I believe you bought that dog of yours just to come to this class," she said fiercely to Coffin.

"Not bought. Womble's borrowed." Hearing his name, Womble bared his teeth. "Womble's a well-known character."

Ella Champion went very white. "I was never jealous of Josie. I would never have harmed her."

"But you thought she was going to be married?"

Ella was silent.

"Oh, yes. We have her body now and know what she was wearing. You saw her just before she went off because she borrowed your scarf: a blue suit, a new shirt and a borrowed scarf. 'Something old, something new, something borrowed and something blue.' "

Ella swallowed. "We all wore old things then."

"And your scarf?"

She met his eyes honestly. "All right, you can make

what you like of it. She joked herself about what she was wearing. 'Looks like I'm getting married, doesn't it?' "

"And you believed her?"

"Yes. *Then*. Not now. I've had years to think about it. She didn't mean she was getting married. She didn't intend to marry. I see that now. She was too keen on going off to Oxford and starting her career. 'Now the war's over, I'm free,' she said. 'I can start.' That's not the talk of a girl getting married."

"But you told someone then that she was going to get married?"

"I don't remember. I might have done. But whatever I said was wrong, wasn't it?" She stared at him, beseeching him to absolve her from any guilt she had incurred.

He didn't feel inclined to do so, but he left it there. "Josephine Beaumont was strangled and her body well hidden in a bombed building then undergoing repairs. She must have gone to that bombed building with someone. Perhaps someone who had lived there. That would be a good reason for a visit, wouldn't it? 'Let's have a look round and see what they've done,' someone could have said. You lived there once, didn't you, Bob?"

"As a lad," Bob said briefly. "I never went back to live once it was bombed."

"But your wife did?" Coffin looked at Ann Tweedie. "And you were courting her then?"

Bob was silent.

"Yes, you were, Bob," Ann said loudly. "We were going strong."

Coffin went on: "And there were ginger and white dog hairs found on Josephine Beaumont's jacket. She didn't have a dog herself, but she knew someone who had." He looked at the Jack Russell. "From a dog like that, I'd guess. You've always been a dog lover, haven't you? Your wife says so. And people tend to repeat their dogs. Like their mistakes."

"I did have a terrier then," muttered Bob. He shook

his head, as if shaking an idea out of it. "Josie was strangled, wasn't she?"

"Yes. And the rope had a yellow strand in it."

There were two doors to the room, and their little group was standing by one of them. The rest of the Circle, as if making a common decision, were filing out of the room like jurors who had reached a decision and were passing a verdict with their feet.

Coffin gathered up Womble's lead. Moonlight was lying at his feet. She had abandoned her trophy. Coffin bent down and patted her head.

There were only five of them left in the room now: the Admiral with Moonlight, Miss Champion, Bob and his wife, Ann, with Nancy Sykes, and Coffin with Womble.

The Admiral was looking sad, and his frequent jest that he was so old he could have served with Nelson no longer seemed such a joke. The others were the same. In recmerging into the world, Josie had taken away a little of the life left to those who had once been close to her. "Yellow, eh?" he said. "The old Rogue's Twist."

"That doesn't prove anything," said Ella Champion defiantly.

"You've still got a soft spot for Bob Tweedie, haven't you?" asked Coffin. "No, don't say anything, Bob. I think this rope does prove something. It's a new piece of rope. Or it was in 1947. I mean unused."

"Ah," said the Admiral. "And it had a yellow strand? And yellow in 1947 was used for sisal."

"But this isn't sisal, you see. I've seen it. It is the very best-quality Manila rope."

"I thought you'd say that," said the Admiral. "Inevitable, really. The same thought's been gathering momentum in my own mind since this started."

"You see what it means?"

"I see it," said Bob. "I see that in 1947 Josie was strangled with a piece of pre-1947 rope. And what was the motive?" He was very white.

"The motive was jealousy."

"I'm not a jealous man," said Bob slowly.

"No, but you were in love with her."

He nodded. "It was me she was coming to meet. I thought at first she'd let me down. Then I thought she'd gone off with someone else. Later on I knew that wasn't true, either. She was just gone. But I couldn't have hurt her."

Two of them now had disclaimed violence towards Josephine.

"No, you aren't a violent man. Not even with dogs." Coffin added, "Nor are you a stupid man."

Bob looked up sharply.

"You would never have used a piece of rope that could point so clearly to you. You know about rope. So does Ella Champion. So, God bless him, does the Admiral. But it could have been used by someone who had a piece of rope, a piece brought home by her father before his death. A person who did not understand about the Rogue's Twist." Coffin turned towards Ann Tweedie. "You," he said. "What about you?"

Bob said, "Ann was just a girl then."

"A girl to whom a bit of rope was just a bit of rope. A jealous girl who wanted you, a girl who is not afraid of violence."

"Oh, but that's rubbish," said Ann Tweedie.

"Is it?" Coffin held out the bit of rope that Moonlight had been chewing. Her efforts had opened it up. The yellow strand was clearly to be seen there. "Still just another bit of rope to you, but a piece of evidence to me. You must have had a lot of that rope in your household. I suppose a dockyard policeman was in as good a position as anyone to lay his hands on it."

"Don't say anything, Ann," said Bob, but he could not stop her.

"She won't say anything," said Ella Champion. "But I can say it for her. She hated Josie. She wanted Bob, and Josie just flicked her little finger and got him. And she didn't even want to marry him. He wasn't worth that to her. I can say all this because I felt the same."

Ann said coolly, "I don't think after thirty years you can prove a thing."

Coffin picked up Womble. "I don't know. One jury of a kind has reached a verdict this evening, hasn't it?"

Afterwards to the Admiral he said that he thought that Moonlight had been as good as judge, jury and prosecuting counsel all rolled into one.

"But of course, she only did what you wanted her to do," said the Admiral, who knew something about men and beasts.

Twenty-One Good
Men and True

DICK FRANCIS

Arnold Roper whistled breathily while he boiled his kettle and spooned instant own-brand economy-pack coffee into the old blue souvenir from Brixham. Unmelodic and without rhythm, the whistling was nonetheless an expression of content, both with things in general and with the immediate prospect ahead. Arnold Roper, as usual, was going to the races; and as usual, if he had a bet he would win. Neat, methodical, professional, he would operate his unbeatable system and grow richer, the one following the other as surely as chickens and eggs.

Arnold Roper at forty-five was one of nature's bachelors, a lean-bodied, handy man accustomed to looking after himself, a man who found the chatter of companionship a nuisance. Like a sailor, though he had never been to sea, he kept his surroundings polished and shipshape, ordering his life in plastic dustbin liners and reheated take-away food.

The one mild problem on Arnold Roper's horizon was his wealth. The getting of the money was his most intense enjoyment. The spending of it was something he postponed to a remote and dreamlike future, when he would exchange his sterile flat for a warm, unending idyll under tropical palms. It was the interim storage of the money which was currently causing him, if not positive worry, at least occasional frowns of doubt. He might, he thought, as he stirred dried milk grains into the brownish brew, have to find space for yet another wardrobe in his already crowded bedroom.

If anyone had told Arnold Roper he was a miser, he would have denied it indignantly. True, he lived frugally, but by habit rather than obsession; and he never took out his wealth just to look at it, and count, and gloat. He would not have admitted as miserliness the warm feeling that stole over him every night as he lay down to sleep, smiling from the knowledge that all around him, filling two oak-veneered bargain-sale bedroom suites, was a ton or two of negotiable paper.

It was not that Arnold Roper distrusted banks. He knew, too, that money won by betting could not be lost by tax. He would not have kept his growing gains physically around him were it not that his unbeatable system was also a splendid fraud.

The best frauds are only ever discovered by accident, and Arnold could not envisage any such accident happening to *him*.

Jamie Finland woke to his customary darkness and thought three disconnected thoughts with the first second of consciousness. The sun is shining. It is Wednesday. They are racing today here at Ascot.

He stretched out a hand and put his fingers delicately down on the top of his bedside tape recorder. There was a cassette lying there. Jamie smiled, slid the cassette into the recorder and switched on.

His mother's voice spoke to him. "Jamie, don't forget the man is coming to mend the television at ten-thirty and please put the washing into the machine, there's a dear, as I am so pushed this morning, and would you mind having yesterday's soup again for lunch. I've left it in a saucepan, ready. Don't lose all that ten quid this afternoon or I'll cut the plug off your stereo. Home soon after eight, love."

Jamie Finland's thirty-eight-year-old mother supported them both on her earnings as an agency nurse, and she had made a fair job, her son considered, of bringing up a child who could not see. He rose gracefully from bed and put on his clothes: blue shirt, blue jeans. "Blue is Jamie's favourite colour," his mother would say, and her friends would say, "Oh, yes?" politely and she could see them thinking, how could he possibly know? But Jamie could identify blue as surely as his mother's voice, and red, and yellow, and every colour in the spectrum, as long as it was daylight. "I can't see in the dark," he had said when he was six, and only his mother, from watching his sureness by day and his stumbling by night, had understood what he meant. Walking radar, she called him. Like many young blind people, he could sense the wavelength of light, and distinguish the infinitesimal changes of frequency reflected from coloured things close to him. Strangers thought him uncanny. Jamie believed everyone could see that way if they wanted to, and could not himself clearly understand what they meant by sight.

He made and ate some toast and thankfully opened the door to the television fixer. "In my room," he said, leading the way. "We've got sound but no picture." The television fixer looked at the blind eyes and shrugged. If the boy wanted a picture he was entitled to it, same as everyone else who paid their rental. "Have to take it back to the workshop," he said, judiciously pressing buttons.

"The races are on," Jamie said. "Can you fix it by then?"

"Races? Oh, yeah. Well . . . tell you what: I'll lend you another set. Got one in the van. . . ." He staggered off with the invalid and returned with the replacement. "Not short of radios, are you?" he said, looking around. "What do you want six for?"

"I leave them tuned to different things," Jamie said. "That one"—he pointed accurately—"listens to aircraft, that one to the police, those three are on ordinary radio stations, and this one, local broadcasts."

"What you need is a transmitter. Put you in touch with all the world."

"I'm working on it," Jamie said. "Starting today."

He closed the door after the man and wondered whether betting on a certainty was a crime.

Greg Simpson had no such qualms. He paid his way into the Ascot paddock, bought a race card, and ambled off to add a beer and sandwich to a comfortable paunch. Two years now, he thought, munching, since he had first set foot on the turf; two years since he had exchanged his principles for prosperity and been released from paralyzing depression. They seemed a distant memory now, those fifteen months in the wilderness, the awful humiliating collapse of his seemingly secure pensionable world. No comfort in knowing that mergers and cutbacks had thrown countless near-top managers like himself onto the redundancy heap. At fifty-two, with long success-strewn experience and genuine administrative skill, he had expected that he at least would find another suitable post easily; but door after door closed, and a regretful chorus of "Sorry, Greg," "Sorry, old chap," "Sorry, Mr. Simpson, we need someone younger," had finally thrust him into agonized despair. And it was just when, in spite of all their anxious economies, his wife had had to deny their two children even the money to go swimming that he had seen the curious advertisement:

Jobs offered to mature respectable persons who must have been unwillingly unemployed for at least twelve months.

Part of his mind told him he was being invited to commit a crime, but he had gone nonetheless to the subsequently arranged interview, in a London pub, and he had been relieved, after all, to meet the very ordinary man holding out salvation. A man like himself, middle-aged, middle-educated, wearing a suit and tie and indoor skin.

"Do you go to the races?" Arnold Roper asked. "Do you gamble? Do you follow the horses?"

"No," Greg Simpson said prudishly, seeing the job

prospect disappear but feeling all the same superior. "I'm afraid not."

"Do you bet on dogs? Go to Bingo? Do the pools? Play bridge? Feel attracted by roulette?"

Greg Simpson silently shook his head and prepared to leave.

"Good," said Arnold Roper cheerfully. "Gamblers are no good to me. Not for this job."

Greg Simpson relaxed into a glow of self-congratulation on his own virtue. "What job?" he said.

Arnold Roper wiped out Simpson's smirk. "Going to the races," he said bluntly. "Betting when I say bet, and never at any other time. You would have to go to race meetings most days, like any other job. You would be betting on certainties, and after every win I would expect you to send me twenty-five pounds. Anything you made above that would be yours. It is foolproof, and safe. If you go about it in a businesslike way, and don't get tempted into the mug's game of backing your own fancy, you'll do very well. Think it over. If you're interested, meet me here again tomorrow."

Betting on certainties . . . every one a winner. Arnold Roper had been as good as his word, and Greg Simpson's lifestyle had returned to normal. His qualms had evaporated once he learned that even if the fraud was discovered, he himself would not be involved. He did not know how his employer acquired his infallible information, and if he speculated, he didn't ask. He knew his employer only as John Smith, and had never met him since those first two days, but he heeded his warning that if he failed to attend the specified race meetings or failed to send his twenty-five payment, the bounty would stop dead.

Simpson finished his sandwich and went down to mingle with the bookmakers as the horses cantered to the post for the start of the first race.

From high in the stands, Arnold Roper looked down through powerful binoculars, spotting his men one by one. The perfect work force, he thought, smiling to himself; no absenteeism, no union troubles, no complaints.

There were twenty-one of them at present on his register, all contentedly receiving his information, all dutifully returning their moderate levies, and none of them knowing of the existence of the others. In an average week they would all bet for him twice; in an average week, after expenses, he added a thousand in readies to his bedroom.

In the five years since he had begun in a small way to put his scheme into operation, he had never picked a defaulter. The thinking-it-over time gave the timid and the honest an easy way out; and if Arnold himself had doubts, he simply failed to return on day two. The rest, added one by one to the fold, lived comfortably with quiet minds and prayed that their benefactor would never be rumbled.

Arnold himself couldn't see why he ever should be. He put down the binoculars and began in his methodical fashion to get on with his day's work. There was always a good deal to see to in the way of filling in forms, testing equipment and checking that the nearby telephone was working. Arnold never left anything to chance.

Down at the starting gate, sixteen two-year-olds bucked and skittered as they were led by the handlers into the stalls. Two-year-old colts, thought the starter resignedly, looking at his watch, could behave like a pack of prima donnas in a heatwave in Milan. If they didn't hurry with that chestnut at present squealing and backing away determinedly, he would let the other runners off without him. He was all too aware of the television cameras pointing his way, mercilessly awaiting his smallest error. Starters who got the races off minutes later were unpopular. Starters who got the races off early were asking for official reprimands and universal curses, because of the fiddles that had been worked in the past on premature departures.

The starter ruled the chestnut out of the race and pulled his lever at time plus three minutes twenty seconds, entering the figures meticulously in his records. The gates crashed open, the fifteen remaining colts roared out of the stalls, and along the stands the serried ranks of race glasses followed their progress over the five-furlong sprint.

Alone in his special box, the judge watched intently. A big pack of two-year-olds over five furlongs were often a problem, presenting occasionally even to his practised eyes a multiple dead heat. He had learned all the horses by name and all the colours by heart, a chore he shared every day with the race-reading commentators, and from long acquaintance he could recognize most of the jockeys by their riding style alone, but still the ignominy of making a mistake flitted uneasily through his dreams. He squeezed his eyeballs, and concentrated.

Up in his aerie, the television commentator looked through his high-magnification binoculars, which were mounted rock-steady like a telescope, and spoke unhurriedly into his microphone. "Among the early leaders are Breakaway and Middle Park, followed closely by Pickup, Jetset, Darling Boy and Gumshoe. . . . Coming to the furlong marker, the leaders are bunched, with Jetset, Darling Boy, Breakaway all showing. . . . One furlong out, there is nothing to choose between Darling Boy, Jetset, Gumshoe, Pickup. . . . In the last hundred yards . . . Jetset, Darling Boy . . ."

The colts stretched their necks, the jockeys swung their whips, the crowd rose on tiptoes and yelled in a roar which drowned the commentary, and in his box the Judge's eyes ached with effort. Darling Boy, Jetset, Gumshoe and Pickup swept past the winning post abreast, and an impersonal voice over the widespread loudspeakers announced calmly, "Photograph. Photograph."

Half a mile away in his own room, Jamie Finland listened to the race on television and tried to imagine the pictures on the screen. Racing was misty to him. He knew the shape of the horses from handling toys and riding a rocker, but their size and speed were mysterious; he had no conception at all of a broad sweep of railed racecourse, or of the size or appearance of trees.

As he grew older, Jamie was increasingly aware that he had drawn lucky in the material stakes, and he had become in his teens protective rather than rebellious, which touched his hard-pressed mother sometimes to tears. It was for her sake that he had welcomed the television fixer, knowing that, for her, sound without pictures was almost as bad as pictures without sound for himself. Despite a lot of trying, he could pick up little from the screen through his ultrasensitive fingertips. Electronically produced colours gave him none of the vibrations of natural light.

He sat hunched with tension at his table, the telephone beside his right hand and one of his radios at his left. There was no telling, he thought, whether the bizarre thing would happen again, but if it did, he would be ready.

"One furlong out, nothing to choose . . ." said the television commentator, his voice rising to excitement-inducing crescendo. "In the last hundred yrads, Jetset, Darling Boy, Pickup and Gumshoe . . . At the post, all in a line . . . Perhaps Pickup got there in the last stride, but we'll have to wait for the photograph. Meanwhile, let's see the closing stages of the race again. . . ."

The television went back on its tracks, and Jamie waited intently with his fingers over the quick, easy numbers of the push-button telephone.

On the racecourse, the crowds buzzed like agitated bees round the bookmakers, who were transacting deals as fast as they could. Photo finishes were always popular with serious gamblers, who bet with fervour on the outcome. Some punters really believed in the evidence of their own quick eyes: others found it a chance to hedge their main bet or even recoup a positive loss. A photo was the second chance, the life belt to the drowning, the temporary reprieve from torn-up tickets and anticlimax.

"Six to four on Pickup," shouted young Billy Hitchins hoarsely, from his prime bookmaking pitch in the front row facing the stands. "Six to four on Pickup." A rush of customers descending from the crowded steps enveloped him. "A tenner, Pickup—right, sir. Five on Gumshoe—right, sir. Twenty, Pickup—you're on, sir. Fifty? Yeah, if you like. Fifty at evens, Jetset—why not?" Billy Hitchins, in whose opinion Darling Boy had taken the race by a nostril, was happy to rake in the money.

Greg Simpson accepted Billy Hitchins's ticket for an even fifty on Jetset and hurried to repeat his bet with as many bookmakers as he could reach. There was never much time between the arrival of the knowledge and the announcement of the winner. Never much, but always enough. Two minutes at least. Sometimes as much as five. A determined punter could strike five or six bets in that time, given a thick skin and a ruthless use of elbows. Greg reckoned he could burrow to the front of the closest of throngs after all those years of rush-hour commuting on the Underground, and he managed, that day at Ascot, to lay out all the cash he had brought with him: all four hundred pounds of it, all at evens, all on Jetset.

Neither Billy Hitchins, nor any of his colleagues, felt the slightest twinge of suspicion. Sure, there was a lot of support for Jetset, but so there was for the three other horses, and in a multiple finish like this one a good deal of money always changed hands. Billy Hitchins welcomed it, because it gave him, too, a chance of making a second profit on the race.

Greg noticed one or two others scurrying with wads to Jetset, and wondered, not for the first time, if they, too, were working for Mr. Smith. He was sure he'd seen them often at other meetings, but he felt no inclination at all to accost one of them and ask. Safety lay in anonymity; for him, for them, and for John Smith.

In his box, the Judge pored earnestly over the black-and-white print, sorting out which nose belonged to Darling Boy and which to Pickup. He could discern the winner easily enough, and had murmured its number aloud as he wrote it on the pad beside him. The microphone linked to the public announcement system waited mutely at his elbow for him to make his decision on second and third places, a task seeming increasingly difficult. Number two or number eight. But which was which?

It was quiet in his box, the scurrying and shouting among the bookmakers' stands below hardly reaching him through the window glass.

At his shoulder a racecourse official waited patiently, his job only to make the actual announcement, once the decision was made. With a bright light and a magnifying glass, the Judge studied the noses. If he got them wrong, a thousand knowledgeable photo-readers would let him know it. He wondered if he should see about a new prescription for his glasses. Photographs never seemed so sharp in outline these days.

Greg Simpson thought regretfully that the judge was overdoing the delay. If he had known he would have so much time, he would have brought with him more than four hundred. Still, four hundred clear profit (less betting tax) was a fine afternoon's work; and he would send Mr. Smith his meagre twenty-five with a grateful heart. Greg Simpson smiled contentedly, and briefly, as if touching a lucky talisman, he fingered the tiny transistorized hearing aid he wore unobtrusively under hair and trilby behind his left ear.

Jamie Finland listened intently, head bent, his curling dark hair falling onto the radio with which he eavesdropped on aircraft. The faint hiss of the carrier wave reached him unchanged, but he waited with quickening pulse and a fluttering feeling of excitement. If it didn't happen, he thought briefly, it would be very boring indeed.

Although he was nerve-strainingly prepared, he almost missed it. The radio spoke one single word, distantly, faintly, without emphasis: "Eleven." The carrier wave hissed on, as if never disturbed, and it took Jamie's brain two whole seconds to light up with a laugh of joy.

He pressed the buttons and connected himself to the local bookmaking firm.

"Hullo? This is Jamie Finland. I have a ten-pound credit arranged with you for this afternoon. Well . . . please, will you put it all on the result of the photo finish of this race they've just run at Ascot? On number eleven, please."

"Eleven?" echoed a matter-of-fact voice at the other end. "Jetset?"

"That's right," Jamie said. "Eleven. Jetset."

"Right. Jamie Finland, even tenner on Jetset. Right?"

"Right," Jamie said. "I was watching it on the box."

"Don't we all, chum," said the voice in farewell, clicking off.

Jamie sat back in his chair with a tingling feeling of mischief. If eleven really had won, he was surely plain robbing the bookie. But who could know? How could anyone ever know? He wouldn't even tell his mother, because she would disapprove and might make him give the winnings back. He imagined her voice if she came home and found he had turned her ten pounds into twenty. He also imagined it if she found he had lost it all on the first race, betting on the result of a photo finish that he couldn't even see.

He hadn't told her that it was because of the numbers on the radio he had wanted to bet at all. He'd said that he knew people often bet from home while they were watching racing on television. He'd said it would give him a marvellous new interst, if he could do that while she was out at work. He had persuaded her without much trouble to lend him a stake and arrange things with the bookmakers, and he wouldn't have done it at all if the certainty factor had been missing.

When he'd first been given the radio which received aircraft frequencies, he had spent hours and days listening to the calls of the jetliners thundering overhead on their way in and out of Heathrow; but the fascination had worn off, and gradually he tuned in less and less. By accident one day, having twiddled the tuning knob aimlessly without finding an interesting channel, he forgot to switch the set off. In the afternoon, while he was listening to the Ascot televised races, the radio suddenly emitted one word. "Twenty-three."

Jamie switched the set off but took little real notice until the television commentator, announcing the result of the photo finish, spoke almost as if in echo. "Twenty-three . . . Swanlake, number twenty-three, is the winner."

How *odd*, Jamie thought. He left the tuning knob undisturbed, and switched the aircraft radio on again the following Saturday, along with Kempton Park races on television. There were two photo finishes, but no voice of God on the ether. Ditto nil results from Doncaster, Chepstow and Epsom persuaded him, shrugging, to put it down to coincidence, but with the rearrival of a meeting at Ascot, he decided to give it one more try.

"Five," said the radio quietly; and later, "Ten." And duly, numbers five and ten were given the verdict by the judge.

The judge, deciding he could put off the moment no longer, handed his written-down result to the waiting official, who leaned forward and drew the microphone to his mouth.

"First, number eleven," he said. "A dead heat for second place between number two and number eight. First, Jetset. Dead heat for second, Darling Boy and Pickup. The distance between first and second a short head. The fourth horse was number twelve."

The judge leaned back in his chair and wiped the sweat from his forehead. Another photo finish safely past . . . but there was no doubt they were testing to his nerves.

Arnold Roper picked up his binoculars, the better to see the winning punters collect from the bookmakers. His twenty-one trusty men had certainly had time today for a thorough killing. Greg Simpson, in particular, was sucking honey all along the line; but then Greg Simpson, with his outstanding managerial skills, was always, in Arnold's view, the one most likely to do best. Greg's success was as pleasing to Arnold as his own.

Billy Hitchins handed Greg his winnings without a second glance, and paid out, too, to five others whose transistor hearing aids were safely hidden by hair. He reckoned he had lost, altogether, on the photo betting, but his book for the race itself had been robustly healthy. Billy Hitchins, not displeased, switched his mind attentively to the next event.

Jamie Finland laughed aloud and banged his table with an ecstatic fist. Someone, somewhere, was talking through an open microphone, and if Jamie had had the luck to pick up the transmission, why shouldn't he? Why shouldn't he? He thought of the information as an accident, not a fraud, and he waited with uncomplicated pleasure for another bunch of horses to finish nose to nose. Betting on certainties, he decided, quietening his conscience, was not a crime if you come by the information innocently.

After the fourth race he telephoned to bet on number fifteen, increasing his winnings to thirty-five pounds.

Greg Simpson went home at the end of the afternoon with a personal storage problem almost as pressing as Arnold's. There was a limit, he discovered, to the amount of ready cash one could stow away in an ordinary suit, and he finally had to wrap the stuff in the *Sporting Life* and carry it home under his arm, like fish and chips. Two in one day, he thought warmly. A real clean-up. A day to remember. And there was always tomorrow, back here at Ascot, and Saturday at Sandown, and next week, according to the list which had arrived anonymously on the usual postcard, Newbury and Windsor. With a bit of luck, he could soon afford a new car, and Joan could book the skiing holiday with the children.

Billy Hitchins packed away his stand and equipment, and with the help of his clerk carried them the half mile along the road to his betting shop in Ascot High Street. Billy at eighteen had horrified his teachers by ducking university and apprenticing his bright mathematical brain to his local bookie. Billy at twenty-four had taken over the business, and now, three years later, was poised for expansion. He had had a good day on the whole, and after totting up the total, and locking the safe, he took his betting-shop manager along to the pub.

"Funny thing," said the manager over the second beer. "That new account, the one you fixed up yesterday, with that nurse."

"Oh, yes . . . the nurse. Gave me ten quid in advance. They don't often do that." He drank his Scotch and water.

"Yeah . . . Well, this Finland, while he was watching the telly, he phoned in two bets, both on the results of the photos, and he got it right both times."

"Can't have that," said Billy, with mock severity.

"He didn't place other bets, see? Unusual, that."

"What did you say his name was?"

"Jamie Finland."

The barmaid leaned towards them over the bar, her friendly face smiling and the pink sweater leaving little to the imagination. "Jamie Finland?" she said. "Ever such a nice boy, isn't he? Shame about him being blind."

"What?" said Billy.

The barmaid nodded. "Him and his mother, they live just down the road in those new flats, next door to my sister. He stays home most of the time, studying and listening to his radios. And you'd never believe it, but he can tell colours, he can really. My sister says it's really weird, but he told her she was wearing a green coat, and she was."

"I don't believe it," Billy said.

"It's true as God's my judge," said the barmaid, offended.

"No . . ." Billy said. "I don't believe that even if he can tell a green coat from a red, he could distinguish colours on a television screen with three or four horses crossing the line abreast. You can't do it often even if you can see." He sat and thought. "It could be a coincidence," he said. "On the other hand, I lost a lot today on those photos." He thought longer. "We all took a caning over those photos. I heard several of the other bookies complaining about the run on Jetset. . . ." He frowned. "I don't see how it could be rigged. . . ."

Billy put his glass down with a crash which startled the whole bar.

"Did you say Jamie Finland listens to radios? What radios?"

"How should I know?" said the barmaid, bridling.

"He lives near the course," Billy said, thinking feverishly. "So just suppose he somehow overheard the photo result before it was given on the loudspeakers. But that doesn't explain the delay . . . how there was time for him—and probably quite a lot of others who heard the same thing—to get their money on."

"I don't know what you're on about," said the barmaid.

"I think I'll pop along and see Jamie Finland," said Billy Hitchins. "And ask who or what he heard . . . if he heard anything at all."

"Bit far-fetched," said the manager judiciously. "The only person who could delay things long enough would be the judge."

"Oh, my God," said Billy, awe-struck. "What about that? What about the judge?"

Arnold Roper did not know about the long fuse being lit in the pub. To Arnold, Billy Hitchins was a name on a bookmaker's stand. He could not suppose that brainy Billy Hitchins would drink in a pub where the barmaid had a sister who lived next door to a blind boy who had picked up his discreet transmissions on a carelessly left on radio which, unlike most, was capable of receiving 110 to 140 megahertz on VHF.

Arnold Roper travelled serenely homewards with his walkie-talkie-type transmitter hiden as usual inside his inner jacket pocket, its short aerial retracted now, safely out of sight. The line-of-sight low-powered frequency he used was in his opinion completely safe, as only a passing aircraft was likely to receive it, and no pilot on earth would connect a simple number spoken on the air with the winner of the photo finish down at Ascot, or Epsom, or Newmarket, or York.

Back on the racecourse, Arnold had carefully packed away and securely locked up the extremely delicate and expensive apparatus which belonged to the firm that employed him. Arnold Roper was not the judge. Arnold Roper's job lay in operating the photo-finish camera. It was he who watched the print develop; he who could take his time delivering it to the judge; he who always knew the winner first.

Verdict of Three

MICHAEL GILBERT

On that Wednesday morning when the messenger from the Home Office arrived at my flat, I was reading the account, splashed across the front page of the *Daily Telegraph,* of my Uncle Alfred's suicide. It seemed that he had taken poison at his house in Chessington Street. His body had been found by his sister.

I can't say that his departure caused me any sorrow. The fact that he was my relation had been a source of embarrassment to me from my schooldays onwards. Laming was a man who delighted in taking the unpopular side in any public controversy and sometimes compounded his offence by being right. In 1939 he had declared himself a virulent supporter of Stalin and had been interned under Regulation 18B, until the arrival of the Russians in the war on our side had caused him to be released with apologies. After that he had enjoyed innumerable brushes with the authorities. The week before he killed himself, he had penned an open letter to the Home Secretary accusing him of systematic and malicious persecution. The details he gave sounded pretty convincing, too.

I signed a receipt for the buff-coloured envelope and waited until the messenger had taken himself off before I opened it. I had a premonition of what it would contain. It was a three-line communication. It required me to present myself at No. 5 Richmond Terrace at eleven o'clock that morning and it was signed by the secretary to the Cabinet Office.

It crystallized all my recent suspicions and apprehensions.

You cannot work in the inmost circles of government without sensing when something has gone wrong; particularly when that something may affect you.

I reasoned that it must be connected with the American note, because the American note was the most important piece of work which had ever been entrusted to me. It was only by chance that it had come my way at all.

The Prime Minister of that period had four private secretaries. (Nowadays he has six, but these are more spacious times.) We divided the work among us. The senior dealt with patronage and appointments; the next senior, Tom Rainey, with foreign affairs; the two newest, myself and Bill Anstruther, with home affairs. In the ordinary way, the drafting of a note from the Prime Minister to the British Ambassador in Washington, a note which was to form the basis of discussions between the Ambassador and the President of the United States, would have been Tom's job, had he not been whipped off to hospital at the last moment with an inflamed appendix.

So the lot had fallen on me. I had taken the lift down to Registry Filing, had signed for the three green folders which were to form the basis of the note, and had taken them up, in the lift, to my room on the second floor of the Cabinet Office building in Whitehall. I was by then no novice in the inner workings of government, but I must confess that those folders had opened my eyes.

They were verbatim accounts, taken down in the well-known handwriting of the Chief, of conversations earlier that year which he had held with the prime ministers of Canada, Australia and New Zealand, whose presence in London had been carefully, and successfully, concealed. In them the steps to be taken in certain circumstances had been set out with brutal clarity.

When top people talk directly to each other, they do so without any of the euphemisms and half-truths which soften their public utterances. (I recalled some of the unpublished and unpublishable comments made by Churchill to Roosevelt at critical moments during the war.) I could well imagine the effect if a single one of the unvarnished sentences from those folders had been allowed to get into the wrong hands.

If I had needed any further reminder of their importance, I received it when, leaving my office for a quick lunch, I caught a glimpse of Patrick Regan at the end of the corridor. I'm not sure if he saw me, but I knew what his presence there signified. Patrick is a month or two older than I. I first met him when we arrived at our prep school at Broadstairs on the same day. He preceded me to our public school by a single term. During the war I lost touch with him. I was a plodding infantryman. He was in a number of irregular and dashing outfits suited to his Irish temperament. After the war, as I knew, he had joined M15 and I didn't doubt that it was part of his job to patrol the corridors and ensure that no unauthorized eyes saw those three green folders.

Since it was a fine morning in late autumn and since there was plenty of time, I decided to walk from my flat, which is near Lord's, to Whitehall. Before I left, I packed a few things into a suitcase. When you went into No. 5 Richmond Terrace, it was not always certain that you would come out again. It has an underground exit which leads straight to Cannon Row police station.

As I walked down Baker Street and through the maze of little lanes behind Oxford Street, I was being followed by a memory.

The schoolhouse fag was a cheerful shrimp of my own age called Edgecumb. Curious that I could remember his name and face when so many, more important, have been rubbed out by the passage of time.

"Ashford wants you in his study," he said. "I shouldn't hang about. He's in a frightful bait about something."

I sped along those stone-paved passages until I reached and knocked on the door of the large study at the end. Even now I sometimes see that door in my dreams.

A hoarse roar told me to come in.

A table had been pulled out from the wall and my three judges sat behind it. It was a hanging court. Ashford, in the middle, was head of house. Captain of rugger, red in hair and temper. On his right was a tall boy, called Major, a cross-country runner and one of the school racquets pair. The third was something of an unknown quantity, a boy called Collins, who wore pebble glasses and was reputed to have a brain. He might, I felt, be inclined to take a more tolerant view of whatever crime it was I was supposed to have committed, but I hardly saw him standing up to the other two.

"I've been hearing stories about you," said Ashford. "You seem to think you can get away with anything. You may have been a big bug at your prep school, but in this place you're a worm."

To this evident truth no comment seemed possible and I made none.

"You were reported last week for cheek to head of the prep room."

The head of the prep room, a fat boy called Clover, had slipped on a cake of soap in the bathroom and fallen on his backside. I had been rash enough to laugh.

Result, six with a gym shoe.

"I ought to have dealt with you myself that time. Then you might have thought twice about . . . this."

Ashford slapped down on the table in front of me a piece of paper on which was printed, in block capitals, the words: CLOVER IS A SHIT.

"But," I said, "I know nothing about that. Me? I never saw it before."

"Then how is it that Blackie saw you at nine o'clock last night putting something up on the house notice board?"

"I should watch where you're going, sir," said the policeman. "If you step off the curb like that, without looking first, you'll be in trouble."

"Sorry, officer," I said. "I was thinking about something else."

"Lucky he had good brakes. . . ."

Collins said, in his dreamy voice, "Blackie didn't actually say that. He said he saw him in front of the notice board."

Blackie was the youth who cleaned our boots.

Ashford glared at Collins and then swung round on me again. "And anyway, what were you doing out of your dormitory at nine o'clock? You know the house rules."

"Barnes, the head of the dormitory, sent me down to get something for him. It was only just nine o'clock. He said if I hurried I'd be back in time. The clock was striking as I went down the stairs."

Major said, reluctantly, "I did have a word with Barnes. He confirmed that bit."

"All right," said Ashford. "Barnes confirms that you went down and Blackie confirms that you were hanging about in front of the notice board. What were you doing?"

"I did stop for a moment. I wanted to see if I was in the under-fifteen game."

"I think you're a liar. You had it in for Clover and you thought you'd get your own back in this—in this disgusting way."

"Isn't that man Laming your uncle?" said Major. "The man who wrote that letter to *The Times*? He sounds a Bolshy sort of sod."

I admitted that Sir Alfred Laming was my uncle. I had read the letter, too. It was the one in which he said that Baldwin ought to be impeached for neglecting our air defences. A view which found quite a few supporters six years later.

"All right," said Ashford. This seemed to conclude the case for the prosecution. All that remained was to pass sentence. Major nodded. Collins had taken off his glasses and was polishing them gently.

He said, "By the way, when you looked at the notice board, was this paper on it?"

Imminent danger must have tuned up my mental processes to concert pitch, because I saw all the implications of that question as soon as it was asked. If I said "Yes," then why hadn't I reported it to someone in authority? If I said "No," then since all other junior boys were safe in their dormitories by nine, if left me as the last and most likely culprit.

In desperation, I decided to tell the truth.

I said, "I'm sorry, Collins, but I simply can't remember. All I was looking at was the games list."

There was a moment of grim silence. Collins seemed to have lost interest. Ashford said, "You can wait outside."

In the corridor I found Patrick. His Irish blood made him a volatile boy, easily roused to extremes of passion and sentiment. He grabbed me by the arm and said, "Are they going to beat you?"

I croaked out, "I don't know." We were both close to the door and had to talk in whispers.

"If they try to do it, you've got to appeal to old Flathers."

Flathers was Mr. Flatstone, our housemaster.

"I can't do that," I said, aghast.

"You must. It'd be totally unfair. They haven't got a scrap of proof it was you."

"Hold it," I said.

I was listening unashamedly at the door. What I was afraid I was going to hear was the scrape of two chairs being put together, back to back. It would be my lot to kneel on one and put my head down on the seat of the other.

Instead, I heard Ashford's voice. He said, "I don't quite see the point of it."

"It was a test question," said Collins. "The easiest thing would have been for him to have said that it *was* there and he saw it."

Major said, and there was unexpected deference in

his voice, "I still don't see. How do you know he didn't see it?"

"He can't have done," said Collins. "I took it down myself, at five to nine."

"Then why on earth," said Ashford, "didn't you say so before?"

"I was interested to see if he was going to tell a lie," said Collins. He sounded amused. "He jolly nearly did, too. But people usually tell the truth under pressure."

"I think it's all right," I said to Patrick.

The commissionaire at No. 5 greeted me with such a sombre look that I felt that he, at all events, had already found me guilty. He escorted me up in the lift and led me along to the room at the end of the corridor. I felt his hand metaphorically on my collar.

He knocked at the door and held it open. There were two men in the room. One was Lord Cherryl, the man who had headed the inquiry into the Security Services. The other was Mr. Justice Rackham; a most appropriate name, as more than one journalist had pointed out, since he seemed to conduct his cases in a manner reminiscent of the Star Chamber.

Lord Cherryl said, "Please sit down. You must understand that this is an unofficial and preliminary inquiry. We have been asked by the Home Secretary to put some questions to you. No record will be kept of what is said. Nevertheless, although it is unofficial and off the record, you have the right to be represented by a lawyer of your own choosing, if you wish."

"I think I'd better find out what it is I'm being accused of first," I said. "That is, if I am being accused of something."

"It's your decision," said Lord Cherryl. There was a long moment of silence. I didn't say anything. Lord Cherryl turned to the papers in front of him.

"I'd like to clear up one or two preliminary matters first. When you left school in 1937 you went to Oxford, with an open scholarship at Balliol. You were there for two years and left in 1939, without taking a degree, to join the Royal West Kent Regiment."

I nodded.

"Whilst you were at Oxford you were a member of a club called the Barricade Club. A club which professed extreme left-wing views."

"They didn't only profess them," I said. "A number of our members fought in the Spanish Civil War. On the popular side."

"But since you joined the armed forces with such commendable promptitude in 1939—at a time when Soviet Russia was our official enemy—it would seem that your feelings had altered."

"One tends to be volatile at the age of twenty."

"Of course. You fought throughout the war as an infantry soldier, attained the rank of major, were wounded in the North African fighting and were mentioned in dispatches."

I had no quarrel with that.

"After the war you were called to the bar, Gray's Inn, and joined Maurice Pastor's chambers."

"As a pupil," I said. "I never actually achieved a tenancy."

Mr. Justice Rackham said, "That was the Maurice Pastor who was disbarred for sedition in 1950."

I nearly said, "You know bloody well it was. You were chairman of the Bar Council at the time and chiefly responsible for getting him chucked out." However, I still had myself in hand and simply said, "Yes."

"You gave up the bar in 1950 and joined the Home Office under the special arrangements then in force for ex-servicemen. You were given accelerated promotion through the principal grade and in 1952 were an assistant secretary in the Department of Establishment and Organization."

"Officially, I still am," I said. "My next step was a posting, not a promotion."

"I was coming to that," said Lord Cherryl smoothly. "Two years ago you were offered, and accepted, the post of private secretary to the Prime Minister."

"Did it ever occur to you to wonder," said Mr. Justice Rackham in his gravelly voice, "why you were selected for such a position?"

"Frequently," I said. "The only solution which occurred to me was that the P.M. himself had fought as an infantry soldier through the First World War."

This was an unkind sideswipe at Rackham, who was quite young enough to have served in 1939, but had preferred his career at the bar. I wasn't feeling kind. I thought this dissection of my early life impertinent and wished they would come to the point.

Lord Cherryl did so, with unexpected suddenness. He said, "Your duties would not normally have covered foreign affairs. It was only owing to the chance indisposition of Mr. Rainey, I believe, that you were charged with drafting a note for the P.M. to Sir Neville Stokes in Washington."

Here it came.

"That's correct," I said.

"And in order to draft this note you were given access to three folders of documents of the highest security classification."

"I had them in my room for one complete working day," I said.

"And were they ever out of your sight?"

"Only when I went down to lunch in the canteen. When I locked them in my filing cabinet. I also locked the door of my room."

"Then you will no doubt be surprised," said Mr. Justice Rackham, "when you learn that photocopies of the documents in all three folders were in the possession of your uncle, Sir Alfred Laming, twenty-four hours later."

"But—" I said.

"Just to keep the record straight," said a third voice, "Sir Alfred isn't actually your uncle, is he?"

He had come into the room so quietly and I had been so intent on what was being said that he might have been there for some moments without my noticing him.

I had seen him on one occasion only since I left

school, but I recognized him at once. The same pebble glasses, the same downward-turning mouth. Time had taken away some of his hair and had put a stamp of authority on his face, but he had the same stooped shoulders and unathletic figure.

"I called him my uncle," I said. "He was really only my mother's cousin."

Lord Cherryl did not seem too happy about this interruption, but was clearly in no position to resent it. Collins pulled up a chair and added himself to the tribunal. He had a folder of papers, which he put down on the table as carefully as if they had been new-laid eggs. He said, "Please don't recap for me. I'm fully in the picture."

"Then," said Lord Cherryl, "perhaps you would deal with Mr. Justice Rackham's question."

The interruption had given me time to get some part of my wits back.

"If I remember it correctly," I said, "he asked me if I was surprised to know that copies of these documents had found their way into the hands of my uncle. It would be an understatement. I am not surprised. I am flabbergasted."

"You can offer no explanation?"

"Before I say anything more, I should like to know exactly what happened to my uncle."

Lord Cherryl looked at Collins, who gave a very slight nod. I knew then that he was really conducting the interview.

"Home Security have had Sir Alfred under observation for some time. Yesterday morning he made an arrangement, on the telephone, to meet a man, in the afternoon, in Kensington Gardens."

"What man?"

Lord Cherryl didn't like being interrupted and he didn't like being asked questions, but after another glance at Collins he condescended to deal with this one. He said, "He is—or was, until that moment—the Third Secretary, for Economic Planning, at the Russian Embassy. As a result of what happened, his credentials have been withdrawn."

Collins said, with a very slight smile, "He returned to Moscow, by air, yesterday evening. I don't imagine we shall see him again. I beg your pardon, Lord Cherryl; I interrupted you."

"As I was saying, Sir Alfred kept this rendezvous. He was in the act of handing over a packet when he was apprehended and taken into custody. He must have been prepared for such a contingency. He swallowed a cyanide capsule when he was in the car on the way to the police station."

"The report in the papers said that he died at home."

"We agreed on this minor variation with his sister. There seemed no point in distressing the family further by announcing that he was under arrest at the time of his death."

I was conscious, suddenly, of a very cold feeling.

The world, at that time, was balanced between a war which had just finished and a new war which might break out at any moment. Those particular documents would be embarrassing if they were published even now. At that time they could have been deadly. The prompt action of the Security Service had prevented the papers from getting into the wrong hands. But they would argue that Sir Alfred had read them and could probably reproduce them. *Was that why he was dead?* He had never seemed to me to be the sort of man who would commit suicide. He had far too great a sense of his own importance.

I had no illusions about M15. Their motto was *Salus Populi Suprema Lex*. A single life was unimportant where the safety of the state was in the balance. And if they convinced themselves that I was the only other outsider who had read those papers . . .

I became aware that Lord Cherryl had been speaking for some moments and the silence suggested that he had asked me a question and was waiting for an answer.

I said, "I'm sorry. Would you mind repeating that?"

"You must agree that the timing is significant. You

had the papers under your control all day on Monday. When you had finished with them by six o'clock, you returned them to Registry Filing. Their records show that these papers have not been removed by anyone else since. Yet on the following morning we find copies in the possession of your uncle."

There was nothing to say but "No comment." I guessed this would be thought flippant and said nothing.

Mr. Justice Rackham now took a hand. He said, in his Star Chamber voice, "Surely you can see the strength of the case against you?"

Again I said nothing.

"Unless you are going to suggest that there is some leakage in Registry Filing."

I knew better than to suggest that. The two middle-aged ladies who controlled our security filing system were of the utmost respectability. One was the daughter of an admiral and the other was the sister of an air vice-marshal. The only crime one could conceive either of them committing was assaulting someone they found being unkind to an animal.

"And in any event," said Lord Cherryl, "since neither of the officials concerned had, as far as we know, any connection with Sir Alfred Laming, even if, inconceivably, one of them had extracted these papers, they would have had no reason to hand them to him."

"Well?" said Mr. Justice Rackham.

At that point, regrettably, I lost my temper. I said, "It's no good saying 'Well,' as if I was an obstinate juryman. This tribunal may be unofficial, but I imagine it's meant to observe some of the elementary rules of law and procedure. All you're saying is that I could have taken these papers and no one else *as far as you know* could have done so. Therefore I've got to prove that I'm innocent. You ought to know better than that. You've got to prove me guilty."

Lord Cherryl started to say, "Where a strong presumption—" but Collins cut him off with a tiny movement of his hand.

Collins said, "The case against you isn't quite as watertight as you seem to be assuming. After all, there was a full hour when you were at lunch."

I rounded on him in turn.

"There's no need to try and lead me into that trap. I know perfectly well that you had one of your watchdogs in the corridor during the whole time I was away."

"You mean . . . ?"

"I mean Patrick Regan. I happen to know him. We were at school together. And I knew he was a member of your outfit."

"Yes," said Collins, with another of his ten-percent smiles. "I remember you both, very well indeed."

It was difficult to explain quite how it happened, but from that moment the feeling of the meeting altered. The atmosphere lightened. The few remaining questions which Lord Cherryl put were couched in a much more friendly tone. Mr. Justice Rackham seemed subdued.

When I was shown out, even the commissionaire seemed to have caught the prevailing spirit. He positively smiled at me as he let me out. I walked down Whitehall gulping great lungfuls of air and wondering what to do next.

Perhaps I was being subjected to the traditional hard-soft-hard treatment. Was the next thing a hand on my shoulder? Was I being kept under observation?

I suddenly felt that I didn't care.

I had a good lunch at my club and then went for a walk. If I was being followed, I would give my followers some exercise.

I started from central London, walked up to Hampstead, made a complete circle of the heath and came back down Fitzjohn's Avenue in the dusk. There were bonfires in the gardens and the smell of burning leaves filled the misty autumn air.

I was surprised to see a light on in my flat and had a word with the porter.

"The gentleman arrived half an hour ago. He said you were expecting him and I took the liberty of letting him in. I hope I did right, sir."

"Quite right, Stokes."

I had guessed it would be Collins before I found him sitting primly on the edge of one of my armchairs.

"Do you know," he said, "there were moments this morning which took me back twenty years."

He sounded entirely friendly.

"Me, too," I said with feeling. "Would you mind telling me what it was all in aid of? And would you care for a drink?"

I poured a drink out for both of us. Collins watched me in silence. Then he said, "Regan was arrested this afternoon."

I put my own drink down carefully on the table.

"We've had our doubts about him for some time. What we wanted was one clear piece of proof that he was lying. He'd committed himself, beyond the point from which he could retract, to a statement that he had not been inside the Cabinet Office on that day, or any other day. We still don't know how he got in, without passing the security guard, or how he got out again. It's possible that he used the kitchen entrance and took a chance on not being spotted."

"He got into my room and opened my filing cabinet and photographed the papers? Whilst I was at lunch?"

"I don't suppose the locks gave him much trouble. We teach our people these tricks."

"And didn't realize that I'd seen him?"

"Even if he'd suspected it, he'd have taken a chance on it, I think. You assumed he was there on duty. You wouldn't necessarily have said anything about it. You very nearly didn't, either."

"That's right," I said. "I very nearly didn't."

"I'd concluded that he must have been there and that you might have seen him. I thought that if we went about it the right way, you'd probably blurt it out. You were in such a bad temper by the time you got round to it that it convinced us all."

People usually tell the truth under pressure, said a voice from the past.

When Collins was putting his coat on in the hall, he said, "Incidentally, did it never occur to you that it was Regan who put that notice up on the board? That was why he was so worried about you getting beaten for it. In those days he had a conscience, I suppose."

Cloud Nine

CHRISTIANNA BRAND

During the latter half of the nineteenth century, three attractive ladies suffered—by no means inconsolable— bereavement. In 1857 Miss Madeleine Smith of Glasgow, aged twenty-one, was deprived of the further attentions of her blackmailing lover, allegedly by means of a cup of cocoa laced with arsenic, passed to him from her bedroom window. In 1886 Adelaide Bartlett, aged thirty-one, of Pimlico, London, was widowed thanks to a large dose of chloroform, internally administered, she being at the time sentimentally entangled with a young Wesleyan minister. And in 1889, in Liverpool, Florence Maybrick, from Alabama, aged twenty-six, lost her husband through arsenical poisoning, to which aphrodisiac drug, however, he had long been addicted. The two other ladies went free, but poor Florence, confessedly involved in an extramarital love affair, served fifteen years of a commuted life sentence.

" . . . and on your way, child, flip across to Cloud Number Nine and tell those ladies to break it up and get on with some harping. Honestly, Gabriel, Heaven's no place for eternally—well—harping on murder."

" 'Did I ever tell you about *my* operation?' But seriously, Peter, I never could think why you let that lot in so easily."

"It's this wretched computer. It came up with 'Angel,' but when he arrived he turned out to be that shocking little blackmailer L'Angelier. So if *he* was in, I could hardly keep out La Belle Madeleine—and with Maybrick and Bartlett already in and on Cloud Nine. Mind you, she's been waiting a bit, you know. Eighteen fifty-seven, that L'Angelier affair, and she's only just got here."

On Cloud Nine, the two ladies in residence welcomed the newcomer with modified rapture. "Arsenic for the boyfriend in a cup of cocoa," hissed Adelaide, aside. "You remember? Years before our time, of course: thirty years, at least." She held out a gracious hand and her accent, as in moments of extra refinement it always did, reverted more strongly to her native French. "Mees Madeleine Smeeth? Me, I am Adelaide Bartlett. Permit me, I present Mrs. Maybreek."

"Just call me Florence. I was raised in Alabama and in my country we don't stand on ceremony."

"So I found. You know that I went to America—"

"Dear Madeleine set up a little business there, Florence. So enterprising! Selling coffee and . . . hot chocolate."

"Well, what's so amusing? Even if I had. I passed him an innocent cup; of course there was no arsenic in it."

"From your bedroom window, *ma chère,* a young, unmarried lady. That was not so *comme il faut!*"

"And that's why I got a Not Proven verdict instead of a clean acquittal. That and some letters."

"What is this Not Proven?"

"It means when they know you did it, honey, but they think you didn't. Peculiar to Scotland. And typical," said Mrs. Maybrick loftily, "of the British."

"What was typical all round was that all they really tried me on was my morals. You, Florence—you should understand that."

"None better. My husband was no good in bed; he was treating himself with huge doses of arsenic as an aphrodisiac. And just because I soak a few flypapers and use the solution for my complexion—"

"Just what I used mine for," said Madeleine. "Only I bought it in powder form, 'for rats.' "

"—they condemn me to death for murder. But they really condemned me for having a lover."

"If your husband was as dud as all that," said Madeleine sympathetically, "what else were you to do?"

Mrs. Bartlett's maiden name had been Adelaide Blanche de Tremoille and it took some living up to. She now remarked piously that even with her own husband, there had been none of that sort of thing, none at all; yet they didn't find *her* resorting to vulgar infidelities. . . .

"Oh, come off it, Adelaide! You were canoodling all day long with that Reverend Dyson, pretending to take geography lessons—"

" 'Oh, my Americans, my new-found land,' " murmured Madeleine, looking down her beautiful nose.

"And not so new-found after all. Her husband's pockets were stuffed full of contraceptives when he died. Besides, Adelaide, you even started a baby."

"One act took place, Florence, so that I might have this child. One act, one time. As for Mr. Dyson, that was nothing, no impropriety at all."

"Then why dose your poor old man with chloroform? Tipped it down his throat, Madeleine, when he was lying ill and helpless. Not very nice, was it?"

"I did no such thing. Nobody could do it. It was not possible; all the doctors said so—his throat would be burned, he would make the big outcry, but he did not and there was no sign of burning. After all," said Adelaide, none too lovingly, "I was found Not Guilty, which is more than either of you can say."

" 'Now that Mrs. Bartlett has been acquitted,' " quoted Florence, " 'it seems only fair that, in the interests of science, she should tell us how she did it.' "

"I do nothing, but nothing!"

"You sent your precious Dyson running around for chloroform, buying it up secretly a bit at a time in little bottles."

"*I* did not say to buy it secretly. I wanted it for . . ."

Adelaide's charming face lit up with a delicate blush. "Poor Edwin, he was not then so . . . attractive, you understand. The teeth very bad, gums spongy and sloughing; breath not very nice—"

"And crawling with lumbricoid worms, poor chap," said Madeleine. "What is a lumbricoid worm?"

"I'm happy to say I never heard of such a thing," said Florence. "Not at all what Adelaide herself would call *comme il faut*."

"Very well. So naturally I did not care to—"

"But you say that you never did, anyway."

"I might kiss my husband good night," said Adelaide resentfully, "without all that you ladies found so . . . necessary that you must run about taking your lovers. But even to kiss was not very agreeable. So I would put on a cloth a little drop of chloroform and wave it under his nose and he would go off to sleep. I did not put any down his throat," she insisted. "Such a thing was not possible. Besides, why should I? Very soon he would die, he said so himself; and then, if I wished, I could marry with Mr. Dyson."

"What, run off with a reverend the minute your husband turned up his toes? In the eighties! If it had been nowadays—"

"Ah, if it had been nowadays . . . What would have happened to us three if it had all happened nowadays? For my part, I'd never have got beyond the Procurator Fiscal."

"What is this Procurator Fiscal?"

"More of Madeleine's Scotch peculiarities. He conducts the first examination of the accused." Florence leaned back against a fold in the cloud, crossed her legs with an air of importance and, ever a good mimic, assumed a strong Glaswegian accent. "Y'r name is Madeleine Smith and ye live in Blythswood Square?"

"Great!" said Madeleine. "You've got him to the life. But—as it would have been nowadays?"

"Yes, yes, a hundred years afterwards. So—come along wi' ye! Y'r name is Madeleine Smith and ye live in Blythswood Square?"

"Yes, of course," said Madeleine pertly. "You know perfectly well I do."

"And y'r faither's verra well tae dae and respeckit a' through the community?"

"He's a rich old square, if that's what you mean."

"Ay, well. And the daid mon, Emile L'Angelier—how cam ye to meet wi' *him?*"

"Picked him up on the street. We just fancied one another on sight."

"Did the wee mannie not in fact rather fancy the family moneybags?"

"Yes, he did—the snake; and when I took up with someone else, tried on a bit of blackmail, saying he'd show my letters to my pa."

"And were the letters no' what ye might call a wee bittie hot stuff?"

"They were what *you* might call a wee bittie hot stuff; and my pa certainly would. But so what? He'd have stamped about and said he didn't know what young people were coming to, but what more could he do?"

"Tairn ye oot the hoose mebbe—"

"So what? I'd just have shacked up with the latest and got myself a job."

"—and cut ye oot his will?"

"A voice of awe as to that, Florence," suggested Madeleine, coming back for a moment to Cloud Nine. "No Scotsman would speak so calmly of being done out of dough."

Florence obliged with an extremity of dismay. Madeleine climbed back metaphorically into sweater and jeans, elaborately shrugging. "What would I care? There's always lovely social security, and by the time the old boy died, we'd probably be making a bomb out of lopsided pots or home-blown glass or something. I'd just have told him what to do with his precious will, and thankfully hopped it. You don't know what it was like in that dump in Blythswood Square. They weren't *hu-man.*"

"No need at a', then, tae have resorrted to murrrrder?"

"No, of course not. Emile came round that evening and started a scene, I told him not to be stupid and passed him a hot drink out of the window—it was freezing outside, but I wasn't going to let him in and have even more fuss—and sent him packing. So off he trotted and I suppose went back home and took an overdose. He was always threatening to; he was madly neurotic and this time he just went too far, the silly gumph." Madeleine resigned jeans and sweater altogether and returned to white nightie and wings, lounging back, relaxed and complacent, against a resilient balloon of cloud. " 'Not Proven,' indeed! The whole thing was ridiculous. There was nothing against me, no actual proof, in fact, that he'd ever even been to the house, let alone that I'd put anything into any drink. I was tried on the letters and these days they'd never even have got me into court. Would they? Well, I mean— you two, be my jury: *would* they?"

"Not nowadays, Madeliene; no, of course not."

"All right," said Madeleine. "Good. The verdict of you both—Not Guilty."

"But a hundred years ago . . ."

"I was tried on my letters," repeated Madeleine, "and even then it was Not Proven. These days they'd never have got off the ground."

"Ah, Madeleine, very well for you, *ma chère,* but with me they would get off the ground, even nowadays; they would have me in their court."

"Well, then—defend yourself. I've defended *my*self. You do ditto!"

"I could not then speak in my defence. The accused could not go into the witness box."

"The same applied to all three of us. Counsel had to do it for us. So be your own counsel. My Lord, members of the jury—the speech for the defence!"

Adelaide considered it doubtfully. She agreed at last. "Well—I try," and stood up, rather rocking the cloud as she did so, grasping with two small plump hands at the edges of her paradisal robe. The French intonation sat somewhat comically upon an assumption of courtroom pomposities, but she ploughed manfully on. "Members of the jury, my client, Mrs. Adelaide Bartlett, as you have heard, lived with her middle-aged husband, Edwin, in Pimlico, London. This Edwin was one who has many strange ideas," said counsel, rolling his *r*'s a little in his intensity. "He believes that a man should have two wives. One is for use, he says, and one for companionship. And I—I mean my client—she is the one for use. Therefore"—the large brown eyes looked down with some reproach upon her listeners—"therefore if when he dies contraceptives are found in his pockets, does not this suggest the existence of this 'second wife'? A man does not keep in the pockets of his outdoor suits something which he uses at home."

"Good point," acknowledged Madeleine, nodding to her fellow juror.

"So, members of the jury, there is in his life another woman; and if this poor wife is to be deprived of her husband's affections, must we be surprised if she forms elsewhere an . . . attachment? A sentimental attachment, not more," insisted counsel firmly, "the gentleman being a clergyman and very rrrespectable. And the husband, he is absolutely approving. He says if he shall die, then the wife should be marrying with George Dyson. You have heard this in court; it was quite understood between them, all three."

"Good one again," agreed Florence. "O.K., honey, you're doing fine. Carry on!"

"But if he died or not—is it not true that if she wished to marry with George, she was free enough to do so? Her husband has not been to her so much of a husband, he has his 'second wife.' He was ill, yes, but she need not too much worry; he has an old father, very devoted, always coming to take care of him if she is there or not—she need have no bad conscience for leaving him. Mr. Dyson is not rich, but she had brought to her marriage a very handsome *dot* and in these days—we speak now of these days—a wife's money re-

mains her own. So what motive could she have to risk
murdering a man who anyway probably soon would
die? Even if she could have administered the chloroform," said Adelaide, letting go her clutch on the edges
of her legal gown, "which I say again I could not."

"Nowadays they'd probably know how it could have
been done."

"No one has ever so far demonstrated it," said Florence reasonably.

"And anyway, it was *not* done. I had no reason to do
it."

"You did want to marry this man of God—"

"Hey, Madeleine, watch it!" said Florence. "Remember where you are. The very clouds have ears."

"Oh, Lord!—I mean, oh, dear!" said Madeleine,
looking uneasily about her. "But still—what's so dreadful? So he was—a man of God."

"He was a crrrraven little rrrrat," said Adelaide, rolling the *r*'s like a drumbeat. "The minute there is
trrrrouble, off he goes and leaves me holding the baby."

"*Now* she tells us!"

"Madeleine, you are not nice. You are unkind and
silly. I wish now I had not given you the Not Guilty."

"You couldn't help yourself."

"Not as things are now. But then—"

"Even then, without those stupid letters . . . In
fact, the new boyfriend wasn't a boyfriend at all; it was
a 'suitable match.' I could still just have run off with
Emile and in the end my pa would have arranged for us
to be married secretly and given us enough income at
least for respectability—anything rather than bring dis-
grace upon the family! But you, Adelaide, in those days
you wouldn't have had your own money, and your
wretched Dyson would have lost his job; his Wesleyans
would have chucked him out neck and crop. You just
couldn't have left your old man. You had to get rid of
him."

"Oh, come off it, Madeleine!" said Florence, anxious
to get on with her own exposition. "Why should she

even want to leave him? He was perfectly happy; he encouraged all this canoodling—"

"What if they weren't content with just canoodling?"

"I have many times told you, nothing so vulgar; all was—was platony," said Adelaide stoutly.

"All I'm saying," said Florence, "is that either way, he wouldn't have minded. Then or nowadays—there was no reason for you to kill him."

"And I couldn't have killed him."

"Yes; well, honey—we both know perfectly well that you didn't kill him. None of us killed anybody, and here we are in Heaven to prove it."

"Madeleine's taken a long time getting here," said Florence, not to be smoothed down immediately.

"*They* didn't approve of the letters, either," said Madeleine with a nod of the head towards the major concentration of light. "I had to copy them out a million times each, with a red-hot pen. Mind you," she added, "it brightened things up in Purgatory no end; every soul had a copy, the letters were passed round and round."

"Madeleine, for Heaven's sake!"

"Oh, Chri—Oh, dear, I keep forgetting!" said Madeleine. She bent a meek eye upon Florence. "You were saying?"

"I was saying that you and Adelaide are clear of murder. *You* had method but no motive; Adelaide had neither motive nor method. Come on, Madeleine, admit it! She didn't need to kill poor old Edwin, and what's more, she couldn't have."

"O.K., O.K.," agreed Madeleine, surrendering to reason. "Verdict of the present-day jury upon Mrs. Adelaide Bartlett—Not Guilty."

"Which was the verdict anyway," said Adelaide smugly.

"So now me," said Florence. "And I was found Guilty. And so I *was* guilty—of having a lover. You had your letters, Madeleine; Adelaide had her tame pussy cat—but me, my honeys, I had a real live lover complete with hotel bill to prove it. And you just hear what the judge had to say about that!" As with Adelaide's rolling *r*'s, the judicial thunderings were overlaid with the accents of the Deep South. " 'You must remember, members of the jury,' he said, 'the intrigue she was carrying on with this man, Brierly. And how horrible, how incredible it was'—those were his very words!—'that a woman should be plotting the death of her own husband in order that she might be left at liberty to follow her own degrading vices.' Degrading vices! A perfectly ordinary tumble in bed with a gentleman who, unlike my dear husband, just happened not to be impotent. 'The propensities which lead people to vices of that kind,' the judge said—his own words, honestly!—'do kill all the more tender, all the more womanly feelings of the human mind.' To the jury—and they hadn't even considered the verdict yet. If I'd been on that jury . . ." The cloud rocked again as she in her turn scrambled to her feet. "Well—I'll *be* my jury. Madeleine has been her own prosecutor, Adelaide's been her own counsel; I'll be my own jury." And she launched into argument, the soft Alabama coo forced into variations of the deep growlings of twelve good men and true. "All right, so she had a feller. Her husband was no use to her. . . ." "Give him his due, he was doing his best, poor beggar, dosing hisself with all this stuff. . . ." "Yes, and what stuff? Arsenic. His room was crammed full with it, hidden in hat boxes, lord knows where else. . . ." "But if there was all that in the house, then why—?" "Yes, why should she go out and buy more of it, to kill him with?" "Well, we know that in fact she did buy more of it. . . ." "And was seen messing about with white powder . . ." "But it was flypapers I bought," said Florence, coming back to cases for a moment, "and made them into a solution. I had this rash on my face—"

"Yes, well, you shut up, love; you're supposed to be down in the cells below, awaiting the verdict."

"Oh, yes, so I am," said Florence. She resumed the assorted deep voices. "Fact remains, she had this Brierly. If she'd wanted to marry him . . ." "Well, what was to stop her? She had money of her own; her dad's a rich man back home in the States. . . ." "There was kids to be considered, mind. . . ." "The courts would have given the kids to their ma; they weren't going to leave two small children with an elderly father doping hisself with arsenic and strychnine and the lot. . . ." "Right. So who'd blame her, walking out, kids and all, to the man wot she loved?" "In other words . . .?" "In other words, no cause to kill her husband. All agreed, yes? She bought the stuff for her face, like she says; she never killed him, for the simple reason she had no cause to kill him. . . ." "So," said Florence, back on Cloud Nine again, "there's the answer. I'm my own jury and I agree with myself and this is the verdict of me all—Not Guilty. I've tried myself and I've found myself Not Guilty."

"We'd all be found Not Guilty nowadays. In none of our cases was it actually proved that we'd administered poison; they were driven to dragging in motive, and the motives all amounted—in their eyes—to immorality, which nowadays nobody would care two hoots about."

"Mind you, Madeleine, these days they'd be smarter over the poisons. Fingerprints and x-rays and all the rest of it. I mean, you could rinse out that cocoa cup till hell froze over; they'd still find signs in your basin or sink or wherever."

"Well, thanks very much, Florence dear. How many cups did *you* rinse out in the course of your ministrations to poor dying Maybrick? And what'll you bet," said Madeleine, nettled, "that there's ways enough been invented by now of discovering how chloroform could have been forced down a man's throat?"

"Oh, *girls!*" protested Adelaide. "Don't start all over again! Haven't we this minute all declared one another to be innocent?"

Irritability dissolved into cagily penitent smiles. "Well, sorry—I was only teasing." "And I didn't really mean that, honey."

"Because," said Adelaide earnestly, "we're going to be here a very long time, aren't we? Shall we not talk of things more agreeable? No more of murder. We agree, after all—we've all gone into it—we've proved that none of us would do such a thing. So let us—" But she peered down suddenly over the edge of the dangerously tipping cloud. "Oh, *mon Dieu!*"

"*Oui?*" said a very deep voice.

She was deaf to it. "Madeleine! Florence! Look down there!"

Three gentlemen, robed in white, strolling along the golden path beneath them, their harps—the handy, everyday, smaller ones—tucked underneath their arms. "It's Edwin!"

"It's Maybrick!"

"It's that little swine Emile!"

Emile L'Angelier, neat and dandyish as ever in his well-fitting white robe (most people, men anyway, took whatever was handed to them from the store, but Emile would have winked and ogled at the angel and got her to find him something just right) . . . And Maybrick, fit and well and obviously free from his aphrodisiac addictions—which anyway, in Heaven, might have brought about complications . . . And Edwin Bartlett, glowing with health, no spongy gums now and presumably no lumbricoid worms . . . Their voices carried up to Cloud Nine, which seemed rather curiously to be losing its buoyancy, down on a par with Cloud Seven or even Six. "Hush! Let's listen!"

Trust L'Angelier, the little tick, to be boasting. "What eyes, my dear friends; what shoulders, what a bosom! And what a papa! Rich as Croesus. If I'd got to him with those letters . . . He had a *parti* for her and, say what she would, she was keen as mustard. Love in a cottage had suddenly lost all its charms—just one glance at one of the letters would have finished all that; the old man would have paid out a fortune. But there you are! She beat me to it. Coaxed me round to her room, all sweetness and light again all of a sudden. 'Oh, my little Emile, what a night! You're so wet and cold, you must have a cup of cocoa to warm you up!' 'I don't think much of your cocoa these days,' I said. 'It's bitter as all hell.' 'No, no, darling, drink it up—you'll catch your death of cold.' Well, I did catch my death, but not of cold. I caught my death of the Scotch Disease; I caught my death of Belle Madeleine.''

And Maybrick. "And so did I—let us make a pun and say of the Italian Disease: I caught my death of Florence. 'Oh, Bunny,' I said to her—Bunny I used to call her, so pretty and charming—and as for the rest, well, I was taking more and more of the stuff to keep up with her, but nothing was enough. She found this other fellow and he was too cautious to start off a regular affair with another man's wife. 'Oh, Bunny,' I said to her, 'is it true what they're telling me, that you've been soaking flypapers to extract the arsenic?' 'Yes, but that lot I really *am* using for my skin,' she said, and clapped her hand to her mouth and stood there, staring at me. Well, it was too late by then; it was all up with me. What was the point of saying anything?" He shook his head sadly, shifting the harp to reach for a handkerchief. "Fancy her finding where I kept the stuff! Such a clever creature! Yours, too, Edwin?"

"The cleverest of all. Couldn't wait to be off with that curate fellow. I tried to make the best of it: 'I'll soon be dead,' I said. 'You can marry each other then—no, *do!* I insist.' But I took a turn for the better. So . . . Yes, she was clever. Or was it just first time lucky? We shall never know. Poured out a tot of brandy, poured a tot of chloroform into that. The chloroform hung suspended in the brandy like the yolk in the white of an egg. I never dreamed what it was; I was taking all sorts of doses at the time. I just swallowed it down, and the stuff never touched my throat. 'Thank you, my dear,' I said. 'And now if you'll just sit awhile and hold my toe.' She used to sit and hold my big toe. I found it very soothing; it sent me off to sleep. But of course it was something else that sent me off to sleep that night. You can make your jokes about Scotland and Italy. My joke's a bit deeper. My joke's Down Under. *I* died of Adelaide. . . ."

The voices faded; the three figures, amiably chatting,

passed out of sight. Up on the cloud, there was a rather long silence. Then all three ladies spoke at once. "I was only going to ask," said Madeleine, whining, "can't we do something about this cloud? All of a sudden it seems to have gone very limp."

"Just what I was thinking. Pull out that stopper beside you, Florence, and let a little fresh air into it. It'll soon fluff up again."

And so it did. Right back to lovely, happy, carefree Cloud Nine. For as Adelaide had earlier said, they were going to be here together for a very, very long time to come; and it would be a relief, after all, not to have to pretend any more.

Pelly and Cullis

MICHAEL INNES

"And is that the verdict of you all?"

This second question will sometimes take the foreman of a jury by surprise. But on the present occasion the foreman was an instructed person, who knew he would be required to answer it. He was, in fact, an eminent physician in the town, who on the score of other and more important services to the community could have gained exemption from this chore in court had he chosen to do so. Nevertheless—perhaps believing that in a criminal trial one or two trained minds on the jury cannot be amiss—here he was.

The question addressed to Dr. Girdlestone could clearly be answered with a single word—hard upon which the jurymen could go home and dine, comfortable in the feeling that their wisdom had ensured the due punishment of the unrighteous. Dr. Girdlestone, however, resolved upon using two: this from a feeling that "It is," being slightly more emphatic, even weightier, than plain "Yes," better became the gravity of the situation.

"It—" Dr. Girdlestone began.

But the clerk of the court had elevated his right hand the few inches that were required to apprise so alert a man as Dr. Girdlestone that silence was requested of him. The clerk of the court did this because the judge had raised *his* hand and misdoubtingly touched his little wig with his index finger. The clerk had been quite unable to see this gesture, since he could bring the judge

into view only by standing up and turning round. But
tradition having long constrained him to this disabling
situation, he had developed a species of clairvoyant fac-
ulty which made him aware of even the smallest movements on the bench. And now the judge spoke.

"Dr. Girdlestone, you must forgive my interrupting
you." The judge was much too grand to pretend not to
be acquainted with Girdlestone, whom he frequently
met at dinner when a Crown Court was being holden in
the city. He was also the last man—or woman—of all
those present who would deviate for a moment from
that inflexible courtesy to the accompaniment of which
the English legal profession goes on its prosperous way
amidst the wiles of criminals and the agitations of liti-
gants. "I am very conscious," the judge went on (and
he seemed now to be benevolently addressing the jury
at large), "of the strains and fatigues to which you have
been exposed while assisting me today. And you may
justly feel that a stage has been reached at which the
most exigent attention is no longer required of you.
Nevertheless, it seems to me desirable that when a question explicitly involving all of you is propounded, all of
you should be cognizant of the answer that your foreman gives to the court. So would somebody be so very
good as to awaken the gentleman who appears to have
fallen asleep in the middle of the front row? It will be
no great unkindness, since a jury box is scarcely well
adapted to comfortable slumber."

There was laughter in court—subdued perhaps out of
some decent feeling for the man in the dock. Counsel
for the prosecution and counsel for the defence (who
had not only been in the Harrow eleven together but
had actually been its opening pair on a number of aus-
picious occasions) exchanged humorous glances indica-
tive of a common consciousness that old Herriman up
there, although getting on for eighty, could still be
trusted to keep his form. Meanwhile, somebody had
given the peccant juryman a nudge; had given him, indeed, first a gentle and hesitant nudge, and then another, a good deal more vigorous. Dr. Girdlestone, still

on his feet, observed this performance with composure. But it must have been with a sharp-eyed composure, for suddenly he had uttered the words: "If I may have your leave, My Lord," and was edging his way along the line of jurors. He stooped over the slumped and immobile figure, upon whom all eyes were now fixed. And it seemed a long time before he straightened up again and spoke.

"My Lord," he said, "I am a doctor, as you know. In my opinion, this man is not asleep, and so cannot be awakened. And it is desirable that help be called and that he be removed from court at once."

"Let that be done. Dr. Girdlestone, I am most grateful to you."

Without more words, Mr. Justice Herriman rose and bowed. The barristers in court rose and bowed. Sundry other persons felt they ought to do this, too, but were a little slow about it—whereupon they were bellowed at by some functionary to be upstanding in court. But by the time this was achieved, Mr. Justice Herriman had gathered his skirts about him and vanished from the bench.

The two Q.C.s and their respective juniors were in a little clump as Sir John Appleby approached. Appleby had been in court because he was concerned in a case that hadn't been called; he had lingered because the present one interested him; these men had spotted him and caused him to be handed a hospitable message. What had happened in the jury box appeared to have put them in good spirits quite as much as the glass of sherry they were now discussing.

"Odd situation," the first Harrovian said. "If the chap's dead, that is. Take a little thinking out on Herriman's part. Not that he won't have us across there again in no time. He's uncommonly expeditious, as that generation of judges goes. But much too downy an old bird to say anything off the cuff when a thing like that crops up."

"Perhaps he's on the blower," one of the juniors said, "to the Lord Chancellor."

"My dear lad, would you go to a Lord Chancellor for law? Don't make me laugh."

"Or the L.C.J.," the other junior said.

"More likely to be to some fly old crony of his own, who has never strayed out of chambers in his life, but has a useful knack of remembering this and that."

"Is it so complicated?" Appleby asked. "Suppose the man is dead. Isn't it just a question of whether he died before, or after, the verdict was delivered?"

"He certainly didn't die in the jury room," the second Harrovian said. "He must have walked, or at least tottered, back into court. And it's arguable that, up to this very moment, the verdict has *not* been delivered. After 'Guilty,' you know, comes that 'Verdict of you all.' Both questions must receive an answer audible to the whole court."

"What if the judge himself were fast asleep," the first junior asked, "and then woke up and went ahead as if he'd heard what he certainly had not?"

"What, indeed?" The second junior consulted his glass. "But nowadays there's all this business—isn't there?—about when one *is* dead. They may bury that chap in a couple of days' time. But I'll bet you a bottle of claret you'd never get that superior sawbones Girdlestone to give a positive opinion as to whether he was alive or dead when they carried him out of court."

"Mere wandering and maundering, this," the first Harrovian said severely. "Unless the man can be brought back into court alive, and be demonstrably alive when the verdict is formally completed and accepted by the judge, there does seem to be an odd little point of law to be considered."

"And there might have to be a retrial?" Appleby asked. "What about a majority verdict? That's allowed at the discretion of the judge nowadays."

"Perfectly correct, Appleby. Eleven good men and true saying 'Guilty.' And one saying nothing at all, because he's dead. It would be like one of those comical cases you used to read in *Punch*."

As he made this remark, counsel for the prosecution glanced over Appleby's shoulder, and his expression at once registered mild dismay. Counsel for the defence followed his glance—and promptly evinced the same perceptible perturbation. Whereupon the two juniors, becoming aware of the occasion of this, seemed on the verge of giving way to panic. Yet all that had happened was the approach of Dr. Girdlestone.

"Good morning," counsel for the prosecution said smoothly. "But I wonder, my dear sir, whether we ought to permit ourselves the pleasure of your conversation? This vexatious case is not closed, and as a result you have not yet been discharged from your position as a juryman."

"Rubbish," Dr. Girdlestone said brusquely.

"Come, sir," counsel for the defence expostulated, coming to the support of his learned colleague. "You must be aware that, absurd though it may be, it is held to be an awkward thing should jurymen be found in talk even with officers of the court—which is what barristers and solicitors have the honour to be. So let me suggest that my colleagues and I withdraw. We can leave you in the company of Sir John, of course, who hasn't the slightest connection with the case."

"Then I hope he will have."

"I fail to understand you, Dr. Girdlestone."

"What I mean to say is that this affair appears to have turned into just his sort of thing. And I think we can forget that punctilio about jurymen having to be treated like lepers, sir. Neither the judge nor anybody else is likely to make a point of it. In view, that is to say, of what has now happened. That unfortunate man is indeed dead. Precisely when he died, I should not care to say." Dr. Girdlestone paused for a moment and frowned, having unfortunately detected a wink passing between the two junior barristers. "But dead he is."

"These sudden things are always rather shocking," counsel for the prosecution said, easily but with proper sobriety. "A heart attack, was it? Or one of those treacherous cerebral embolisms?"

"Nothing of the kind, sir. Decidedly nothing of the kind."

"Then just what did he die of?"

"I have very little idea. Doubtless the pathologists will inform the world in due season. But if you are content for the moment with a very rough answer, I believe I can afford it you."

"And it is?"

"Strong poison. *Very* strong poison. Just that."

An acquaintance of Appleby's, Colonel Hargreaves, had been nominated as high sheriff of the county in the previous November, and was still treating his duties very seriously. "I'm afraid I'm rather tied up at the assizes," he would say—a shade anachronistically—in answer to friends inviting him to play golf or shoot pigeons. And on the present occasion he had seen to it that the reading of the judge's commission had been a properly ceremonious affair, and then settled in at a respectful distance on the bench to see the Queen's justice dispensed. And now, since the late mysterious event had taken place within the precinct of the court, he felt that he had a part to play (perhaps in a manner equally mysterious) in its unravelment. This persuasion annoyed the police inspector who had turned up to discover what the fuss was about. He understood about judges, and was prepared to be properly deferential to them on the wholesome basis of having had much opportunity of watching them at work on criminal cases. But a high sheriff he clearly regarded as a piece of medieval flummery having no title to waste his time. There was, of course, the vexatious fact that Colonel Hargreaves's elder brother, Lord Lumbercraft, was the chairman of the County Council, and therefore in an absurd and remote sense Inspector Roach's employer. But this didn't make Inspector Roach any more pleased with Colonel Hargreaves's fussing around. And it was thus that the retired John Appleby, merely because his name happened to be legendary among the police forces of the land, came to be drawn into a composing role during the perplexed affair that centred upon the trial and conviction— only was it to *be* a conviction?—of Pelly. Pelly was the little rat of a man (although, indeed, a certain physical strength had to be posited of him) who had killed the girl—or who had done so if the prosecution was to be believed. Pelly, it was maintained, had failed to leave ill alone. He had killed the girl after ineffectively attempting to rape her. It was a story nobody had particularly liked listening to.

"I suppose," Hargreaves asked Appleby, "this disgusting Pelly is for the nick for keeps—without, I mean, the nonsense of a second trial and all that?"

"It's hard to say."

"Dash it all, Appleby, anything of the kind would be the most empty formalism! Nothing but a confounded waste of public money and the time of busy people."

"At the moment, one can't be quite sure."

"Dash it all, he did it, didn't he?"

"The jury said so. Or half said so, and was about to say so fully."

"Good God, man—it's the most utter rot! Do you believe some pal of this filthy Pelly was imbecile enough to think he could muck up the whole case by poisoning a juror?"

"It's conceivable, except for the use of poison. Pelly's devoted friend—if he had one, but why should he?—would be more likely to do a tip-and-run murder in the street, or a quick job with a gun in this very building."

"Aren't jurymen guarded better than that?"

"No, they are not. Or only when it's some sort of showpiece that's going ahead."

"Have they found out anything about this poor bastard Cullis yet?"

"Not much, I gather." The man to whom Colonel Hargreaves had thus disparagingly referred was the unfortunate poisoned juror. "He must have been a householder, or on some electoral roll or the like. Roach is after all that now."

"I didn't think that fellow Roach was any too civil."

"No more he was, Hargreaves. But the fact's irrelevant. He struck me as quite a competent man. And here he is."

Inspector Roach was a burly officer, who would clearly have done a good job helping to shove one crowd of senseless demonstrators out of reach of another. Colonel Hargreaves was disposed—most unwarrantably—to treat him as one who was probably out of his depth in this affair. And he scarcely waited until the inspector had put his flat cap down on a table.

"Well," he barked, "anything to report?"

"Not a great deal, so far." Roach, although entirely clear that he had no duty whatever to report to Hargreaves, only some disposition to confer with Appleby, was impassively polite.

"Story all over the place yet?"

"I think not. Of course, there were two or three newspapermen in court. But all they know is that the trial was adjourned when a juror was taken ill. They may be inquiring at the hospital. But it needn't be until the judge returns to the bench tomorrow morning that the manner of Cullis's death becomes public property. By that time, incidentally, the judge will have decided how to proceed."

"No doubt. Meanwhile, what have you discovered about Cullis?"

"A certain amount—and without much difficulty. It turned out that Dr. Girdlestone knew him."

"Knew his fellow juror?" It was Appleby who asked this question, apparently in some surprise. "Girdlestone didn't give that impression when he was coping with the moribund Cullis in the jury box."

"I think it was simply that it came to him afterwards that he knew the fellow. But only slightly, and by sight. Cullis was a porter at the hospital."

"One of the crowd that runs the place, eh?" Hargreaves asked dryly. "A law unto themselves. Have even the consultants right under their thumb."

"Possibly so, sir." Roach seemed to indicate that this

sort of disorder in society was one with which, happily, he was not called upon to deal. "A quiet little man, Cullis seems to have been. Married, but no children. We went to his house, of course, and broke the thing to his wife. I did that myself."

"Ah!" Hargreaves got a certain quality of respect into this ejaculation, as if one had to give it to a man whose duty imposed that sort of task on him. "Did she know anything about Pelly?"

"Nothing at all—except that he was being tried today, and what he was being tried for."

"These sort of people," Hargreaves said, "read the local newspapers, which always tell you more or less what is coming along in the courts. So Cullis knew what he was in for."

"Did Mrs. Cullis," Appleby asked, "afford the slightest suggestion that what had happened was something she feared might happen?"

"No, she didn't, Sir John—and of course it's a point one always looks out for." Roach hesitated. "There was something there, all the same."

"In this woman?"

"Well, yes—and in the whole house as well. I found myself just not liking the place. But that's not a helpful thing to report."

"One never knows, Inspector. But stick to the woman for a moment. Was she frightened about something?"

"Yes."

"It wasn't just a matter of being scared by the sudden appearance of a police officer in uniform—even before you gave her the news of her husband's sudden death?"

"No. One always has to allow for that, even among educated and what you might call sophisticated folk."

"Perfectly true. So what was it?"

"Well, there are people who have to live in dread of they don't at all know what—which must be a good deal worse than being in dread of what you can put a precise name to. And then something bad happens, and they still can't quite relate it to this nebulous anxiety with any precision." Having delivered himself of this,

Inspector Roach picked up his cap again. "And now," he said briskly, "I'm going to see if the pathology people have any preliminary finding. It does sometimes happen they just have to take a sniff and they're there in one. And precisely what killed the poor beggar is certainly the next information we want."

With this, Inspector Roach took his leave. And Colonel Hargreaves shook his head dubiously.

"Viewy fellow, wouldn't you say, Appleby? All that about nebulous anxiety, and so forth. Nebulous itself, if you ask me."

"It may sound a bit like that. However, I've no doubt that what you might call the routine inquiries are going on pretty vigorously at the same time."

"Such as?"

"Just what happened in that jury room. Who had access to it, and when. Do you know, Hargreaves, it sounds rather like the title of a detective story. *The Case with Eleven Solutions.* Something like that."

"I never read the things." The high sheriff chuckled suddenly. "But I see what you mean. One dead juror, and eleven who might have done the job."

"But of course, it doesn't exhaust the possibilities. For instance, why not twelve? What about the woman who brought in the tea?"

"The tea? Would there have been tea?"

"Elevenses, Hargreaves. It's a prescriptive thing. Or it might have been a man, you know. Twelve cups of tea, and in one of them a fatal pinch. And he'd see that the one with the pinch got to the right person."

"Good heavens, my dear Appleby—what a horrible idea!"

"Or of course, it mightn't matter *who* got it. *Any* juror would do. Because with one dead, the whole trial would have to be put off till the next sessions. And that would give time for this or that to happen."

"My dear fellow, you can't believe . . ."

"Well, no—I'm afraid I can't." Most improperly in face of the heinous crime under discussion, Appleby appeared amused by his own extravagance. "But there's something to be said for a play of imagination, you know. It turns up sober truth from time to time."

Appleby was not due home until the next day. So he dined with Burland, the prosecuting Harrovian.

"Would you have been inclined," he asked, "to call that an open-and-shut affair?"

"No."

"You put on a fairly good show of seeming to see it that way."

"My dear Appleby, I was simply carrying out my duty of assisting the court. It's how our odd forensic system works, isn't it? And it was up to Nicky Boxer to do his damnedest t'other way on." Nicky Boxer was the second Harrovian. "And Nicky didn't do a bad job, did he? He made a lot of capital out of all this current talk about the hazardousness of accepting evidence of identity too readily. Pelly, by the way, has a shocking record, which would have been heard about once that verdict was on the books. And he looks it, wouldn't you say? Even so, I thought he had a chance of getting off. Only unidentified fingerprints on that weapon, for instance— and no jury is happy without pukka fingerprints these days. Comes of reading crime stories. Then again, it was a deed of darkness in every sense. The blanket of the dark—as Shakespeare says—fairly smothering the whole thing. I tell you, Appleby, I was surprised at getting a verdict."

"Do you think Herriman was surprised?"

"It would take a lot to surprise *him*. Besides, he may have known a thing or two about friend Pelly already."

"Quite so. And of course, Burland, there is no difficulty about a motive in a case like that. We're all supposed to be rapists at heart. And in the wake of rape— or a shot at it—murder is the most natural thing in the world."

"It's a persuasive conventional view. And I agree we weren't put to a stand in the matter of motive. But when we come to the death of this little chap Cullis, it's a different matter. We know nothing about him, of course—and all sorts of people may have been wanting to kill him for all sorts of reasons. But why do the deed in these very odd circumstances?"

"But we don't know when it was done, do we? It's a matter for the toxicologists. If something comparatively slow-acting was involved, it may have been dropped into Cullis's tea at breakfast by his wife."

"Perfectly true, Appleby—and these small marital disharmonies do occur. But I favour what might be called a more structured view of the thing. Have you thought about Girdlestone?"

"Why should I think about Girdlestone?" This question came from Appleby with perhaps too much innocence. Indeed, it wasn't likely that he hadn't been thinking of Girdlestone, since the physician was the only one of those eleven jurors he knew anything about so far.

"I hear that a link has been established between him and the unfortunate Cullis."

"That's really a slightly coloured way to put it, Burland. Girdlestone merely recalled, it seems, that Cullis was a porter in the hospital where he, Girdlestone, is a consultant. Girdlestone, in fact, had simply noticed Cullis as in more or less humble employment about the place. That's not much of a link."

"At least it gives scope to imagine one. Suppose, Appleby, that Cullis had been snooping around, and had come upon something discreditable to this eminent leech. . . ."

"A pretty stiff supposition, that."

"Never mind! Entertain it for the moment; infer that Girdlestone decided Cullis must be silenced; reflect that nobody was in a better position than Girdlestone to obtain, and understand how to employ, this poison or that; add the fact that their both having to turn up for jury service afforded an opportunity for close contact such as wouldn't normally be easy to achieve between a top physician and a porter: consider all this, my dear fellow, and the handcuffs ought positively to be jingling in your pocket. By Jove—nine o'clock! But shall we have another glass of port?" Burland laughed robustly.

"Keeping a sharp eye, of course, on the fellow as he pours it out."

Not much later that evening, Appleby, despite the second glass of port, might have been judged to have developed a surprising thirst. He prowled the city—or the quarter of it in which the hospital lay—on the most pertinacious-seeming of pub crawls. Conceivably because such behaviour was highly indecorous on the part of a former Commissioner of Metropolitan Police, Appleby in fact wasn't looking like anything of the kind. One of the great detectives of fiction, disguised as a flower girl or a leering Chinaman, might have felt himself first cousin to this commerical gentleman not doing too well in the world. He was such a one, however, who had resisted turning morose or depressed. In fact, he was of the chatty sort which attaches itself to the fringes of a companionable group and listens patiently until allowed to put in a word or two, or perhaps a question or two, of his own.

This was freakish behaviour on Appleby's part, and essentially of a nostalgic order. Hadn't he, as a young man, often frequented pubs in a false nose and spectacles? Well, perhaps not. But certainly similar unassuming labours in the interest of law and order had been his daily, or nightly, round a long time ago. He was rather pleased at this reassumption of an ancient role.

It was simply a question of finding the right hostelry. The unfortunate Cullis's place of employment (and indeed, Dr. Girdlestone's) was a major teaching hospital with a large staff. Those housemen who were briefly off duty would alone fill more than one public bar. But housemen were no use to him, any more than registrars or nurses or grandees like Girdlestone—or for that matter, the swarms of minor administrative persons to be found in such places nowadays. What he was after, he told himself brutally, were the chaps who trundle you around, living or dead, on trolleys.

Eventually he ran them to earth, appropriately enough, in a small pothouse called The Jolly Waggoner.

Here, without a doubt, were three or four of Cullis's colleagues, already aware of the fate that had overtaken him—or at least aware of his sudden death—and disposed to discuss him in an obituary manner. It was on this colloquy that Appleby successfully edged in.

"In the midst of life we are in death," Appleby said, with the air of one who, in modest degree, would elevate a conversation in the direction of philosophic generality. "It's those sudden calls that tell you the truth of that. Would you have said, now, that his health was bad? You're all in a position to be good judges of that, I'd suppose."

The men addressed stared at Appleby for a moment in a hostile fashion, but then decided to take in good part this promotion to a species of status within the medical profession.

"Nothing wrong with Cullis," one of them said. "Or not from the neck down."

"Close," another said.

"Close and jumpy," said a third. "Chapel-going, and that. You'd expect a hymn to be coming from him far more likely than a song—let alone an honest curse. There was something in his eye, though. Not a doubt of that. Like as if he'd slipped the collection in his pocket from under the preacher's nose, and was feeling none too happy about it."

"Is that so?" Appleby said. "Now, that's a remarkable thing."

"It was more remarkable than that," the first man said. "It was as if he was afraid he'd be doing it again tomorrow. A kind of guilty chap, you might say, Cullis was."

"And I can tell you something," the second man said. He had lowered his voice and was glancing circumspectly around him. "Although it's to say ill of the dead, in a manner of speaking. It came out of his coat pocket in the locker room. He picked it up fast enough—and with what you might call a snarl at me, who was standing beside him. But there it was, open on the floor, and I seed it there."

"You don't say that!" the first man said.

"That I do. And he ought to have been past the age for such things, to my way of thinking. Mind you, any man may take a quick look inside one at a bookstall, or some such place. That's only human nature, after all. But Cullis had paid money for the book, and that's another matter. It was a hot one, too. The pictures, you know. Photographs they'd taken of people actually doing them dirty acts. Whips and the like—but that just to tickle your appetite for other turns to come. Of course, I only got a glimpse of it. But enough's enough. You know the sort of thing."

There was a silence, nobody being disposed to deny that he knew the sort of thing.

"I hope," Appleby said solemnly, "that this Cullis wasn't a married man."

"But that he was. No kids, though—which you might call a merciful dispensation. And do you know what I sometimes wondered?" The second man lowered his voice yet further. "It was whether Cullis had it in him to put a bun in the bloody oven."

Appleby's call on Mrs. Cullis was very brief, perhaps because he had abruptly ceased to enjoy the part he was playing. He was tactful, and he asked no questions of a sort that might have been prompted by the conversation he had taken part in at The Jolly Waggoner. He asked, in fact, only one question that was at all out of the way. And when he got back to his hotel he contacted Inspector Roach on the telephone.

"Tell those chaps in their lab," he said, "not to neglect Cullis's left hand."

On the following afternoon Appleby travelled back to London in the company of Burland.

"You know," Burland said, "I was beginning to take quite seriously that notion of mine that it had been Girdlestone. It would have been deuced odd, but nothing like as odd as what you have pulled out of the hat. The coincidence is amazing, for a start."

"It certainly amazed Cullis. Or astonished him, to use an older and stronger word. There he was, suddenly summoned for jury service in a case in which it ought to have been he who was in the dock. And he wasn't exactly a hardened criminal with an untroubled mind. He was a wretch periodically driven by some insane compulsion to actions which he knew to be hideously evil. It's far from surprising that he possessed himself of that lethal stuff."

"It's surprising that he had access to it—and knew what was what."

"He'd prowled that hospital with his eyes and ears open, no doubt. His original idea must have been to possess himself of the means to suicide if his dealings with that poor girl were found out. But what in the end he couldn't face up to was going scot-free and seeing an innocent man convicted of the crime."

"God, Appleby, was there ever a more blindly selfish death? If he'd even left a signed confession before killing himself . . ."

"Quite so. We must just suppose that the poor devil had got clean beyond all coherent thought."

"He hadn't got beyond quite a neat job on his own teacup, or whatever it was. By the way, Appleby, I must say you showed a certain power of coherent thought yourself."

"Thank you." Appleby received this gratuitous approbation a shade dryly. "It did seem to me that, whether pellet or powder was involved, a human hand must have done the trick with it, and that some trace on the skin might remain to an extent detectable by what is called, I think, microanalysis. It was in my head when I asked poor Mrs. Cullis whether her husband was right-handed or left-handed."

"I doubt whether it would ever have occurred to the lab boys to have a dekko at Cullis's hands—whether right or left. They'd find the stuff in the tummy, and that would be that."

"My dear Burland, perhaps you underestimate the thoroughness of a well-trained forensic scientist. I simply thought it would be civil to let them know what had come into my head. Incidentally, how are you people going to assist Mr. Justice Herriman to sort things out?"

"There's really no doubt that a verdict against Pelly was brought in. It's a fact it would be hair-splitting to deny. So there will have to be an appeal, and then we'll see all the brouhaha of bringing forward fresh evidence. I shouldn't be surprised if Cullis's fingerprints turn out to correspond with the unidentified ones on that axe, or whatever it was." Burland waved a dismissive hand; the details of the case were already fading from the memory of this eminent Q.C. "It will all be mopped up, of course. But I'm afraid it will be rather a bore."

"At least Pelly will be pleased," Appleby said.

Something the Cat Dragged In

PATRICIA HIGHSMITH

A few seconds of pondering silence in the Scrabble game was interrupted by a rustle of plastic at the cat door: Portland Bill was coming in again. Nobody paid any attention. Michael and Gladys Herbert were ahead, Gladys doing a bit better than her husband. The Herberts played Scrabble often and were quite sharp at it. Colonel Edward Phelps—a neighbour and a good friend—was limping along, and his American niece Phyllis, aged nineteen, had been doing well but had lost interest in the last ten minutes. It would soon be teatime. The Colonel was sleepy and looked it.

" 'Quack,' " said the Colonel thoughtfully, pushing a forefinger against his Kipling-style moustache. "Pity. I was thinking of 'earthquake.' "

"If you've got 'quack,' Uncle Eddie," said Phyllis, "how could you get 'quake out of it?"

The cat made another, more sustained noise at his door, and now, with black tail and brindle hindquarters in the house, he moved backwards and pulled something through the plastic oval. What he had dragged in looked whitish and about six inches long.

"Caught another bird," said Michael, impatient for Eddie to take his turn so that he could make a brilliant move before somebody grabbed it.

"Looks like another goose foot," said Gladys, glancing. "Ugh."

The Colonel at last moved, adding a P to SUM. Michael moved, raising a gasp of admiration from Phyllis

106

for his INI stuck onto GEM, followed by NATAL from the N in GEMINI.

Portland Bill flipped his trophy into the air, and it fell on the carpet with a thud.

"Really *dead* pigeon, that," remarked the Colonel, who was nearest the cat, but whose eyesight was not of the best. "Turnip," he said for Phyllis's benefit. "Swede. Or an oddly shaped carrot," he added, peering, then chuckled. "I've seen carrots take the most fantastic shapes. Saw one once—"

"This is white," said Phyllis, and got up to investigate, since Gladys had to play before her. In slacks and sweater, Phyllis bent over with hands on her knees. "Good *Chr*— Oh! Uncle Eddie!" She stood up and clapped her hand over her mouth as if she had said something dreadful.

Michael Herbert had half risen from his chair. "What's the matter?"

"They're human *fingers!*" Phyllis said. "Look!"

They all looked, coming slowly, unbelievingly, from the card table. The cat peered proudly up at the faces of the four humans gazing down. Gladys drew in her breath.

The two fingers were dead white and puffy; there was not a sign of blood, even at the base of the fingers, which included a couple of inches of what had been the hand. What made the object undeniably the third and fourth fingers of a human hand were the two nails, yellowish and short and looking small because of the swollen flesh.

"What should we do, Michael?" Gladys was practical, but liked to let her husband make decisions.

"That's been dead for two weeks at least," murmured the Colonel, who had had some war experience.

"Could it have come from a hospital near here?" asked Phyllis.

"Hospital amputating like that?" replied her uncle with a chuckle.

"The nearest hospital is twenty miles from here," said Gladys.

"Mustn't let Edna see it." Michael glanced at his watch. "Of course, I think we—"

"Maybe call the police?" asked Gladys.

"I was thinking of that. I—" Michael's hesitation was interrupted by Edna, their housekeeper-cook, bumping just then against a door in a remote corner of the big living room. The tea tray had arrived. The others moved discreetly toward the low table in front of the fireplace, while Michael Herbert stood with an air of casualness. The fingers were just behind his shoes. Michael pulled an unlit pipe from his jacket pocket and fiddled with it, blowing into its stem. His hands shook a little. He shooed Portland Bill away with one foot.

Edna finally dispensed napkins and plates, and said, "Have a nice tea!" She was a local woman in her mid fifties, a reliable soul, but with most of her mind on her own children and grandchildren—thank goodness, under these circumstances, Michael thought. Edna arrived at half-past seven in the morning on her bicycle and departed when she pleased, as long as there was something in the house for supper. The Herberts were not fussy.

Gladys was looking anxiously toward Michael. "Get *away, Bill!*"

"Got to do something with this meanwhile," Michael murmured. With determination, he went to the basket of newspapers beside the fireplace, shook out a page of *The Times,* and returned to the fingers, which Portland Bill was about to pick up. Michael beat the cat by grabbing the fingers through the newspaper. The others had not sat down. Michael made a gesture for them to do so, and closed the newspaper around the fingers, rolling and folding. "The thing to do, I should think," said Michael, *"is* to notify the police, because there might have been . . . foul play somewhere."

"Or might it have fallen," the Colonel began, shaking out his napkin, "out of an ambulance or some disposal unit—you know? Might've been an accident somewhere."

"Or should we just let well enough alone, and get rid

of it?" said Gladys. "I need some tea." She had poured, and proceeded to sip from her cup.

No one had an answer to her suggestion. It was as if the three others were stunned, or hypnotized by one another's presence, vaguely expecting a response from another which did not come.

"Rid of it where? In the garbage?" asked Phyllis. "*Bury* it," she added, as if answering her own question.

"I don't think that would be right," said Michael.

"Michael, do have some tea," said his wife.

"Got to put this somewhere overnight." Michael still held the little bundle. "Unless we ring the police now. It's already five and it's Sunday."

"In England do the police care whether it's Sunday or not?" asked Phyllis.

Michael started for the cupboard near the front door, with an idea of putting the thing on top beside a couple of hat boxes, but he was followed by Portland Bill, and Michael knew that with enough inspiration the cat could leap to the top.

"I've got just the thing, I think," said the Colonel, pleased by his own idea, but with an air of calm in case Edna made a second appearance.

"Bought some house slippers just yesterday in the High Street and I've still got the box. I'll go and fetch it, if I may." He went off toward the stairs, then turned and said softly, "We'll tie a string around it. Keep it away from the cat." The Colonel climbed the stairs.

"Keep it in whose room?" asked Phyllis with a nervous giggle.

The Herberts did not answer. Michael, still on his feet, held the object in his right hand. Portland Bill sat with white forepaws neatly together, regarding Michael, waiting to see what he would do with it.

Colonel Phelps came down with his white cardboard shoe box. The little bundle went in easily, and Michael let the Colonel hold the box while he went to rinse his hands in the lavatory near the front door. When Michael returned, Portland Bill still hovered, and gave out a hopeful "Miaow?"

"Let's put it in the sideboard for the moment," said Michael, and took the box from Eddie's hands. He felt that the box at least was comparatively clean, and he put it beside a stack of large and seldom-used dinner plates, then closed the cabinet door, which had a key in it.

Phyllis bit into a Bath Oliver and said, "I noticed a crease in one finger. If there's a ring there, it might give a clue."

Michael exchanged a glance with Eddie, who nodded slightly. They had all noticed the crease. Tacitly the men agreed to take care of this later.

"More tea, dear," said Gladys. She refilled Phyllis's cup.

"M'wow," said the cat in a disappointed tone. He was now seated facing the sideboard, looking over one shoulder.

Michael changed the subject: the progress of the Colonel's redecorating. The painting of the first-floor bedrooms was the main reason why the Colonel and his niece were visiting the Herberts just now. But this was of no interest compared to Phyllis's question to Michael:

"Shouldn't you ask if anyone's missing in the neighbourhood? Those fingers might be part of a *muder*."

Gladys shook her head slightly and said nothing. Why did Americans always think in such violent terms? However, what could have severed a hand in such a manner? An explosion? An axe?

A lively scratching sound got Michael to his feet.

"Bill, do *stop* that!" Michael advanced on the cat and shooed him away. Bill had been trying to open the cabinet door.

Tea was over more quickly than usual. Michael stood by the sideboard while Edna cleared away.

"When're you going to look at the ring, Uncle Eddie?" Phyllis asked. She wore round-rimmed glasses and was rather myopic.

"I don't think Michael and I have quite decided what we should do, my dear," said her uncle.

"Let's go into the library, Phyllis," said Gladys. "You said you wanted to look at some photographs."

Phyllis had said that. There were photographs of Phyllis's mother and of the house where her mother had been born, in which Uncle Eddie now lived. Eddie was older than her mother by fifteen years. Now Phyllis wished she hadn't asked to see the photographs, because the men were going to do something with the *fingers,* and Phyllis would have liked to watch. After all, she was used to dissecting frogs and dogfish in zoology lab. But her mother had warned her before she left New York to mind her manners and not be "crude and insensitive," her mother's usual adjectives about Americans. Phyllis sat dutifully looking at photographs fifteen and twenty years old, at least.

"Let's take it out to the garage," Michael said to Eddie. "I've got a workbench there, you know."

The two men walked along a gravelled path to the two-car garage, at the back of which Michael had a workshop with saws and hammers, chisels and an electric drill, plus a supply of wood and planks in case the house needed any repairs or he felt in the mood to make something. Michael was a free-lance journalist and book critic, but he enjoyed manual labour. Here he felt better with the awful box, somehow. He could set it on his sturdy workbench as if he were a surgeon contemplating a patient, or a coroner a corpse.

"What the hell do you make of this?" asked Michael as he flipped the fingers out by holding one side of the newspaper. The fingers flopped onto the well-used wooden surface, this time palm side upward. The white flesh was jagged where it had been cut, and in the strong beam of the spotlight which shone from over the bench, they could see two bits of metacarpals, also jagged, projecting from the flesh. Michael turned the fingers over with the tip of a screwdriver. He twisted the screwdriver tip, and parted the flesh enough to see the glint of gold.

"Gold ring," said Eddie. "But he was a workman of some kind, don't you think? Look at those nails. Short and thick. Still some soil under them—dirty, anyway."

"I was thinking . . . if we report it to the police, shouldn't we leave it the way it is? Not try to look at the ring?"

"Are you going to report it to the police?" asked Eddie with a smile as he lit a small cigar. "What'll you be in for then?"

"In for? I'll say the cat dragged it in. Why should I be in for anything? I'm curious about the ring. Might give us a clue."

Colonel Phelps glanced at the garage door, which Michael had closed but not locked. He, too, was curious about the ring. He was thinking that if it had been a gentleman's hand, they might have turned it into the police by now. "Many farm workers around here still?" he mused. "I suppose so."

Michael shrugged, nervous. "What do you say about the ring?"

"Let's have a look." The Colonel puffed serenely, and looked at Michael's racks of tools.

"I know what we need." Michael reached for a Stanley knife which he ordinarily used for cutting cardboard, pushed the blade out with his thumb, and placed his fingers on the pudgy remainder of the palm. He made a cut above where the ring was, then below.

Eddie Phelps bent to watch. "No blood at all. Drained out. Just like the war days."

Nothing but a goose foot, Michael was telling himself in order not to faint. Michael repeated his cuts on the top surface of the finger. He felt like asking Eddie if he wanted to finish the job, but thought that might be cowardly.

"Dear me," Eddie murmured unhelpfully.

Michael had to cut off some strips of flesh, then take a firm grip with both hands to get the wedding ring off. It most certainly was a wedding ring of plain gold, not very thick or broad, but suitable for a man to wear. Michael rinsed it at the cold-water tap of the sink on his left. When he held it near the spotlight, initials were legible: *W.R.—M.T.*

Eddie peered. "Now, *that's* a clue!"

Michael heard the cat scratching at the garage door, then a miaow. Next Michael put the three pieces of flesh he had cut off into an old rag, wadded it up, and told Eddie he would be back in a minute. He opened the garage door, discouraged Bill with a *"Whisht!"* and stuck the rag into a dustbin which had a fastening that a cat could not open. Michael had thought he had a plan to propose to Eddie, but when he returned—Eddie was again examining the ring—he was too shaken to speak. He had meant to say something about making "discreet inquiries." Instead, he said in a voice gone hollow:

"Let's call it a day—unless we think of something brilliant tonight. Let's leave the box here. The cat can't get in."

Michael didn't want the box even on his workbench. He put the ring in with the fingers, and set the box atop some plastic jerry cans which stood against a wall. His workshop had proved ratproof so far. Nothing was going to come in to chew at the box.

As Michael got into bed that night, Gladys said, "If we don't tell the police, we've simply got to bury it somewhere."

"Yes," said Michael vaguely. It seemed somehow a criminal act, burying a pair of human fingers. He had told Gladys about the ring. The initials hadn't rung any bell with her.

Colonel Edward Phelps went to sleep quite peacefully, having reminded himself that he had seen a lot worse in 1941.

Phyllis had quizzed her uncle and Michael about the ring at dinner. Maybe it would all be solved tomorrow and turn out to be—somehow—something quite simple and innocent. Anyway, it would make quite a story to tell her chums in college. And her mother! So this was the quiet English countryside!

The next day being Monday, with the post office open, Michael decided to pose a question to Mary Jeffrey, who doubled as postal clerk and grocery salesgirl in the establishment. Michael bought some stamps, then asked casually:

"By the way, Mary, is anybody missing lately in this neighbourhood?"

Mary, a bright-faced girl with dark curly hair, looked puzzled. "Missing how?"

"Disappeared," Michael said with a smile.

Mary shook her head. "Not that I know. Why do you ask?"

Michael had tried to prepare for this. "I read somewhere in a newspaper that people do sometimes . . . just disappear, even in small villages like this. Drift away, change their names or some such. Baffles everyone, where they go." Michael was drifting away himself. Not a good job, but the question was put.

He walked the quarter of a mile back home, wishing he had had the guts to ask Mary if anyone in the area had a bandaged left hand, or if she'd heard of any such accident. Mary had boyfriends who frequented the local pub. Mary this minute might know of a man with a bandaged hand, but Michael could not possibly tell her that the missing fingers were in his garage.

The matter of what to do with the fingers was put aside for that morning, as the Herberts had laid on a drive to Cambridge, followed by lunch at the house of a don who was a friend of theirs. Unthinkable to cancel that because of getting involved with the police, so the fingers did not come up in conversation that morning. They talked of anything else during the drive. Michael and Gladys and Eddie had decided, before taking off for Cambridge, that they should not discuss the fingers again in front of Phyllis, but let it blow over, if possible. Eddie and Phyllis were to leave on Wednesday afternoon, and by then the matter might be cleared up or in the hands of the police.

Gladys had also gently warned Phyllis not to bring up "the cat incident" at the don's house, so Phyllis did not. All went well and happily, and the Herberts and Eddie and Phyllis were back at the Herberts' house around four. Edna told Gladys she had just realized they were

short of butter, and since she was watching a cake . . .
Michael, in the living room with Eddie, heard this and
volunteered to go to the grocery.

Michael bought the butter, a couple of packets of cigarettes, a box of toffee that looked nice, and was served
by Mary in her usual modest and polite manner. He
had been hoping for news from her. Michael had taken
his change and was walking to the door, when Mary
cried, "Oh, Mr. Herbert!"

Michael turned round.

"I heard of someone disappearing just this noon,"
Mary said, leaning toward Michael across the counter,
smiling now. "Bill Reeves—lives on Mr. Dickenson's
property, you know. He has a cottage there, works on
the land—or did."

Michael didn't know Bill Reeves, but he certainly
knew of the Dickenson property, which was vast, to the
northwest of the village. Bill Reeves's initials fitted the
W.R. on the ring. "Yes? He disappeared?"

"About two weeks ago, Mr. Vickers told me. Mr.
Vickers has the petrol station near the Dickenson property, you know. He came in today, so I thought I'd ask
him." She smiled again, as if she had done satisfactorily
with Michael's little riddle.

Michael knew the petrol station and knew how Vickers looked, vaguely. "Interesting. Does Mr. Vickers
know why he disappeared?"

"No. He said it's a mystery. Bill Reeves's wife left the
cottage, too, a few days ago, but everyone knows she
went to Manchester to stay with her sister there."

Michael nodded. "Well, well. Shows it can happen
even here, eh? People disappearing." He smiled and
went out of the post office–grocery.

The thing to do was ring up Tom Dickenson, Michael thought, and ask him what he knew. Michael
didn't call him Tom, had met him only a couple of
times, at local political rallies and such. Dickenson was
about thirty, married, had inherited, and now led the
life of gentleman farmer, Michael thought. The family

was in the wool industry, had factories up north, and had owned their land here for generations.

When he got home, Michael asked Eddie to come up to his study, and despite Phyllis's curiosity, did not invite her to join them. Michael told Eddie what Mary had said about the disappearance of a farm worker called Bill Reeves a couple of weeks ago. Eddie agreed that they might ring up Dickenson.

"The initials on the ring could be an accident," Eddie said. "The Dickenson place is fifteen miles from here, you say."

"Yes, but I still think I'll ring him." Michael looked up the number in the directory on his desk. There were two numbers. Michael tried the first.

A servant, or someone who sounded like a servant, answered, inquired Michael's name, then said he would summon Mr. Dickenson. Michael waited a good minute. Eddie was waiting, too. "Hello, Mr. Dickenson. I'm one of your neighbours, Michael Herbert. . . . Yes, yes, I know we have—couple of times. Look, I have a question to ask which you might think odd, but—I understand you had a workman or tenant on your land called Bill Reeves?"

"Ye-es?" replied Tom Dickenson.

"And where is he now? I'm asking because I was told he disappeared a couple of weeks ago."

"Yes, that's true. Why do you ask?"

"Do you know where he went?"

"No idea," replied Dickenson. "Did you have any dealings with him?"

"No. Could you tell me what his wife's name is?"

"Marjorie."

That fitted the first initial. "Do you happen to know her maiden name?"

Tom Dickenson chuckled. "I'm afraid I don't."

Michael glanced at Eddie, who was watching him. "Do you know if Bill Reeves wore a wedding ring?"

"No. Never paid that much attention to him. Why?"

Why, indeed? Michael shifted. If he ended the conversation here, he would not have learned much. "Because—I've found something that just might be a clue in regard to Bill Reeves. I presume someone's looking for him, if no one knows his whereabouts."

"I'm not looking for him," Tom Dickenson replied in his easy manner. "I doubt if his wife is, either. She moved out a week ago. May I ask what you found?"

"I'd rather not say over the telephone. I wonder if I could come to see you. Or perhaps you could come to my house."

After an instant of silence, Dickenson said, "Quite honestly, I'm not interested in Reeves. I don't think he left any debts, as far as I know; I'll say that for him. But I don't care what's happened to him, if I may speak frankly."

"I see. Sorry to've bothered you, Mr. Dickenson."

They hung up.

Michael turned to Eddie Phelps and said, "I think you got most of that. Dickenson's not interested."

"Can't expect Dickenson to be concerned about a disappeared farm worker. Did I hear him say the wife's gone, too?"

"Thought I told you. She went to Manchester to her sister's. Mary told me." Michael took a pipe from the rack on his desk and began to fill it. "Wife's name is Marjorie. Fits the initial on the ring."

"True," said the Colonel, "but there're lots of Marys and Margarets in the world."

"Dickenson didn't know her maiden name. Now look, Eddie, with no help from Dickenson, I'm thinking we ought to buzz the police and get this over with. I'm sure I can't bring myself to bury that . . . object, even in the woods adjacent, which don't belong to anybody. The thing would haunt me. I'd be thinking a dog would dig it up, even if it's just bones or in a *worse* state, and the police would have to start with somebody else besides me, and with a trail not so fresh to follow."

"You're still thinking of foul play? I have a simpler idea," Eddie said with an air of calm and logic. "Gladys said there was a hospital twenty miles away, I presume in Colchester. We might ask if in the last two weeks or so there's been an accident involving the loss of third and fourth fingers of a man's left hand. They'd have his name. It looks like an accident and of the kind that doesn't happen every day."

Michael was on the brink of agreeing to this, at least before contacting the police, when the telephone rang. Michael lifted the receiver, and found Gladys on the line downstairs with a man whose voice sounded like Dickenson's. "I'll take it, Gladys."

Tom Dickenson said hello to Michael. "I've—I thought if you really would like to see me . . ."

"I'd be very glad to."

"I'd prefer to speak with you alone, if that's possible."

Michael assured him it was, and Dickenson said he could come along in about twenty minutes. Michael put the telephone down with a feeling of relief, and said to Eddie, "He's coming over now and wants to talk with me alone. That *is* the best."

"Yes." Eddie got up from Michael's sofa, disappointed. "He'll be more open, if he has anything to say. Are you going to tell him about the fingers?" He peered at Michael sideways, bushy eyebrows raised.

"May not come to that. I'll see what he has to say first."

"He's going to ask you what you found."

Michael knew that. They went downstairs. Michael saw Phyllis in the back garden, banging a croquet ball all by herself, and heard Glady's voice in the kitchen. Michael informed Gladys, out of Edna's hearing, of the imminent arrival of Tom Dickenson, and explained why: Mary's information that a certain Bill Reeves was missing, a worker on Dickenson's property. Gladys realized at once that the initials matched.

And here came Dickenson's car, a black Triumph convertible, rather in need of a wash. Michael went out to greet him. They vaguely remembered each other. Michael invited Dickenson into the house before Phyllis could drift over and compel an introduction.

Tom Dickenson was blond and tallish, now in leather

jacket and corduroys and green rubber boots which he assured Michael were not muddy. He had just been working on his land, and hadn't taken the time to change.

"Let's go up," said Michael, leading the way to the stairs.

Michael offered Dickenson a comfortable armchair, and sat down on his old sofa. "You told me Bill Reeves's wife went off, too?"

Dickenson smiled a little, and his bluish-grey eyes gazed calmly at Michael. "His wife left, yes. But that was after Reeves vanished. Marjorie went to Manchester, I heard. She has a sister there. The Reeveses weren't getting on so well. They're both about twenty-five, Reeves fond of his drink. I'll be glad to replace him, frankly. Easily done."

Michael waited for more. It didn't come. Michael was wondering why Dickenson had been willing to come to see him about a farm worker he didn't much like.

"Why're you interested?" Dickenson asked. Then he broke out in a laugh which made him look younger and happier. "Is Reeves perhaps asking for a job with you, under another name?"

"Not at all." Michael smiled, too. "I haven't anywhere to lodge a worker. No."

"But you said you found something?" Tom Dickenson's brows drew in a polite frown of inquiry.

Michael looked at the floor, then lifted his eyes and said, "I found two fingers of a man's left hand, with a wedding ring on one finger. The initials on the ring could stand for William Reeves. The other initials are M.T., which could be Marjorie somebody. That's why I thought I should ring you up."

Had Dickenson's face gone paler, or was Michael imagining? Dickenson's lips were slightly parted, his eyes uncertain. "Good Lord! Found it where?"

"Our cat dragged it in, believe it or not. Had to tell my wife, because the cat brought it into the living room in front of all of us." Somehow it was a tremendous relief for Michael to get the words out. "My old friend Eddie Phelps and his American niece are here now. They saw it." Michael stood up. Now he wanted a cigarette, got the box from his desk and offered it to Dickenson.

Dickenson said he had just stopped smoking, but he would like one.

"It was a bit shocking," Michael went on, "so I thought I'd make some inquiries in the neighbourhood before I spoke to the police. I think informing the police is the right thing to do. Don't you?"

Dickenson did not answer at once.

"I had to cut away some of the finger to get the ring off, with Eddie's assistance last night." Dickenson still said nothing, only drew on his cigarette, frowning. "I thought the ring might give a clue, which it does, though it might have nothing at all to do with this Bill Reeves. You don't seem to know if he wore a wedding ring, and you don't know Marjorie's maiden name."

"Oh, that one can find out." Dickenson's voice sounded different and more husky.

"Do you think we should do that? Or maybe you know where Reeves's parents live. Or Marjorie's parents? Maybe Reeves is at one or the other's place now."

"Not at his wife's parents, I'll bet," said Dickenson with a nervous smile. "She's fed up with him."

"Well—what do you think? I'll tell the police? Would you like to see the ring?"

"No. I'll take your word."

"Then I'll get in touch with the police tomorrow—or this evening. I suppose the sooner the better." Michael noticed Dickenson glancing around the room as if he might see the fingers lying on a bookshelf.

The study door moved and Portland Bill walked in. Michael never quite closed his door, and Bill had an assured way with doors, rearing a little and giving them a push.

Dickenson blinked at the cat, then said to Michael in a firm voice, "I could stand a Scotch. May I?"

Michael went downstairs and brought back the bottle

and two glasses in his hands. There had been no one in the living room. Michael poured. Then he shut the door of his study.

Dickenson took a good inch of his drink at the first gulp. "I may as well tell you now that I killed Reeves."

A tremor went over Michael's shoulders, yet he told himself that he had known this all along—or since Dickenson's telephone call to him, anyway. "Yes?" said Michael.

"Reeves had been . . . trying it on with my wife. I won't give it the dignity of calling it an affair. I blame my wife, flirting in a silly way with Reeves. He was just a lout, as far as I'm concerned. Handsome and stupid. His wife knew, and she hated him for it." Dickenson drew on the last of his cigarette, and Michael fetched the box again. Dickenson took one. "Reeves got ever more sure of himself. I wanted to sack him and send him away, but I couldn't because of his lease on the cottage, and I didn't want to bring the situation with my wife to light—with the law, I mean—as a reason."

"How long did this go on?"

Dickenson had to think. "Maybe about a month."

"And your wife—now?"

Tom Dickenson sighed and rubbed his eyes. He sat hunched forward in his chair. "We'll patch it up. We've hardly been married a year."

"She knows you killed Reeves?"

Now Dickenson sat back, propped a green boot on one knee and drummed the fingers of one hand on the arm of his chair. "I don't know. She may think I just sent him packing. She didn't ask any questions."

Michael could imagine, and he could also see that Dickenson would prefer that his wife never know. Michael realized that he would have to make a decision: to turn Dickenson over to the police or not. Or would Dickenson even prefer to be turned in? Michael was listening to the confession of a man who had had a crime on his conscience for more than two weeks, bottled up inside himself, or so Michael assumed. And how had

Dickenson killed him? "Does anyone else know?" Michael asked cautiously.

"Well—I can tell you about that. I suppose I must. Yes." Dickenson's voice was again hoarse, and his whisky gone.

Michael got up and replenished Dickenson's glass.

Dickenson sipped now, and stared at the wall beside Michael.

Portland Bill sat at a little distance from Michael, concentrating on Dickenson as if he understood every word and was waiting for the next installment.

"I told Reeves to stop playing about with my wife or leave my property with his own wife, but he brought up the lease—and why didn't I speak to *my* wife? Arrogant, you know, so pleased with himself that the master's wife had deigned to look at him—" Dickenson began again. "Tuesdays and Fridays I go to London to take care of the company. A couple of times, Diane said she didn't feel like going to London or she had some other engagement. Reeves could always manage to find a little work close to the house on those days, I'm sure. And then, there was a second victim—like me."

"Victim? What do you mean?"

"Peter." Now Dickenson rolled his glass between his hands, the cigarette projecting from his lips, and he stared at the wall beside Michael and spoke as if he were narrating what he saw on a screen there. "We were trimming some hedgerows deep in the fields, cutting stakes, too, for new markings. Reeves and I. Axes and sledge hammers. Peter was driving in stakes quite a way from us. Peter's another hand like Reeves; been with me longer. I had the feeling Reeves might attack me, then say it was an accident or some such. It was afternoon, and he'd had a few pints at lunch. He had a hatchet. I didn't turn my back on him, and my anger was somehow rising. He had a smirk on his face, and he swung his hatchet as if to catch me in the thigh, though he wasn't near enough to me. Then he turned his back on me—arrogantly—and I hit him on the head with the big hammer. I hit him a second time as he was falling, but that landed on his back. I didn't know Peter was so close to me, or I didn't think about that. Peter came running, with his axe. Peter said, 'Good! Damn the bastard!' or something like that, and—" Dickenson seemed stuck for words, and looked at the floor, then the cat.

"And then? Reeves was dead?"

"Yes. All this happened in seconds. Peter really finished it with a bash on Reeves's head with the axe. We were quite near some woods—my woods. Peter said, 'Let's bury the swine! Get *rid* of him!' Peter was in a cursing rage and I was out of my mind for a different reason, maybe shock, but Peter was saying that Reeves had been having it off with his wife, too, or trying to, and that he knew about Reeves and Diane. Peter and I dug a grave in the woods, both of us working like madmen—hacking at tree roots and throwing up earth with our hands. At the last, just before we threw him in, Peter took the hatchet and said . . . something about Reeves's wedding ring, and he brought the hatchet down a couple of times on Reeves's hand."

Michael did not feel so well. He leaned over, mainly to lower his head, and stroked the cat's strong back. The cat still concentrated on Dickenson.

"Then—we buried it, both of us drenched in sweat by then. Peter said, 'You won't get a word out of me, sir. This bastard deserved what he got.' We trampled the grave and Peter spat on it. Peter's a man, I'll say that for him."

"A man. And you?"

"I dunno." Dickenson's eyes were serious when he next spoke. "That was one of the days Diane had a tea date at some women's club in our village. The same afternoon, I thought: My God, the fingers! Maybe they're just lying there on the ground, because I couldn't remember Peter or myself throwing them into the grave. So I went back. I found them. I could've dug another hole, except that I hadn't brought anything to dig with and I also didn't want . . . anything more of Reeves on my land. So I got into my car and drove, not caring where, not paying any attention to where I was, and when I saw some woods, I got out and flung the thing as far as I could."

Michael said, "Must've been within half a mile of this house. Portland Bill doesn't venture farther, I think. He's been doctored, poor old Bill." The cat looked up at his name. "You trust this Peter?"

"I do. I knew his father and so did my father. And if I were asked, I'm not sure I could say who struck the fatal blow, Peter or I. But to be correct, *I'd* take the responsibility because I did strike two blows with the hammer. I can't claim self-defence, because Reeves hadn't attacked me."

Correct. An odd word, Michael thought. But Dickenson was the type who would want to be correct. "What do you propose to do now?"

"Propose? I?" Dickenson's sigh was almost a gasp. "I dunno. I've admitted it. In a way it's in your hands or —" He made a gesture to indicate the downstairs. I'd like to spare Peter—keep him out of it—if I can. You understand, I think. I can talk to you. You're a man like myself."

Michael was not sure of that, but he had been trying to imagine himself in Dickenson's position, trying to see himself twenty years younger in the same circumstances. Reeves had been a swine—even to his own wife—unprincipled, and should a young man like Dickenson ruin his own life, or the best part of it, over a man like Reeves? "What about Reeves's wife?"

Dickenson shook his head and frowned. "I know she detested him. If he's absent without tidings, I'll wager she'll never make the least effort to find him. She's glad to be rid of him, I'm sure."

A silence began and grew. Portland Bill yawned, arched his back and stretched. Dickenson watched the cat as if he might say something; after all, the cat had discovered the fingers. Dickenson broke the silence awkwardly but in a polite tone:

"Where are the fingers, by the way?"

"In the back of my garage, which is locked. They're

in a shoe box." Michael felt quite off balance. "Look, I have two guests in the house."

Tom Dickenson got to his feet quickly. "I know. Sorry."

"Nothing to be sorry about, but I've really got to *say* something to them because the Colonel—my old friend Eddie—knows I rang you up about the initials on the ring and that you were to call on us—me. He could've said something to the others."

"Of course. I understand."

"Could you stay here for a few minutes while I speak with the people downstairs? Feel free with the whisky."

"Thank you." His eyes did not flinch.

Michael went downstairs. Phyllis was kneeling by the gramophone, about to put a record on. Eddie Phelps sat in a corner of the sofa reading a newspaper. "Where's Gladys?" Michael asked.

Gladys was deadheading roses. Michael called to her. She wore rubber boots like Dickenson, but hers were smaller, and bright red. Michael looked to see if Edna was behind the kitchen door. Gladys said Edna had gone off to buy something at the grocery. Michael told Dickenson's story, trying to make it brief and clear. Phyllis's mouth fell open a couple of times. Eddie Phelps held his chin in a wise-looking fashion and said, "Um-hm," now and then.

"I really don't feel like turning him in—or even speaking to the police," Michael ventured in a voice hardly above a whisper. No one had said anything after his narration, and he had waited several seconds. "I don't see why we can't just let it blow over. What's the harm?"

"What's the harm, yes," said Eddie Phelps, but it might have been a mindless echo for all the help it gave Michael.

"I've heard of stories like this—among primitive peoples," Phyllis said earnestly, as if to say she found Tom Dickenson's action quite justifiable.

Michael had of course included the resident worker Peter in his account. Had Dickenson's hammer blow been fatal, or the blow of Peter's axe? "The primitive ethic is not what I'm concerned with," Michael said, and at once felt confused. In regard to Tom Dickenson he was concerned with just the opposite of the primitive.

"But what else is it?" asked Phyllis.

"Yes, yes," said the Colonel, gazing at the ceiling.

"Really, Eddie," said Michael, "you're not being much of a help."

"I'd say nothing about it. Bury those fingers somewhere—with the ring. Or maybe the ring in a different place for safety. Yes." The Colonel was almost muttering, murmuring, but he did look at Michael.

"I'm not sure," said Gladys, frowning with thought.

"I agree with Uncle Eddie," Phyllis said, aware that Dickenson was upstairs awaiting his verdict. "Mr. Dickenson was provoked—*seriously*—and the man who got killed seems to have been a creep!"

"That's not the way the law looks at it," Michael said with a wry smile. "Lots of people are provoked seriously. And a human life is a human life."

"*We're* not the law," said Phyllis, as if they were something superior to the law just then.

Michael had been thinking just that: they were not the law, but they were acting as if they were. He was inclined to go along with Phyllis—and Eddie. "All right. I don't feel like reporting this, given all the circumstances. . . ."

But Gladys held out. She wasn't sure. Michael knew his wife well enough to believe that it was not going to be a bone of contention between them, if they were at variance—just now. So Michael said, "You're one against three, Glad. Do you seriously want to ruin a young man's life for a thing like this?"

"True; we've got to take a vote, as if we were a jury," said Eddie.

Gladys saw the point. She conceded. Less than a minute later, Michael climbed the stairs to his study, where the first draft of a book review curled in the roller of his typewriter, untouched since the day before yesterday. Fortunately, he could still meet the deadline without killing himself.

"We don't want to report this to the police," Michael said.

Dickenson, on his feet, nodded solemnly as if receiving a verdict. He would have nodded in the same manner if he had been told the opposite, Michael thought.

"I'll get rid of the fingers," Michael mumbled, and bent to get some pipe tobacco.

"Surely that's my responsibility. Let me bury them somewhere—with the ring."

It really was Dickenson's responsibility, and Michael was glad to escape the task. "Right. Well—shall we go downstairs? Would you like to meet my wife and my friend Colonel—"

"No, thank you. Not just now," Dickenson interrupted. "Another time. But would you give them . . . my thanks?"

They went down some other stairs at the back of the hall, and out to the garage, for which Michael had the key in his key case. He thought for a moment that the shoe box might have disappeared mysteriously, as in a detective story, but it was exactly where he had left it, atop the oil jerry cans. He gave it to Dickenson, and Dickenson departed northward in his dusty Triumph. Michael entered his house by the front door.

By now the others were having a drink. Michael felt suddenly relieved, and he smiled. "I think old Portland ought to have something special at the cocktail hour, don't you?" Michael said, mainly to Gladys.

Portland Bill was looking without much interest at a bowl of ice cubes. Only Phyllis said, "*Yes!*" with enthusiasm.

Michael went to the kitchen and spoke with Edna, who was dusting flour onto a board. "Any more smoked salmon left from lunch?"

"One slice, sir," said Edna, as if it weren't worth serving to anyone, and she virtuously hadn't eaten it, though she might.

"Can I have it for old Bill? He adores it." When Michael came back into the living room with the pink slice on a saucer, Phyllis said:

"I bet Mr. Dickenson wrecks his car on the way home. That's often the way it is." She whispered suddenly, remembering her manners: "Because he feels *guilty*."

Protland Bill bolted his salmon with brief but intense delight.

Tom Dickenson did not wreck his car.

The Postgraduate Thesis

CELIA FREMLIN

The beginning was exactly like the beginning of a story in a women's magazine; so much so, that I actually *felt* tall, dark and handsome, I really did. Well, who wouldn't in the situation I found myself in that afternoon?

Let me quickly give you the synopsis, and you'll see what I mean. Eligible young honours graduate (that's me), all set to rent picturesque country cottage for the summer, finds himself forestalled by beautiful blonde complete with order-to-view from the local estate agent. The two meet (surprise! surprise!) under the honeysuckle entwining the trellised porch; and at first (as is virtually obligatory in these sort of stories) she is a bit sharp with him not to say uppity. But after a few minutes . . .

By now, I am sure, you are feeling that you could go on with the story yourself, blindfolded, right through to the happy ending and the wedding bells. But it so happens, dear reader, that you are wrong. For though, as I say, the whole thing started like a magazine story, the ending was quite, quite different; it was an ending which no women's magazine anywhere—none that I know of, anyway—would countenance for one moment. Readers don't want horrors, we are told; particularly not horrific endings. They want to be assured that everything in the garden is lovely, that all clouds have silver linings, all that sort of thing. And why not, indeed? There is nothing unrealistic about it; lots of things *do* turn out all right in real life; plenty of people *are* quite happy: this, in fact, is something I have to keep reminding myself of when the horror of it all becomes more than I can bear. There *are* such things as happy endings, I keep telling myself; it didn't *have* to end the way it did. . . .

I must apologize. I suppose it is because I am a writer that I am thinking of the thing in these terms—a would-be writer, perhaps I should say, one of those legions of young men who come down from university each year with a good degree in English and a burning ambition not—but absolutely *not*—to teach. And since teaching is the one and only career for which a degree in English is the slightest use, I did what many another foolish and moderately fortunate fellow has done before me: I drew out my modest savings—a next egg left by my fond grandparents—and resolved to give myself a year, just one year, to become a Writer. As is well known, Writers (the ones with a capital *W*, that is) need to Get Away from It All; and so this was how it came about that at the age of twenty-two, on a hot June afternoon, under the honeysuckle of Green End Cottage, I met my destiny.

And everything in the garden *was* lovely. The nasturtiums were out, and the tiger lilies, and the stocks, all in a sweet-smelling, tangled profusion, growing like weeds, as they do in these old-fashioned cottage gardens. And the girl under the honeysuckle was like a flower herself, so straight and slim, her red-gold hair aflame in the midsummer sun. Only her expression was less than flowerlike; that, and the arrogant, possessive way she swung the heavy iron door key from the middle finger of her right hand.

"*I* was here first!" She addressed my belligerently, though in fact I had made no attempt, as yet, to question her prior rights; questioning the rights of beautiful girls is not something that I've ever gone in for much. "*I* was at the estate agent's before nine this morning. *I* spoke to Miss Fry herself. . . ."

way. A girl with whom it would be pointless to argue.

But since when has anyone—particularly anyone with a university education—refrained from argument simply because he knows it to be pointless?

"*I* spoke to Miss Fry, too," I lied glibly (actually Miss Fry was as yet only a name to me, from the estate agent's lists); and I added, for good measure, "She told me I was just the sort of tenant she—"

"No!" The girl was outraged, tossing her blazing head like a flamethrower. "That's what she said to *me!* She said *I* was just the sort of tenant she—"

"She didn't!"

"She did!"

The playground idiocy of the dialogue struck us both simultaneously; together we burst out laughing; and within minutes we were inside the cottage, exploring.

I don't know what Theresa (for this, I learned, was the girl's name) was thinking as she looked around; but for myself, I could see at once that this was the ideal setting for an aspiring writer. You know, the nitty-gritty and all that, starting with a stone-flagged kitchen where nothing worked except, intermittently and with terrible gurglings, a single cold-water tap. On the other side of the passageway was what I suppose you would call a "parlour"—a cavern of green darkness from vegetation overgrowing the cobwebby window and blotting out the midsummer sun. Upstairs—up, that is, a narrow flight of creaking wooden steps—there was a long, low attic bedroom, with one tiny grimy window and a sloping ceiling. For anyone planning to starve in a garret, this was the garret *par excellence:* only ten minutes away from the village pub, and everything inches thick in dust; no one had done any cleaning here in years, and so why should *I* be expected to start?

All this was wasted on a woman: a woman's first instinct would be to get at the place with a bucket and broom.

I began trying to explain this to Theresa; but when I saw that familiar Women's Lib look coming over her face, I hastily changed my tactics. There were other forms of dissuasion.

"You do know, don't you," I said (and I'll swear that at that moment I honestly had no idea that I was telling anything more than a light-hearted lie), "you do know, don't you, that this place is supposed to be haunted?"

Looking back, I can't think what reaction I expected to evoke by this bit of invention. I could hardly have expected a girl like Theresa to go all pale and trembly at the idea, and to say that as in that case nothing would induce her to rent the cottage, I could have it all for my own; but all the same, I was a bit deflated when she merely laughed.

"Well, of course I know!" she retorted. "That's why I'm so anxious to live in it for a bit. I'm doing a thesis, you see, on Rural Superstitions, and so . . ."

And so the afternoon shadows were reaching far across the tangled, overgrown garden, and the scent of the flowers was almost gone, by the time she'd finished telling me about her thesis, about her sociology degree, and about her boyfriend, who might, or who on the other hand might not, be coming to join her in the cottage, sooner or maybe later.

And after that it was my turn. I told her about my ambitions, and about the awfulness of having an English degree and already being twenty-two; but when it came to the question of how I could afford to get away from it all like this, I found I just couldn't bring myself to tell her about my grandfather's legacy. Well, you know how my generation feels about inherited wealth; I was just too ashamed. And so I told her instead (improvising on the spur of the moment, as one has to on these occasions) that I had already written one novel, and that my publishers were so confident it was going to be a best seller that they'd given me this huge advance. . . .

Well, of course, if I'd understood Theresa then as I came to understand her later, I would never have dreamed of telling her this pack of lies; but at the time she was simply an attractive stranger whom I was setting out to impress. I had no idea, then, that our relationship was going to develop as it did—nor, indeed, that we were ever going to see each other again after that one afternoon.

But you know how it is: one thing leads to another, and by the end of that long midsummer day, I had not only totally relinquished my own (admittedly tenuous) claim to the cottage, but had offered to help her move in; which, two days later, she did.

By this time, I couldn't see a reason in the world why I shouldn't move in with her, cobwebby attic bedroom and all. But what about the boyfriend, Colin? she said. Well, what about him? I replied. I mean, he wasn't here, was he? And who'd helped her move in, anyway, him or me? You don't have to be nasty about him, she'd retorted. He's probably coming down this very weekend—on the Friday evening, very likely, or possibly not till Saturday. . . .

And so, in the end, rather than waste in argument the sunshine, and the scent of the cow parsley, and the way it felt to be walking hand in hand with her through the long summer grass—rather than put all these present delights at risk, I shrugged, and agreed to keep my room at the pub for the time being. I promised, too, to keep away from the cottage over the weekend. She insisted on this.

It was a setback, but I wasn't unduly bothered. There was, after all, something rather special about falling in love slowly like this. We had the whole summer ahead of us, and with this Colin character only around for odd weekends, time was clearly on my side.

Or so I thought. . . .

And that, I suppose, was the end, really, of the women's magazine part of the story, though I did not realize it at the time. On the contrary, when I arrived at the cottage on Monday morning and learned that Colin hadn't turned up after all, I was jubilant. I remember standing there under the honeysuckle, breathing in the news of Theresa's disappointment as if it was yet another of the sweet scents of summer, mingling with the scent of the stocks and of the sweet williams. I felt, in that moment, as if the whole golden summer was on my side, leaning up against me like a great, warm, purring cat, edging me towards some new and incomparable happiness.

Perhaps even then, even in that very moment of joy and triumph, I should have realized that something was amiss. I can only say that I didn't. I simply felt an immense and uncomplicated delight that my rival seemed to have been so easily and painlessly eliminated, and it never even occurred to me to ask Theresa what had gone wrong. Still less did it occur to me to condole with her on her disappointment, or to wonder why, in that first second when she opened the door to me, something had flashed into her eyes that looked for a moment like fear. . . .

Anyway, it was all over in a moment; and there was no doubt at all that once she had taken in who it was, she was pleased to see me. Smiling, she took my hand and led me into the cool, sunless kitchen at the back of the cottage, and began talking, almost at once, about her thesis. It was going well, she said, filling the old iron kettle and preparing to make coffee; she felt that she was really getting somewhere—and since this was precisely where my own writing currently *wasn't* getting, I had to suppress a sharp and painful stab of envy.

But suppress it I did. For one thing, I still didn't want Theresa to know that I was something less than the established and successful writer I'd pretended to be; and for another, I wanted to keep her talking, in that husky, eager voice, and to watch her as she moved about the kitchen, her bright hair now red, now gold, among the changing shadows.

Right from the start, the subject of Theresa's thesis had struck me as slightly bizarre—though not outstandingly so, I suppose, sociology being the sort of subject that it is; and certainly, the earnestness with which she applied herself to it, and to the collecting of the necessary data, seemed to me to be touching rather than ma-

cabre. Her work, if such it may be called, seemed to
consist mainly of wandering around the village in the
pleasant June weather asking old gaffers what they'd
heard from their grandfathers about the "haunted" cottage: getting the vicar to show her some bones, or
something, out of the crypt; and then writing it all up in
her round, rather childish handwriting and filing it under headings like "Bones, Hallowed and Unhallowed,"
"Vampires, Miscellaneous," and so forth.

To me, during the long summer days, it all seemed
perfectly harmless, and rather sweet. All these legends
she was managing to unearth about the cottage—
bricked-up brides, gibbering skeletons, all that sort of
thing—roused in me nothing more than a sort of awed
wonderment that she should actually be getting *paid* for
it. I even began to wonder whether I shouldn't have
gone in for postgraduate work myself.

But I must be fair. It wasn't *all* headless monks and
unhallowed corpses mooching around the centuries like
bored teenagers on a Sunday afternoon; here and there
a dollop of real, actual history would raise its uneasy
head.

"In the reign of Henry IV," I remember her reading
out excitedly one golden noontime, with the bees buzz-
ing in and out of the marigolds and the lupines, "in the
rign of Henry IV, it was decreed that the Juries, after
they had been sworn, should not see nor take cognizance of any other evidence than that which had already
been laid before the open court. . . ."

What with the bees, and the sunshine, and the music
of her eager, slightly breathless voice only inches from
my ear, it is not to be wondered at that I was not apply-
ing any very deep critical attention to the vagaries of
fourteenth-century judicial practice; but to the story to
which all this proved to be a preamble I did listen. It
concerned an unhappy damsel whose lover was on trial
for a murder he hadn't committed—*couldn't* have committed, for he had been in her arms throughout the fateful night—so that now it was she, and she alone of all
the world, who had in her possession the evidence

which would have saved him. Torn between the maidenly modesty appropriate to those times, and fear for her lover's life, she dillied and dallied despairingly, wrestling with her medieval conscience, praying to her medieval God, and all the time hoping against hope that the poor fellow might somehow get let off without her intervention. Only when it came to the very last day before the verdict was to be given did she summon up the courage to reveal her shameful secret.

But by this time it was too late. The jury, to their despair and fury (for the accused man was a merry fellow, and well liked in the village), were not permitted to "take cognizance" of this belated though conclusive bit of evidence, and were compelled, knowing that he was innocent, to declare the young man guilty.

They never forgave her. The night after he was hanged, they came in a body to the cottage, all twelve of them, seeking vengeance; but lo and behold, the girl had vanished, never to be seen again.

And very sensible of her, too, you may say—the first sensible thing she'd done throughout the whole sorry business—but of course, that wasn't how they saw it in the fourteenth century. Having searched the cottage and the surrounding fields and woods all that night and for many days after, they finally settled, in the absence of her physical body, for a ceremonial cursing—priest, candles, the whole bit—with solemn prayers for her soul, that it should never find rest.

Which it didn't, of course (well, it wouldn't have been much use to Theresa's thesis if it had, would it?), and neither did the souls of those twelve jurors, whose rage, frustration and sense of justice outraged went with them to their graves . . . so that sometimes, on that stretch of lonely lane that winds from the churchyard to the cottage, you may still see the shadowy outlines of cloaked men in the moonlight, hear the tramp, tramp of long-dead feet—the feet of men still reaching out for vengeance from a distance of nearly six hundred years.

Theresa, of course, was thrilled by this dismal little

tale, and anxious to get it down as quickly as possible, while the details were still fresh in her mind. In the end she dictated it to me, as she said she could think better that way, and we filed it, I remember, under "Apparitions, Multiple," and then we went down to supper.

I was used to it by now, of course, but at the beginning I'd been amazed at the nonchalance with which Theresa could thus thrust her day's gruesome findings into their appropriate files and then, apparently, think no more about them. Didn't she ever feel frightened, I used to ask her, all alone in the creaking, ancient cottage after I'd left her and gone back to my lodgings?

She seemed quite surprised at such a notion.

"But I'm *studying* the subject, don't you see?" she would explain. "You can't be frightened of something you're *studying*. You can't really feel anything much about it at all."

And remembering my own experiences of getting up *Hamlet,* say, or *Macbeth,* for some imminent exam, I did know exactly what she meant. I suppose this is one of the occupational hazards of the academic life, this draining away of emotion in the interests of exact knowledge; but it has its advantages as well as its disadvantages. It certainly had for us: it meant that Theresa wasn't frightened, I wasn't worried about her, and in this peaceful ambience our relationship seemed to be blossoming smoothly, easily, and without trauma or anxiety.

And so when, a week or so later, Miss Fry, the owner of Green End Cottage, marched up to me one morning in the village street and accused me of deliberately terrorizing her new tenant with stories of the cottage being haunted, I was completely thrown.

By now I knew Miss Fry quite well by sight, though this was the first time we had actually engaged in conversation. She was not a lady who looked easy to converse with—sixty if she was a day, and very tough, pounding around the neighbourhood on a bicycle, her thick, muscular legs taking the hills at a speed which put my own effete and pleasure-loving generation to shame.

So when she skidded to a stop and strode across the street towards me, all tweeds and weather-beaten indignation, I could find at first absolutely nothing to say. The accusation was so wild, you see, and so absurdly wide of the mark, that I simply could not orientate myself. It was *I* who had been putting all this superstitious nonsense into Theresa's head? *I* who had been filling her imagination with gruesome fancies, so that she was scared to death every time she spent a night alone in the cottage? The sheer idiotic injustice of the charges took my breath away.

"But it's *she* who——" I began angrily, and then stopped. For Theresa had, right at the beginning, extracted from me a promise that I would tell no one—absolutely no one—about the subject of her thesis. She'd explained that she was employing the "depth interview" technique, which meant that she had to engage her victims in conversation, and get them to answer her questions, without their realizing what she was up to; and naturally, if it once got around the village that she was interviewing them for her thesis and writing up everything they said about the "haunted" cottage, then their reactions to her questions would no longer be "spontaneous and unbiased."

Her phrase, not mine. For it seemed to me (though of course I didn't tell her so) that their reactions were probably pretty suspect, anyway. Not that I'd ever seen her in action: the hours she spent on "fieldwork" (as she called this business of chatting up startled yokels leaning over gates) seemed always to be just exactly those same hours that *I* spent brooding over my typewriter in my room above the saloon bar, and so I can't speak with authority; I can only guess. But my guess was that the yokels, having recovered from their first stupefaction, would have fixed their rustic gaze on that smashing head of hair and on those wide, green-flecked eyes, and would have proceeded to do whatever it seemed necessary to do to keep the goods around. Yokels aren't stupid—that I *have* learned—and as soon as they discovered that what kept her chatting them up was a bit of well-chosen grue about Green End Cottage, why, then, a bit of grue they'd give her, tailored to the occasion. They wouldn't be short of plots; after all, they all watched television, and their knowledge of village superstitions probably matched hers easily, werewolf for werewolf.

But I am digressing. The validity or otherwise of Theresa's research methods was irrelevant to my immediate predicament. The point is that I had promised, no matter how light-heartedly, that I would keep the subject of her thesis a secret; and so now, confronted by Miss Fry and her outrageous accusations, I was left with no way of defending myself. To have pointed out to Miss Fry that if Theresa *was* scared (and I happened to know she wasn't), then she must be scaring herself with her own research project, would have been a breach of trust of which I'm not capable: not when the trusting is done by a beautiful girl, anyway.

So, "Er . . ." I said; and, "Um . . . well . . . you see . . ." I must have sounded guilty as hell. Miss Fry simply overrode my feeble protestations, and in a loud, overbearing voice, which carried from one end of the village street to the other, she got on with the case against me. How dared I use my talent for fiction (yes, it had got around that I had come here to write)—how dared I use this talent for the perverted purpose of terrifying a susceptible young girl (Theresa susceptible? I should be so lucky!) and trying to frighten her into giving up her tenancy of the cottage! Only a couple of mornings ago, before Miss Fry was even out of bed, it seemed that the poor girl had come knocking on her door in a state of near hysteria, babbling of disembodied voices, of skeleton knuckles rapping on the window, of phantom footsteps and demonic howlings round and about the cottage. . . .

And so on and so on. I knew it was all lies, because I'd seen Theresa both yesterday and the day before, and hadn't heard a word about any of it. *Why* Miss Fry should go to the trouble of concocting this ludicrous rigmarole I couldn't imagine; maybe old maids of sixty were like that? The one thing that *did* get me on the raw, though, was the implication that *I,* a serious up-and-coming novelist in the Social Realism tradition, could possibly, in any circumstances whatever, have employed my "talent for fiction" on such a load of outdated Gothick balderdash! I was outraged, I felt professionally insulted, and I turned on Miss Fry in a sort of impotent fury—impotent because I couldn't say any of the things I really wanted to without breaking my promise to Theresa.

Still, I did my best. I didn't exactly call her a meddling old fool—something in those snapping, colonel's-daughter eyes precluded such language—but I think the idea must have got across, because when she mounted her bicycle again she was actually trembling with rage.

"You'll be sorry for this!" was her parting shot, as her well-brogued foot drove against the pedal. "You'll be sorry! As the dear vicar was telling me only last week . . ."

I wish, now, that I'd listened more carefully to what the dear vicar *had* been telling her. But how was I to know then that it would be worth hearing? I had met the Reverend Pinkerton only once since taking up my residence here, and I had formed the opinion—a snap judgement, I have to admit—that he was crackers. Either that, or he was a very, very holy man indeed.

It was on that first Monday morning that our encounter had taken place. I was on my way up the lane that led to Green End Cottage, full of dark thoughts about the weekend boyfriend (I didn't know then, of course, that he hadn't turned up after all), when I heard footsteps round the bend ahead of me—quick, loud footsteps, almost running—and a moment later, down the lane towards me, black as a crow in his clerical garb, the Reverend Pinkerton came striding. He was muttering as he came, and as he drew near I heard the words:

"Evil! Before my very eyes . . . the embodiment of Evil!"

I thought at first that he was addressing me personally; and I was just trying to think of the right reply—I mean, "And good morning to you, too, sir," didn't seem to strike quite the right note—when I realized he wasn't speaking to me at all; hadn't, indeed, actually seen me, for all that his pale, wild eyes seemed to be staring right into mine. He was in some sort of trance, or state of prayer, or something, I decided; and when he strode on past me without a backward look, I breathed a sigh of relief. The last thing I wanted this morning was a lecture on the Nature of Evil.

And so, naturally, I'd written him off, poor old chap (well, not *so* old really—around fifty, I'd guess, but you know what I mean). And equally naturally, when Miss Fry invoked his name to clinch her crazy argument, I'm afraid I could only laugh. I wish now that I hadn't; as I say, I wish that I'd actually listened to those parting shots of hers, but how could I have guessed—how could I possibly, at that time, have conceived—that above Mr. Pinkerton's grim clerical collar and beneath his sparse greying hair dwelt the only brain which already knew the secret which would have saved me? I didn't even know there *was* any secret; there had been nothing in Miss Fry's melodramatic maunderings to make it cross my mind, even for a moment, that there might *actually* be something mysterious about Green End Cottage; that those ancient walls really *might* be harbouring forces of evil; that in that cottage where Theresa spent her days and her solitary nights there might be danger—real, deadly danger—lurking.

And so, as I say, I laughed. After all these humiliating and unfounded accusations, to which I was debarred from replying, it was good at the end to have the last laugh. I laughed as Miss Fry angrily hoisted her great tweed-clad bottom into the saddle; and I was laughing still as I watched her pedalling umbrageously down the street, her front wheel wobbling with temper.

Theresa thought it was all very funny. And I suppose it was, really. Certainly, I tried to make it sound so, because I didn't want Theresa to imagine that I had for one moment taken Miss Fry's far-fetched allegations seriously—particularly the bit about Theresa having knocked on Miss Fry's door in such an uncharacteristic state of nervous alarm. Reassuringly, this was the bit that made her laugh most of all, though not until she had ascertained, with a couple of sharp questions, that I had at no point given away to Miss Fry the subject of her thesis. Reassured as to this, she relaxed, and I'll never forget the fun we had that afternoon, lying in the long grass behind the cottage, my arm thrown lightly across her lissome body (the nearest to lovemaking that she would so far allow, on account of Colin, the Vanishing Wonder), and talking about Miss Fry.

Not a very romantic topic, you may object? Ah, dear reader, you don't understand! When you are young, and carefree, and in love, there is something infinitely satisfying in the contemplation of all the people who are none of these things. People like Miss Fry, old and ugly and alone—and all through her own fault, because she had never had the courage to grasp at happiness when it was offered . . . had never lain in the long June grass with a man's arms around her . . . never heard his whispered words of love. . . .

I don't know why we were so sure that she hadn't. We'd "typed" her, I suppose (in the jargon of Theresa's colleagues); the stereotype of the village old maid was just what we needed on that golden afternoon, to enhance by contrast our own sense of triumphant and eternal youth. The mere contemplation of Miss Fry's primness and old-maidishness made us feel deliciously and quite effortlessly abandoned, though in fact we were both limp with the heat.

"The poor old thing's half crazed with jealousy, you see," Theresa explained, in her psychological-insight voice, playing smugly with the lobe of my ear as she spoke, to show how different she was from Miss Fry. "You see, having heard that I was a Ph.D. student, she must at once have pictured the sort of frumpish, lumpish creature that female students were in *her* young days. But now that she's actually *seen* me, and . . . well . . . noticed that I've found myself a rather nice young man—What? . . . Oh, but yes, sweetie, you *are* nice, of course you are, I never said— No, look, darling, stop it. Remember we agreed. . . ."

"We" was an overstatement, but I let it pass. As I say, it was so *very* hot, and it was nice to hear Theresa's earnest, husky voice going on and on so close to my ear.

"You see," she was explaining, "she's got you cast as the villain. A real, old-fashioned villain, like the ones in the novelettes of her youth. She thinks you're plotting a fate worse than death for me—"

"I am," I interrupted, but Theresa carried on as if I hadn't spoken, psychoanalyzing Miss Fry and her repressed urges, her fantasy sex substitutes, until, to tell the honest truth, I was nearly asleep.

I got the gist of it, though. Miss Fry, for all these complex reasons that I hadn't really listened to, now had me cast as the friendly neighbourhood rapist, whose life style consisted of first persuading innocent girls that the cottage they'd rented for the summer was haunted, and then offering to come and protect them from the ghostly visitations of the night. . . .

"That's an idea!" I interposed, tightening my arms round her. "Grrrrrr—rrrr! Whoo-ee-ooo! Come on! Be terrified! Don't you recognize a ghost noise when you hear it? And you an expert on village superstitions?"

"Silly!" She struggled free of my embraces; and a few minutes later, we went indoors to make tea. And even now, when I know all too well, and with exact and dreadful clarity, exactly what was to follow, I still have to say that that pot of tea we took out into the garden was the most delicious I have ever tasted. Boiling hot, as tea should be, and yet refreshing as iced water on this scorching afternoon. I remember, too, what fun we had while we drank it—laughing, throwing bits of grass at each other, and generally fooling around.

And that night, for the first time, Theresa did not send me away when dusk fell.

How can I describe what happened next? Where can I begin? Not with our lovemaking, because it still hurts to remember how marvellous it was, and how close it seemed to bring us, beyond anything I had ever experienced. Perhaps the place to begin is afterwards—just a few minutes afterwards; half an hour at most.

"Let's make some tea," said Theresa, swinging her legs out of bed and feeling around for her slippers on the dusty floor. "I always seem to feel like a cup of tea at this stage."

From the depths of the bed I murmured something which was neither yes nor no. It wasn't that I disliked the idea of a cup of tea; it was just that I wanted to go on lying here, feeling perfect, for a bit longer. And I wanted her to go on lying here, feeling perfect, too.

But already this was no longer an option. Once one of you has said, "Let's make some tea," then it's been said, and there is no going back. Theresa found her slippers and padded off out of the room; and as for me, I pulled the blankets up a bit and simply went on lying there, utterly content, watching the stars coming out one by one through the small dusty square of the window. This is it, I remember thinking. This is what life is all about. This is total, absolute happiness.

From where I lay, I could hear Theresa moving about downstairs: the faint clink of crockery . . . the thump of the big kettle . . . the opening and shutting of a dresser-drawer . . . the nostalgic, heartwarming sound of a woman's footsteps back and forth across a kitchen floor.

And then, suddenly, I heard her scream.

I was out of bed and down those stairs before she could have drawn a second breath; and I found her, not in the kitchen, but in the "parlour," that gloomy little front room that by day was bathed in eternal dim green light from the rampant vegetation over the windows, and which now, by night, was almost completely black, only a thin tracery of moonlight finding its way through the tangle of leaves, and throwing a sort of silvery basketwork of light across the old warped boards. By this faint, irregular illumination I was just able to make out Theresa's figure—still whitely naked, she had not troubled to add a dressing gown to the slippers when she got out of bed—crouched in a corner of the room.

"Darling!" I cried, stumbling towards her through a dim clutter of intervening furniture. "Darling, what . . . ? Who . . . ?"

By now I had reached her, my hand was on her shoulder, and I was aware that she was shuddering from head to foot, racked (as I thought for a moment) by violent sobbing.

But it was laughter. The relief was almost as big a shock as the screaming itself had been. I half-shook her, in a mixture of thankfulness and indignation.

"What the *hell* . . . ?" I began.

"I—I'm sorry, darling," she gasped, between paroxysms of laughter, "but it was so *funny,* you see! First finding this awful great knife—" Here she brandished before my eyes an evil-looking weapon nearly a foot long and glinting dreadfully in the moonlight. "It was in the dresser drawer, I'd never seen it before, it really gave me a shock; and then, suddenly, I couldn't help myself thinking: Miss Fry!" Here she was once more overcome by giggles. "Poor old Miss Fry—if only *she'd* found it! She'd have been absolutely certain that it was the very weapon with which you threatened me when you raped me this evening!"

I was laughing, too, by this time. I found myself catching her mood, and in a moment—both of us still stark naked—we were giggling and fooling.

"Your honour or your life!" I yelled, in a melodramatic, villainous sort of voice, brandishing the knife in mock savagery. "You are at my mercy, gentle maiden! Tonight I shall have my will of you!"

Her screams were most convincing; as also was her portrayal of a panic-stricken virgin defending her honour. Louder and louder she shrieked, dodging in and out among the shadowy furniture, while I followed in pursuit. A chair went crashing over . . . then a vase. The sound of splintering glass sobered me.

"Enough, darling!" I exclaimed, reaching out a restraining hand towards Theresa, who was still shrieking, and darting hither and thither, as though quite carried away by her own playacting. I tried to grab her by her arms . . . by her waist . . . but each time she somehow slithered from my grip. I began to feel alarmed.

"Enough, Theresa! Really!" I repeated urgently. "We'll be smashing the place up if we aren't careful! And if you keep screaming like that, they really *will* think I'm raping you. . . ."

"Of course they will." Theresa was suddenly standing motionless, completely quiet and controlled. "That's the whole idea. And unless you promise me, here and now, to give me two thousand pounds—"

At first, naturally, I thought she was still fooling.

"And cheap at the price!" I cried gaily; and added, laughing, "What a shame that our own dear Miss Fry wasn't at the window watching our little skirmish just now! She'd have had me in jail on a rape charge before I could have said 'extenuating circumstances!' "

"She was; and she will," Theresa replied quietly. "I saw her face at the window just exactly when you started chasing me round the room with the knife: the timing was perfect. You see, I knew it would take her just about that long to get here on her bicycle after she heard my first scream. Sounds carry well in the country, you know, especially at night.

"Besides, she's been expecting it, ever since I told her about your weird rape fantasies—all that stuff about the fourteenth-century jurymen, in your own handwriting. . . .

"Yes, *of course* it was a rape fantasy: what do you *think* they'd have done to her, those twelve enraged medieval peasants? They'd have raped her, naturally, before they murdered her, if only to make sure that she'd go to Hell. Anyone knows *that* much about the Middle Ages—certainly Miss Fry does, though I daresay she's too much of a lady to put it into words. Oh, she understood, all right . . . and she agreed with me that a young man with his mind stuffed full of such peculiar and sadistic fantasies could easily become dangerous. If ever you threatened me, she said, or frightened me in any way, then I was to scream out, as loud as I could, and she'd be here on her bicycle within a couple of minutes. . . . And she was, too; just nicely in time to see everything she needed to see, and to go for help. By now she'll have roused half the village . . . and so you really *will* hear that tramp, tramp, tramp of avenging feet, won't you? You thought it was all nonsense, didn't you?

"And so which is it to be, my dear? Six years for rape? Or two thousand pounds by tomorrow afternoon? And don't tell me you haven't got it! That bloody best seller of yours . . . !"

Which was, of course, exactly where she'd miscalculated. No doubt the thing had worked well enough on the poor harmless old vicar, whose whole livelihood was put in jeopardy on that unlucky day when he'd innocently shown her those interesting old bones in the crypt. I recalled that stunned, unbelieving look in his eyes as he stumbled back from handing over the hush money that Monday morning: he'd never believed before in the power of Evil, but he did now, all right.

And so did I. In how many other remote villages, on how many other gullible vicars and besotted young men, had she played this same trick, complete with the nonexistent "thesis"? Or maybe with some other ploy, according to the educational level of her victim?

"Well, which is it to be?" she demanded once more, her white, naked body straight as a candle among the shadows. "I can tell them we were just fooling, or I can tell them . . . the other story! Choose quickly. They'll be here in a minute, or less . . ." and indeed, I could already hear the crunch of tires, the clamour of voices, at the end of the lane. Already the first of the headlights were sweeping across the garden.

"Quick! Make up your mind!" she snarled; but of course my mind was already made up.

For the Reverend Pinkerton, surrender may have been inevitable; his whole career was at stake.

But mine wasn't. And that was just where Theresa had gone so very wrong in her calculations—and not merely through believing my cock-and-bull story about the best seller, either. Naturally, I don't *want* to serve a prison sentence on a false charge of rape, any more than I wanted to have my heart broken and my faith in human nature shattered forever; but by God, if that's the way it goes, I really *shall* have a best seller on my hands, right slap in the mainstream of Social Realism at its starkest.

Or maybe, now I come to think of it, I might try my hand at an old-fashioned Gothick.

Why ever not?

Gup

H. R. F. KEATING

At ease in the shade on a warped wooden bench outside a tea stall in the bazaar, Sudhir Naik, the telegraph operator, blew skillfully across the milky liquid in his saucer.

"Yes," he said, "I sent the cable. To U.K. To the beautiful Webster Gardens, London W.5."

For the benefit of those of his listeners who did not speak the language of the Angrezi-log, he translated the word "Gardens." "With many, many flowers," he added. "And the scent also of much frangipane. Beautiful."

His hearers wagged their heads in appreciation. No one asked what had been said in the cable. They knew that in his own good time Sudhir Naik would tell them.

He did better. From the pocket of his uniform he drew out the crumpled sheet which he had had before him when he had operated his Morse key. There was a craning forward of faces shining with delighted interest.

"Ah, yes," said old Laloo, who was a servant at a bungalow on the outskirts of the hill station and was sometimes concerned that he did not get to hear the news as quickly as others did. "Yes, I knew Cadogan Sahib must be dead. I knew it at once when my memsahib was saying to my sahib, 'But it's only a rumour, Peter, just bazaar gup.'"

He had imitated to a nicety the strident voice of his mistress and received an appreciative chuckle from

those members of the circle who came into direct contact with the English.

From the opposite pocket of his uniform Sudhir Naik
then drew out his spectacles. He polished them on the
loose corner of the jacket, taking delicate care with the
lens that was cracked, and placed them with ceremony
upon his nose. He picked up the telegraph form,
cleared his throat, looked round at them all and at last
read out the English words.

"Mahadharwar, 13 September, 1935. Miss Elizabeth
Cadogan, 18 Webster Gardens, London W.5. Have to
inform you with greatest regret your nephew Rupert
passed away effects malaria. Letter follows. All condol-
ences. Anketell Brown, Chairman Mahadharwar Club."

He left a pause after the reading so that those of
them with good enough English could fully savour what
they had heard. Then he explained to the others that
"passed away" was what the Angrezi-log said when
they meant "died," and that Anketell Brown Sahib was
the burra sahib at the club, and that "effects malaria"
was a lie.

Moti was only a boy. But there was always one of
the long-established club servants to explain things to
him in the long, sun-slowed hours while the sahibs slept
in their homes under the burring drone of their new
electric fans. Sometimes even the butler, Ram Lal,
heavy brass-badged sash and stiff white turban laid
aside, would enlighten his ignorance.

"Now, Cadogan Sahib is Assistant Secretary Sahib.
But Major Johnson Sahib, also known by the name of
Horrible Horace, is Secretary Sahib. Understand that,
little fool."

"Oh, yes, khitmagar sahib. But if Cadogan Sahib is a
burra sahib also, why is Major Johnson Sahib always
angry against him?"

Ram Lal looked grave.

"That is because of Cadogan Sahib's *cigarette case*,"
he said, laying down the words, vernacular and English,

one by one so that at last they formed an edifice that would stand up against even a hurricane.

Puzzled, Moti looked down for comfort to the lump of dirty rag with which he cleaned the floors of the club's corridors, his particular charge.

"But, khitmagar sahib, why is this *cigarette case* making Secretary Sahib always angry. Is it because Cadogan Sahib has stolen?"

The butler laughed.

"Oh, little one, you have plenty to learn. Cadogan Sahib is a true Angrezi sahib. Such a one does not steal. No, no. It is because on the *cigarette case* there is *crest*. A *crest*, you know, is a very strong magical sign that is saying that Cadogan Sahib comes from a very, very great family across the black water."

"But then," asked the boy, who knew so little, "why is not Cadogan Sahib the Secretary and Major Johnson Sahib Assistant Secretary only?"

"Ah, that is because, although Major Johnson Sahib is not at all from a great family and was ranker officer only before he was retiring and becoming Secretary of Mahadharwar Club, Cadogan Sahib's family is losing all, all their money. So Cadogan Sahib is having to come to India to take job. Because in U.K. now there are no jobs for foolish young men, even though they are from great families, like Cadogan Sahib."

The boy Moti sighed, as did the other servants who were sitting or lying in this coolest spot in the club's servant quarter.

"Yes," said the butler, "so that is why Major Johnson Sahib, whom the burra sahibs are calling Horrible Horace when it is behind his back, is always angry with Cadogan Sahib."

"And it is for that reason," added Gopal, Major Johnson's bearer, who had come across from the Johnsons' bungalow on the other side of the club compound to join in talking the afternoon away, "that soon after Cadogan Sahib had come, Major Johnson Sahib was telling him that the servant he had got was a great bad-mash, when everybody is knowing he is altogether hon-

est and good at his work also, and making him instead
take that fellow Mangu, who would steal from his own
mother."

"Yes, yes," agreed Ram Lal. "That is what Major
Johnson Sahib is always doing. Moti, my boy, keep out
of the way of Major Johnson Sahib. He is *not quite a
gentleman.*"

Moti gratefully inclined his head at the advice.

The evening before, Mangu, the thief, had been present at a small gathering of servants from here and
there around the station who would meet, when they
could, in the potting shed in the corner of the garden at
Ethel Cottage. Kanni, the mali whose responsibility the
garden was, lived in the shed and liked to extend its
hospitality to cronies whose special delight lay in discussing the sexual peccadilloes of the Angrezi-log.

"Maisie the Man-Eater," Mangu had just proclaimed
to them in English.

The others sitting round, comfortably cross-legged,
all knew well that this was the name the European community had bestowed on the wife of Major Johnson,
Secretary of the Mahadharwar Club. But they appre-
ciated Mangu's reference with as much chuckling and
elbow-digging as if this was the first time they had
heard it.

"Maisie the Man-Eater," Kanni repeated when the
original impulse had at last died away.

He wagged his head marvellingly.

"And now," added Mangu, "she is beginning to gob-
ble up Cadogan Sahib. In his sleep I have heard him
mutter her name even. 'Maisie, Maisie.' "

His imitation was considered extraordinarily droll
and he was pressed several times to repeat it.

"And," asked Kanni at last, with a fearful leer, "have
the jaws snapped yet? Eh? Eh? Eh?"

"Ah," Mangu answered, "that is tonight. Tonight.
Snap."

And he brought his own stumpy and red betel-stained teeth together with a shomp that reverberated from side to side of the close, earth-smelling shed.

"Yes," he went on after the laughter, "I heard her say to him yesterday, 'Darling, Horace always plays in the Diwali Night bridge tournament. So tomorrow we can be together, at last.' And afterwards she is telling him that always Major Johnson Sahib puts his own name on top of the pile when Anketell Brown Sahib is making draw. And next he puts Hitchman Sahib's just underneath, so that in that way he makes sure of becoming partner with the best player in whole Mahadharwar Club. 'Darling, we will have hours together, hours,' she is saying. And Cadogan Sahib is saying, 'Oh, Maisie.' "

The laughter at Mangu's imitation of lonely, lovelorn Rupert Cadogan's voice was tremendous. It quite drowned the pops and bangs from the many crackers and rockets with which are celebrated Diwali, when with lights and fireworks of every sort of goddess Lakshmi is begged to bring modest prosperity to all in the year ahead.

That same firework-popping night, Ram Lal, the butler, and Chandra, the club billiards marker, chanced to pass each other in a dark passage as they went about their duties. They exchanged a few brief words.

"Oh, oh, great trouble, khitmagar sahib."

"What trouble, Chandra bhai?"

"Anketell Brown Sahib has done a terrible thing."

"What thing, Chandra bhai?"

"When he was offered mighty bridge cup by Major Johnson Sahib to make draw for Diwali Night tournament, he was not taking top piece of paper in customary manner."

"Aiee," said the butler, at once grasping the implications. "So Major Johnson Sahib has not drawn Hitchman Sahib for partner?"

"Oh, khitmagar sahib, it is worse than that."

"Worse than that, Chandra bhai?"

"Khitmagar sahib, he was drawn Murdoch Sahib."
The butler patted his cheeks in dismay.

"Murdoch Sahib, whom all are calling 'rabbit,' " he
exclaimed.

"Already, khitmagar sahib, Major Johnson Sahib is
saying, 'Sorry, you chaps, beastly headache, must take a
stroll.' But he is going, of course, back to his bungalow."

The butler darted a glance along the passage. Beyond
the open doors of the dining room he could see that all
his waiters seemed to be properly busy laying their tables. Perhaps he could afford to linger one moment
more.

"And Johnson Memsahib?" he asked the billiards
marker. "Is Maisie the Man-Eater playing mah-jongg
tonight at Hitchman Memsahib's bungalow, as she told
Major Johnson Sahib, or not?"

He hurried off then to the dining room. His question
was not one that needed an answer.

Busy going to and fro with his arrangements for the
late Diwali Night dinner—there were to be special flowers on each table as well as paper streamers crisscross-
ing the big dining room this way and that—the butler
did not at first believe little Moti when out in the
smoky kitchen he told him that Major Johnson Sahib
had returned to the club.

"Nonsense, boy, nonsense. Secretary Sahib is having
a headache tonight. Secretary Sahib drew rabbit partner
in Diwali Night bridge tournament. Keep a thousand
times out of Secretary Sahib's way tomorrow, I warn
you."

But the boy persisted.

"Khitmagar sahib, I have seen. He was coming back.
He was going again into card room. Chandra, who is on
duty there tonight because nobody is playing billiards,
told that Major Johnson Sahib is coming in there and
he is saying, 'Ha, need new score cards, I see; half a
mo' and I'll fetch some.' "

The butler was impressed by this wealth of detail.

"Very good, Moti," he said. "But all the same, keep clear of Secretary Sahib tonight and tomorrow. I have told you."

"Yes, khitmagar sahib. And Chandra is saying that score cards were there all the time. Cadogan Sahib himself put many there before he was going."

"Ah, Cadogan Sahib," the butler said with a sigh.

The story of what happened when, within two minutes of leaving the card room to go and fetch fresh score cards from the store cupboard in his own bungalow, Major Johnson suddenly and unexpectedly returned was all over the bazaar at an early hour next day.

A huddle of boys sitting on the ground behind a flower stall busy threading garlands passed the news to and fro among themselves.

"Major Johnson Sahib came running into club. 'My wife, my wife,' he was shouting."

"Yes, 'my wife, my wife, she has been shot.' "

"Yes, yes. 'She has been shot dead.' Bang, bang. And the safe—"

"Yes. The burra safe of the club in Major Johnson Sahib's bungalow, it was open. All the great cups were gone. All the money."

"Yes, yes. Ten lakhs of rupees stolen."

"No. Twenty. Twenty lakhs, and the memsahib shot. Oh, that was done by terrible terrible goondas."

"No, no. You are a fool only, Budhoo. That is what Anketell Brown Sahib is saying. 'Might be the work of some damned native,' he is saying. But then Major Johnson Sahib is saying, ' 'Fraid not, Anketell Brown— I mean, damn it, you saw that cigarette case there."

"Yes, yes. It is the *cigarette case* of Cadogan Sahib. The *cigarette case* with the magic, magic sign upon it to say what a great man is Cadogan Sahib. It was there by the safe."

In the little group of women standing watching with mild envy as the bangle-seller works with his strong fingers on the hand of the young bride squatting in front of him, flexing the green glass bangle over the pliant bones, Sundari, wife of Gopal, Major Johnson's bearer, relays from time to time choice items from the unprecedentedly rich store that her husband has just acquired in the course of his duties.

"Anketell Brown Sahib thought it might be a thing done by a damn-native."

Her hearers sighed gustily at this. But with a proud lift of her bosom, sending the red sari slipping a little, Sundari immediately trumps her own ace.

"But no, they are saying. It cannot be the work of some goonda because look, here is the *cigarette case* that the thief has left and it is the *cigarette case* of Cadogan Sahib."

Such indrawn breaths, such tongue cluckings at this. Such glances from one to the other. The traditional moment of triumph when the banglewallah at last gets the thin ring of green glass over the mounded knuckles and on along in a rush to join its fellows at the slim wrist goes quite unmarked.

And Sundari has yet more to dole out.

She waits till the young bride has risen to her feet, modestly drawn her sari over her head and slipped to the outer edge of the circle, looking downwards always at her new acquisition. And she waits yet longer, until the bangle-seller's first burst of noisy salesmanship has petered away. And only then does she release the next morsel.

"My husband says it was Major Johnson Sahib himself who suggested what they should do."

"Aiee, and what was that, Sundari behn?"

Sundari looked round to make sure that every person in her audience was hanging on her lips, not exluding the bangle-seller, from whom she hoped before all was told to get the offer of a bangle at even as little as half the regular price, and at last when she saw the moment was right she told them.

"Major Johnson Sahib is saying to Anketell Brown Sahib, 'My dear chap, do you think that is wise?'"

The old woman nearby who sold plantains, her little stock carefully laid out on a piece of gunny in front of her, each separate banana of the ten given its exact best place in the pattern, actually broke in on the circle at this point, her curiosity was so whetted and her understanding so bemused.

"What was wise? What was not wise? Oh, kind one, clear a poor old person's head."

Sundari felt then that this was indeed a day of days. She pretended to ignore the old woman, turning elaborately to her neighbours on the other side.

"Yes," she said, "Major Johnson Sahib himself was saying that. Him it was and not another, as that Mangu fellow is trying to make out."

"Oh, aiee, that one is a thief, a goonda of goondas."

Such loyalty earned from Sundari a prompt reward.

"Yes," she said. "Very quietly Major Johnson Sahib is saying, 'Do you think it is wise? To make it a police matter?' And then Anketell Brown Sahib answered, 'But we have to tell them.' And Major Johnson Sahib said then, 'But if he gets into the hands of the police, there'll have to be a trial. And think who the judge might be: a damned Indian. And what a field day it's going to make for the Indian papers, whoever's on the bench.' "

Sundari, playing from strength, gave a little sigh.

"I am not knowing what 'field day' means," she said. "And neither is my husband. But it is bad. Very bad."

Devi, the wife of the sweetmeats merchant, who was making a concession by stopping to listen to such people as Sundari and her friends—but with such a story to be heard, the story of a lifetime even, some dignity had to be sacrificed—weighed in with a comment here, the comment of a woman of experience.

"Oh, the Angrezi-log, they are not at all liking that they should be written about in the Indian papers. It gives them what they call *a bad name*. It is as if there had been painted many times on a wall: 'Down with British Sarkar.' But papers cannot so easily be tarred over."

There was a great deal of wise nodding and murmuring over that. Rather more than was necessary, only it was seldom one got a chance of agreeing with the wife of the sweetmeats merchant.

Sundari, feeling that attention was beginning to slip away from her, offered another juicy morsel to be gulped.

"Yes," she said, "so then Anketell Brown Sahib and Hitchman Sahib and all the great ones of the club are agreeing. 'We'll flush the blighter out ourselves and settle the matter between gentlemen.' "

"So they are hunting, hunting Cadogan Sahib?" asked one of the less well informed wives.

Sundari waited to give her answer, that yet more appetizing gobbet than any before. She waited to feel the whole weight of everyone's curiosity tugging at her. Waited too long.

"Oh, no," said the sweetmeats merchant's wife. "Everybody well knows how hunting and punting was not necessary. Not at all necessary."

And she laughed her jolly, well-fed, sugar-sweetened laugh, rolling up from deep in her rounded belly and lasting long and long.

The manager of Rivoli Talkies, the station's single cinema, came out to the sweetmeats shop himself instead of sending a boy to buy his customary midday badam halwa. He discussed the price of sugar with the sweetmeats merchant and the merits of replacing the cinema's great flapping punkahs with the new electric fans. He had hoped that Bhabi Rani might himself refer first to the subject of real interest. But before long he had to admit that that would have been too much to expect.

He took a breath.

"And what is all this about Cadogan Sahib?" he asked. "They are saying that the hunt for him never found."

The sweetmeats merchant wagged his many chins in agreement.

"Yes, yes, that is perfectly true, Manager Sahib. They did not find. They did not need to find. Because although Cadogan Sahib did not return to his bungalow all night, in the morning he came into the club daftar just as if it was an ordinary day. 'Good morning, Chatterjee,' he said to that Bengali clerk they have there. Just as he always does. He is not long from England, you know."

"Yes, yes. To me also when I am showing him into best armchair seats he is saying always, 'Thank you, Manager Sahib.' But what after he came into the office, Mr. Rani? What did they do to him then?"

It was galling to have to ask right out, but he had been away arranging the new films—there was the newsreel of the King Emperor's Silver Jubilee, something that was bound to bring in customers, both European and Indian—and he had missed too much of the talk.

Bhabi Rani was generous.

"Manager Sahib," he said as a preliminary, "please try some of this new sweet my cook has made only this morning. I think you would find it very good."

The cinema manager accepted graciously.

"Yes," Bhabi Rani said, watching the fat pink tongue explore the crisp golden strands. "Yes, all their hunting and punting had gone for nothing. In came Cadogan Sahib. At first they did not know at all what to do. So Cadogan Sahib went, with no one saying a word, into his own chota daftar where he works every day and he began as usual to do his accounts. Outside, they were having a long, long discussion with Anketell Brown Sahib till in the end they were deciding just to lock him in where he was, and he was all the time protesting and exclaiming and saying, 'Why is this?' "

"Yes, yes. Well, well. But he could do nothing but protest, a proved thief. Yes, he should be kept under lock and key. And a murderer also."

"Yes, yes. That is what they are saying one to another. 'The chap is a murderer, after all, damn it.' And so then they sent messages to all members of the Club Committee. One I have read myself. The boy they sent much enjoyed that new sweet you are enjoying also, Manager Sahib."

"Yes, yes?" inquired the manager, between hasty licks.

"Ah, yes. This is what the message said: 'I hereby summon you to a Special Extraordinary Meeting of the Committee of the Mahadharwar Club to be held this day at 2 P.M. Agenda: private.' "

"Yes," said the manager, the last of the new sweet disposed of. "That was very good, Mr. Rani. Very good. Excellent.'" He sucked at his teeth. "And we are well knowing what is that 'private,' " he added.

"Yes, yes," said the sweetmeats merchant. "It is the trial and execution of Cadogan Sahib, no less."

Old Laloo, out in the bungalow—well called Heathview—on the outskirts of the station, where, he was always afraid, the news penetrated much too slowly, took what compensatory pleasure he could for his isolation in instructing the ayah whom the sahibs had brought with them from the Punjab. But since they shared only a few words in various languages, communication was not easy.

However, he did his best.

"Now, Bhagwati, listen. This is what I heard with my own ears. I heard it from Subhir Naik, who is a big, big telegraph operator."

Here a little work on an imaginary Morse key and an assumed air of tremendous dignity conveyed much.

"So listen, Bhagwati, and hear. This is the cable Anketell Brown Sahib himself was sending across the black water to the beautiful Webster Gardens."

The pretty Punjabi ayah's eyes were wide and expectant as dark parched pools in a dried-up riverbed.

" 'Nephew Rupert'—that is Cadogan Sahib, you are understanding—'Nephew Rupert is passing out from very bad malaria. Many bitter tears. Anketell Brown Sahib, Chairman of Mahadharwar Club.'"

The girl repeated with carefully moving silent lips the awkward English words. When old Laloo thought they had thoroughly sunk in, he explained laboriously that "very bad malaria" was not the cause of Cadogan Sahib's death.

Bhatu, the sweeper at Major Johnson's bungalow, was the hero that day of the whole sweepers' colony tucked away in a narrow cleft at the edge of the station well downwind of the other inhabitants.

"Now I am telling you," he said to the squatting group outside his dark little tumble-down hut. "It was this way. There in the dark in the garden Cadogan Sahib was kneeling on the ground behind a big bed of tall canna plants. He had come running, running out when they had heard the heavy steps of a sahib in shoes coming near. 'Please go. Go,' Maisie the Man-Eater had cried. And then came the noise of a gun shooting."

"Yes, yes," agreed Bhatu's friend Jai, the sweeper at Cadogan Sahib's bungalow. "A shot from a gun. Only a fool would think that was a Diwali cracker or a rocket. Like my sahib, Cadogan Sahib."

"Yes, yes, yes," Bhatu said. "I was there, seeing all, and I knew that it was a gun. It was the gun Major Johnson Sahib had in the drawer of his bedside teapoy, the one that no damn-native is supposed to know about. But Cadogan Sahib, on the ground making his white, white trousers all dirty, he thought it was another rocket only and that Maisie the Man-Eater would lie and lie for him and all would be well."

"But what was it that you did, Bhatu bhai, when you heard the gun?" asked Jai.

He knew, of course. But he was aware, too, of his duty as the storyteller's best friend.

"Oh, bhai, then at once I was going quietly, quietly to see what had happened in bungalow."

"Good, good. And what was it that you saw?"

Bhatu's eyes shone. This was the best bit of all. His utter triumph.

"Oh, Jai bhai, what did I see? I saw Maisie the Man-Eater shot dead, with what she is calling 'my kimono' only just dragged onto her naked, naked body. And then . . . And then . . ."

"Yes? Then?"

"Then I saw Major Johnson Sahib pull off that kimono and instead pull on first those clothes the memsahibs wear under their clothes and then the dress of the memsahib."

"Yes, yes," Jai explained to the others. "It was necessary for Major Johnson Sahib to do that so that it was looking as if Maisie Memsahib had just come back from playing the game of mah-jongg with Hitchman Memsahib and she had found Cadogan Sahib stealing from safe."

"That is so," Bhatu agreed gravely. "He had to do that, and he had also to move *cigarette case* with magical crest, which in the end is not very strong magic, from bedside teapoy, where Cadogan Sahib had left, to a place next to the safe, which he had also opened wide, so that there Anketell Brown Sahib would see. Oh, yes, Major Johnson Sahib is very clever sahib, very clever sahib indeed."

It had taken a long time for little Moti, to whom almost everything that went on among the sahibs in the club where his whole duty lay was so much arcane mystery, to learn the news. And even longer for him to acquire any glimmerings of an idea of its meaning. But at last now he had his questions to ask.

"Oh, Chandra, tell me, please."

The billiards marker, still buzzingly happy from all the things he knew, condescended to take notice.

"Tell what, little one? There is much, much, much to tell."

"Oh, Chandra, say is it true that they have locked up Cadogan Sahib in his own daftar?"

Chandra smiled, a grim smile.

"Yes, in the chota daftar he is under lock and key."

"But, Chandra, is it not that he is saying, and shouting even, 'What is this? Why are you doing this?' "

"Oh, yes, little boy. Saying and protesting and repeating, that is what Cadogan Sahib was doing."

Out in the bungalow called Heathview, that most distant of bungalows from the hub of activity, Bhagwati, the pretty little ayah, was reduced from lack of hearers capable of understanding her Punjabi to telling the little kicking white baby she looked after all about everything.

"And they are sending cable, babyji. Yes, cable they are sending to the beautiful, beautiful Webster Gardens where there is a marble baradari in the middle of a big, big tank. And in the cable they are saying, 'Very bad malaria,' and what is that meaning, babyji?"

She cooed at the little kicking pink-skinned creature.

"It is meaning they have made him shoot with his own gun, babyji. Bang, bang, bang, bang."

But it was actually little Moti who turned out to have after all perhaps the best tale of them all to tell. Because it was he, too insignificant to be noticed squatting in the passage swirling his lump of grey rag round on the floor, hopping at intervals from one side to the other, who had seen, in the middle of the luncheon hour when none of the white sahibs was anywhere about, Major Johnson come quickly along, hastily pull from his pocket the key of the chota daftar where Rupert Cadogan was a prisoner awaiting trial, slip it into the lock, open the door a crack and slide rapidly in.

And it was Moti who, crouching up against the door, heard what that low intense voice on the far side had said.

"Oh, khitmagar sahib, this is how Major Johnson Sahib talked. This and this only, I am telling you."

"Yes, yes. Repeat to me just what you heard, boy. And tell the truth. 'Tell the truth; you are not in court.' "

"Yes, khitmagar sahib. This is, in truth, what Major Johnson Sahib said: 'Now listen to me, Cadogan, because I shan't give you another chance.' "

The boy's sharp ear had caught every nuance of the hardly understood English and he repeated the words now faithfully as a gramophone.

"And, 'Yes?' Cadogan Sahib said. Then Major Johnson Sahib said, 'You know Maisie shot herself? Yes, shot herself from the sheer shame of it.' And Cadogan Sahib is saying, 'Oh, my God. I seduced her, Johnson. I seduced her.' "

"Maisie the Man-Eater," the butler murmured, but only to himself.

"Then Major Johnson Sahib is saying this," the boy went on. "He is saying, 'Do you want what you did, and what she did, to become so much common knowledge? Do you want everybody to know, even the servants, perhaps?' And Cadogan Sahib is saying, 'No, no. Not that. My God, not that.' "

"And then?" the butler asked, all dignity forgotten.

"Then, khitmagar sahib, Major Johnson Sahib is saying, 'Then you must do the decent thing, Cadogan. Plead guilty when the Committee sit, and take the gentleman's way out when they offer it.' And then he gave a little laugh like this, khitmagar sahib."

In the quiet of the compound where the two of them were standing in the shade of a darkly green neem tree, there came into the hot, still air, extraordinarily lifelike, the sound of Major Johnson's curtly brutal laugh.

The boy looked up to the imposing figure of the butler.

"Then Major Johnson Sahib said, 'In any case, man, you won't be believed if you do tell the truth. And if you don't take the chance that's offered you, I can tell you twenty years in an Indian gaol's a whole lot worse than a clean death.' "

In the bazaar afterwards a score of versions of the trial by committee were retailed. The embroidery differed. But the essentials were always there. Not one version, for instance, omitted the moment when Anketell Brown Sahib had said, "A thief. That's what I can't get

over. No more than a common thief." And there had
followed a general murmur of sad assent.

And like every other one, the version told by the bar-
ber, a sharp, much-travelled man who had picked up a
good deal of English, though much of it appallingly mis-
pronounced, had of course included what was really the
climactic moment of the whole trial.

Squatting on his heels, working his thin-as-a-wafer
cutthroat razor round the lean square jawbone of the
astrologer whose place of business was in the porch of
St. Thomas's Church, the fellow had paused the proper
length of time and then had quoted with exact solemnity
Anketell Brown's most solemnly uttered words:

"And that is werdict of you all?"

Murder at
St. Oswald's

MICHAEL UNDERWOOD

"I think he should be sentenced to be boiled in oil," said Wace, who was aged eleven.

His friend, Webster, nodded enthusiastically. "Yes, then be thrown into a pit full of poisonous spiders and scorpions."

Nigel Kilby frowned impatiently. He was the recognized leader of their form and the acknowledged foreman of their self-constituted jury, for it so happened that middle school (the name of their form) had exactly twelve pupils.

"That's silly," he said scathingly. "Where'd you get enough oil?"

"And where would you find poisonous spiders and scorpions?" inquired Marsden, the form's best all-rounder.

"I'd steal them from a zoo," Webster said robustly.

"And I'd get oil from a garage," added Wace, "and heat it in a cauldron."

Nigel Kilby was still frowning. "We've got to think of some terribly clever way of killing him," he said. "Something that can never be detected."

"I was reading in a magazine about a tribe in some jungle who kill their enemies with poison darts. They use blowpipes and the poison is so deadly that the person dies immediately." This contribution came from Perry mi, who was the smallest and, at ten, the youngest boy in the form.

Kilby nodded. "Poison is definitely the best way."

"We could push him over the cliff on a walk," Marsden said. "We'd say it was an accident, that he went too close to the edge and it crumbled."

"That'd be all right if we could be certain it'd kill him," Kilby conceded. "But supposing he was only injured. Supposing he managed to hang on to something. . . ."

A silence fell as each of them contemplated the full horror of such a plan going awry. The existing tyranny would be nothing compared with what would inevitably follow.

There was no doubt that Mr. Cheeseman was the most unpopular master at St. Oswald's and the boys of middle school, of which he was the form master, were further convinced that he must be the most hated master in any of the preparatory schools strung out along the Sussex coast in that year of 1929. Whenever they compared notes with boys from neighbouring schools, it served to confirm their morbid conviction that "Cheescpot" was Attila the Hun, Genghis Khan and Fouquier-Tinville rolled into one. They accepted from Kilby that you couldn't find a nastier trio in history.

Mr. Cheeseman—Cheesepot behind his back—was a tall, lean man with a heavy moustache and a deep voice which could sound more threatening than any roll of thunder. He had drifted into teaching after coming out of the army in 1919 and had been at St. Oswald's for six years. Like many of his sort at the time, he had no academic qualifications, merely a basic knowledge of the subjects he taught, and an ability to maintain discipline and lend a crude hand at games. Even allowing for the boys' natural exaggeration, a dispassionate adult eye could not have failed to notice that he took a distinct relish in tormenting his pupils. He was not only a bully; he was also unfair. For example, just recently he had kept Webster behind and made him late for prayers and had then told the headmaster there was no reason why Webster should not have been there on time. When Webster had made a muted protest, Mr. Cheeseman had given a nasty sort of laugh and said, "Life *is* unfair, boy. The sooner you realize it, the better."

"I bet Mrs. Cheeseman'll be glad when he dies," Wace said, breaking the silence that had fallen.

The Cheesemans lived in a cottage on the edge of the school grounds and Mrs. Cheeseman helped Matron with the boys' clothes. She was a small, pale, soft-spoken woman, who appeared to be as much dominated by her husband as were the boys of his form. She aroused their sense of chivalry and they had little doubt that she would welcome her husband's demise as much as they would.

"I bet he pulls her hair," Webster added.

"How are we going to poison him, Kilby?" Marsden asked, getting the discussion back on course again.

"What we need," Kilby said slowly to his now attentive audience, "is a poison that'll take a bit of time to work. I mean, we can mix it with his porridge at breakfast, but we don't want him to drop dead until later, so that no one will guess when he took it."

"Like when he's in the shed mending the mower," Marsden remarked.

One of Mr. Cheeseman's responsibilities was looking after the school's large motor mower. He appeared to have a far greater affinity for its oily workings than he did for his pupils and he was forever tinkering with its engine.

"But where'll you get the poison, Kilby?" Wace asked.

"I'll have to look in my book. It'll probably mean making our own poison. There are all sorts of poisonous things in the school wood."

"It'd have to be tasteless," Marsden observed.

"That's not difficult," Kilby said confidently. "And anyway, the porridge is so revolting, no one could tell whether it'd been poisoned or not."

Perry mi gave a sudden frightened start and bent studiously over his desk. One or two boys turned their heads and then quickly followed suit, for standing in the doorway with a disagreeable gleam in his eye was Mr.

Cheeseman. How long he had been there and what, if anything, he had overheard they were not to know, but a chilly fear gripped each of them.

They sat in two rows of six and it was Mr. Cheeseman himself who had sardonically likened them unto a jury. They now gazed at him with expressions of anxious innocence as he mounted the small dais and faced them across the top of his desk.

The silence which followed became quickly oppressive, so that Wace felt compelled to break it.

"Good morning, sir," he said.

Mr. Cheeseman now focused his attention on Wace. His moustache twitched.

"Is it, Wace?"

Wace was nonplussed and gave a nervous giggle.

"What's the joke, Wace? Come on, share it; don't keep it to yourself," the deep voice boomed.

"Joke, sir? There isn't any joke, sir."

"But you giggled, Wace. There must be a joke. Or are you so featherbrained that you giggle at nothing?"

"I didn't know I did giggle, sir," Wace said in a tone of alarm, endeavouring to extricate himself from a rapidly deteriorating situation.

"I didn't hear him giggle, sir," Webster said loyally.

"Webster and Wace, our twin buffoons," Mr. Cheeseman observed, glancing at the faces turned towards him. Then in his most sepulchral tone he added, "But buffoonery can be a dangerous sport, so take warning!"

He picked up the top exercise book from the pile he had brought into the classroom with him. It was their French composition of the previous afternoon, which he had corrected.

"Brook?"

"Here, sir."

"Evans?"

"Here, sir."

"Perry mi?"

"Here, sir."

As each boy answered to his name, his exercise book

was skimmed at him like a quoit. Anyone failing to catch was made to stand with the book balanced on his head.

"Everyone got their books?" Mr. Cheeseman asked in a doom-laden tone.

"No, sir, you haven't given me mine," Wace said nervously.

"Nor I have, Wace. I've kept yours back for special presentation. Just step up here, will you?"

Wace rose and made his way slowly round the end of the desks, an expression of apprehension on his face. He paused when he reached the edge of the dais.

"Stand here, Wace," Mr. Cheeseman said, pointing at the floor beside his desk, "and face the rest of the class."

Mr. Cheeseman rose and stepped across to stand behind him. In one hand he held the exercise book; his other hand seized the hair on the nape of Wace's neck.

"What gender is *maison*, Wace?"

"Er . . . feminine, sir."

"Then why did you put *le maison*?" he barked, giving the hair a vicious tweak.

"Ouch!"

"And what is the plural of *hibou*?"

"I can't think, sir—you're hurting, sir."

There was another tweak, followed by a further cry of pain.

"Come on, Wace, the plural of *hibou*?"

"*H-i-b-o-u-s.*"

This time there was a shriek as Mr. Cheeseman jerked his head back.

"*H-i-b-o-u-x*, you ignorant boy! There are more mistakes in your composition than there are pips in a pot of raspberry jam. You're lazy, Wace, and you don't pay attention."

"I do, sir."

"Don't argue with me," Mr. Cheeseman thundered, slowly rotating the hand which held the hair.

By now Wace was scarlet and tears were tumbling down his cheeks.

"Crying doesn't cut any ice with me, Wace. You'll stay in this afternoon and copy out the first ten pages of your French grammar. Later I shall come and hear you, and there'd better not be any mistakes. Now get back to your desk!" As he spoke he slapped him across the top of his head with the exercise book and then flung it after him.

A grim silence ensued in which only Wace's strangulated sobs could be heard. Webster tried to comfort his friend by picking up the book for him and helping him look for his pen, which had rolled off the desk.

The rest of the lesson was passed in a more oppressive atmosphere than ever and it was not until the school bell had been rung to signal the end of the period and Mr. Cheeseman had swept out that anyone dared speak.

"Don't worry, Wace," Kilby said. "It won't be for much longer."

"Couldn't we put a spell on him?" Perry mi asked.

"What sort of spell?" Marsden inquired with interest.

"A spell to make him fall down and break both his legs."

"How do you do that?"

"I'm not really sure. But if we formed a sort of circle and held hands and closed our eyes and muttered an incantation, it might work."

"What's an incantation?" Webster asked.

"It's words for casting spells," Kilby broke in. "But I doubt if we could make it work. I still think poison's the best way. I tell you what. I'm excused games this afternoon because of my new spectacles, so I'll go into the wood and collect poisonous things. I'll look in my book first and see what would make the deadliest poison."

"I'll come with you," Perry mi said. "Matron's excused me games because of my cold."

Kilby nodded his approval. "We'll go off immediately after lunch, while everyone's changing."

At this, even Wace managed to look more cheerful. Life without Cheesepot came as close to paradise as his imagination could bring him.

Nigel Kilby was the last to enter the classroom when they reassembled just before half-past four. He was carrying a brown cardboard box, which he quickly slipped into his desk.

"What did you get?" Marsden asked.

Kilby removed the lid of the box and they all craned forward to have a look. What they saw was some mysterious pale berries, a root resembling a parsnip, and a number of different leaves.

"Are they all poisonous?" Webster asked eagerly.

Kilby nodded gravely and one or two boys pulled back from the deadly contents. Yarrow even held his breath in case any fumes were being given off.

"But you can't sprinkle that lot on his porridge," Marsden remarked.

"Of course not. The poison's got to be made. The leaves have to be boiled and then the grated root and the crushed berries must be added. It's what left at the end that's the poison." Kilby cast a quick glance towards the door before going on. "I've got a tin and I'll boil the leaves on the gas ring outside Matron's room when she's down at staff dinner tonight. But someone'll have to keep watch at the end of the corridor in case she comes back early."

"I'll do that," Marsden volunteered.

"It'll be better if Perry does it. He's smaller and can hide under the table."

"What'll the poison look like?" Wace asked.

Nigel Kilby blinked behind his spectacles. The truth was that he had no idea, but no leader could possibly make such an admission.

"It'll be a sort of nondescript powder," he said. "We'll put it on his porridge at breakfast tomorrow. You know the way he goes and talks to Mr. Saunders after serving us. I'll do it then."

"Suppose he doesn't have any porridge tomorrow?" Webster asked.

"Then we'll have to wait until the next day. But he always has porridge."

"He didn't one day last week. I remember noticing."

"That was because he'd been out drinking the night before. He's only like that on Mondays." Kilby glanced round at his eleven fellow jurors. "Don't forget we're in this together. We must take an oath of silence and swear never to tell a single soul, whatever happens. If we stick together, nobody'll ever find out."

"Not even the top Scotland Yard detective," Wace added in a burst of confidence.

"So are we all agreed: Cheesepot must die?" Kilby said, looking from face to face.

Everyone nodded, though some a trifle apprehensively.

Shortly afterwards the object of their death sentence strode into the classroom. But for once he seemed preoccupied. It was supposed to be an English lesson, but all he did was to give them an essay subject and then, while they wrote, stare with a glowering expression out the window. He didn't even shout or attempt to cuff Wace when he dropped his pen.

It was almost as if he realized he hadn't much longer to live.

Nigel Kilby was already awake when the school bell rang at half-past seven the next morning. He jumped out of bed, put on his spectacles and ran over to the radiator on top of which he had left his lethal mixture to mature. He noted with satisfaction that it had turned into a greyish paste. He held it to his nose and sniffed, and decided that it smelt of shoe polish, but not too strongly.

Twenty minutes later, the first bell rang for breakfast. In the dining hall, where they sat by forms, middle school was at one end of the room. This meant that the boys on one side had their backs against a wall and those sitting on the opposite side had theirs turned to the rest of the room, which provided Kilby with as much cover as he could hope to have when the crucial moment arrived.

Before leaving the dormitory, he had transferred the mixture to a paper bag, which he put in his trouser pocket.

"How much are you going to give him?" Wace had asked.

"I reckon it's so deadly, it won't need much."

"How are you going to sprinkle it on?" Perry mi had inquired earnestly. "It looks all sticky."

"I'll just put in a few bits. If Cheesepot comes back too soon, you'll have to kick me under the table, Marsden."

"Aren't you frightened of getting some on your own plate, Kilby?" someone else had asked.

He shook his head. "I shall be extra careful and wash my hands as soon as breakfast is over."

The novelty of this struck silence into his audience and a couple of minutes later the second bell rang and they trooped downstairs to the dining hall.

Mr. Cheeseman came in late, just as the headmaster was starting to say grace. He gave the boys a curt nod and began ladling out the porridge. He was never very communicative at breakfast, but this morning there seemed something subtly different about him. Nothing which could be called an improvement, but nevertheless different. His eyes looked as they did when he had a hangover, but there wasn't the usual smell that went with that condition. He had a grimly brooding air.

Kilby wondered whether others had noticed the difference as he watched Mr. Cheeseman through his own quite different eyes. The eyes of an executioner.

When each boy had been served, Mr. Cheeseman filled his own bowl and then, as they had hoped, stalked away to the table presided over by Mr. Saunders.

Kilby had given the strictest instructions that when this moment was reached, everyone must eat normally and not gaze up the table in his direction, as this could give the whole thing away. Despite the warning, he observed Wace leaning forward and staring at him as though about to witness a conjuring trick. He gave him a furious glare, at the same time as Webster kicked him on the ankle. Wace blushed and quickly picked up his spoon.

Removing the crumpled paper bag from his pocket, Kilby slid to the very end of the bench so that his movements would be masked from everyone save those of his own form on the opposite side of the table. Quickly he shook out four pellets of the grey paste onto the waiting plate, where they promptly sank from sight beneath the surface of equally grey porridge.

He was halfway through his own porridge before Mr. Cheeseman returned to the table and sat down. With twelve pairs of eyes trying not to stare at him, he began to eat. At one moment, he made a face and appeared to remove something from the tip of his tongue, but otherwise he ate without comment. Porridge was followed by kippers and the meal ended with a slice of bread and margarine, covered by a film of marmalade.

There was a grating noise as the headmaster pushed back his chair and said, "I'll say grace for those who've finished."

This was followed by a noisy exodus, leaving only the dreamers and slow eaters to continue chewing their wholesome cud.

Mr. Cheeseman had left with the majority, without having spoken a single word during the meal. Kilby was puzzled and Perry mi voiced the theory that their form master had already had a vision of the angel of death.

"How long will it take to work?" Webster asked as he and Kilby went out of the dining hall together.

Kilby shrugged noncommittally. "Difficult to say."

"I hope it means we miss French."

As events turned out, they missed history as well.

History should have been the first lesson of the day and at twenty to nine, five minutes before it was due to start, middle school were at their desks.

"I wonder if he'll come out in spots first," Wace whispered to Webster.

"I don't want to see him actually die in here," Webster said with a slight shiver.

Noise from other classrooms along the corridor began to die away, indicating the arrival of teachers for
the start of the day's work. But there was no sign of Mr.
Cheeseman. A quarter to nine came and went. Then ten
to nine and five to nine. But still no Cheesepot.

"It must have worked already," Marsden said in a
hoarse whisper, and Kilby swallowed nervously. "I
mean, he's never been as late as this before. What are
we going to do?"

"If he hasn't come by the time the school clock
strikes nine, I'll go and have a look around," Kilby said.

It seemed no time at all before nine o'clock struck,
hurling them into a state of high tension such as they
had never experienced.

Kilby rose from his desk. "Everyone stay here. If
anyone comes, say I've gone to look for Cheesepot."

He slipped out of the classroom, half closing the door
behind him. It was doubtful whether middle school had
ever sat in silence for so long. Even Webster and Wace
barely exchanged a whispered word.

It was a quarter of an hour before Kilby returned,
and they could see at once from his expression that
something had happened. His face was white and he
kept on blinking behind his spectacles. With great delib-
eration, he moistened his lips.

"He's dead, all right," he announced in a quavering
voice. "He's lying on the floor of the mower shed."

The news was greeted in stunned silence, apart from
a few quick gasps. Deliverance had come, but their reaction was not as they had anticipated. There was no
urge to cheer or bang their desktops; just a feeling of
fearful unease.

Perry mi was the first to break the silence.

"Did you feel his pulse?" he asked.

Kilby shook his head. "I didn't go into the shed. I
looked through the keyhole and could see him lying
there in a sort of heap."

"How do you know it was Cheesepot?" Marsden
asked.

"I could tell by his jacket. The black-and-white-check one he was wearing at breakfast. He must have been bending over the mower when he collapsed."

"He might have still been breathing," Perry mi remarked in a worried tone.

"No, he was dead, all right. I'd have noticed if he was breathing. His chest would have been going up and down."

"What are we going to do?" Wace asked, a note of panic in his voice.

The question was answered for them by the sudden appearance in the doorway of Mr. Repping, the headmaster.

"What are you all doing?" he asked sharply. "Where's Mr. Cheeseman?"

"We don't know, sir," Kilby replied. "He hasn't turned up."

"Hasn't turned up! But he was at breakfast."

"Yes, sir," agreed a chorus of voices.

"Well, get on with some work while I go and find out what's happened. Now, no talking, do you understand?"

"May I make a suggestion, sir?" Kilby said.

"Well, what is it, Kilby?"

"Mr. Cheeseman often goes to the mower shed between breakfast and first period, sir."

"I'm aware of that, Kilby."

"Sorry, sir. I just thought it might be a good idea to look there. He might have had an accident and be trapped."

Mr. Repping frowned. "That sounds most far-fetched. You're letting your imagination run away with you, Kilby. Now get on with your work while I go and attend to the matter."

It was half an hour before the headmaster returned. Half an hour during which the minutes ticked away with agonizing slowness and very little work was done. When he did reappear in the classroom, they stared at him in fascinated horror while waiting to hear how he would break the news.

"Well, I'm afraid the mystery remains unsolved for

the time being," he said briskly. "I've tried to phone Mr. Cheeseman's home, but can't get any answer, so both he and Mrs. Cheeseman must be out. I believe Mr. Price is free next period, so I'll ask him to come and take you. What is your next period, by the way?"

"French, sir," Marsden said when no one else spoke.

"Very well. Stay in your classroom and I'll go and speak to Mr. Price."

"Excuse me, sir."

"Yes, what is it, Kilby?"

"Didn't you look in the mower shed, sir?"

"As a matter of fact, I did, Kilby. I told you that you were letting your imagination run away with you, lad. There wasn't a single sign of Mr. Cheeseman having been in there this morning."

Fifty minutes of French with the benign Mr. Price would normally have been something of a treat, but middle school agreed afterwards that they had never known the clock to move so slowly. It seemed as if the midmorning break would never come. And when at last it did, Nigel Kilby found himself facing a barrage of questions which would have undermined the confidence of anyone less self-assured. As it was, however, he stuck to his story and remained outwardly unshaken. Cheesepot had definitely been lying on the floor beside the mower, his black-and-white-check jacket being unmistakable. If he was no longer there when Mr. Repping inspected the shed, it meant only one thing. His body had been removed.

"But who'd have done it, Kilby?"

"And why, Kilby?"

To these and similar questions Nigel Kilby did not pretend to have answers, but his trump card, which he played over and over again, was to remind his audience that Cheesepot had indisputably disappeared.

"Body-snatching is not unknown," he added in a tone which hinted at personal experience of the practice.

And so the day dragged by, with Mr. Cheeseman's

twelve jurors fermenting in an agony of feverish speculation.

When bedtime came, still without any news of their
form master, the prospect of sleep could not have
seemed more distant.

It was Perry mi who suggested that, like a wild animal aware of its approaching end, Cheesepot had gone
off to die in a cave. But Kilby crushed this theory by
pointing out that it didn't begin to fit the facts.

"I wish now we'd never sentenced him to death,"
Wace whispered to Webster in the next bed.

"So do I," Webster said. "I'm scared."

At breakfast the next morning, the head boy was de-
puted to sit at the end of their table and serve the porridge. He and Marsden then spent the whole time discussing England's cricket prospects in the coming
season.

When breakfast was over, various masters were to be
observed exchanging conspiratorial whispers, but of Mr.
Cheeseman there was neither sign nor mention.

By twenty minutes to nine, middle school were sitting
at their desks wondering what to expect. Their first lesson was Latin and it seemed possible that the headmaster himself might take it.

Kilby had reminded them all of the need to stand
firm and not break ranks, because they had all been in
it together. Anyone who sneaked could expect a fate
little better than Cheesepot's.

"What have you done with the rest of the poison?"
Perry mi asked.

"I flushed it down the lav last night," Kilby replied.

The sound of approaching footsteps in the corridor
brought them to silence and a moment later the headmaster entered, followed by a stranger. He was dressed
in a tweed suit and had an outdoor appearance. To
Kilby, he looked much more like a farmer than a
teacher. Though teacher he must presumably be.

Mr. Repping mounted the dais and clutched both
sides of the high desk in front of him. The stranger

stood at his side, letting his gaze roam impassively over
the two rows of faces. He had blue eyes which gave the
impression of missing nothing. He certainly didn't look
to be a tyrant in the same mould as Cheesepot; equally,
he didn't give the appearance of being a soft touch.

This line of thought was passing through a number of
heads as the boys sought to assess him. Thus the jolt
they received when the headmaster spoke was like a se-
vere electric shock.

"Boys, this is Detective Inspector Cartwright. He has
some questions he wants to ask you about Mr. Cheeseman's disappearance and I expect you to be completely
truthful in your answers." He turned to the officer. "I
shall be in my study if you want me, Inspector." Glancing back at the two rows of anxious upturned faces, he
added, "Inspector Cartwright has said that he would
like to speak to you alone. That's why I'm leaving the
classroom. But he'll certainly report to me if anyone
misbehaves."

Inspector Cartwright watched Mr. Repping's departure and waited for the door to be closed. Then he
looked at the boys and gave them a broad wink.

"You look just like a jury sitting there," he said in an
amused tone. Kilby gulped and several other boys
blushed, all of which he observed. "As the headmaster
told you, I want to ask you some questions about Mr.
Cheeseman. When did you last see him?"

"At breakfast yesterday, sir," Kilby said when no one
else answered.

"That would have been at eight o'clock. Right? And
he never turned up for your first lesson at eight forty-
five, is that right?"

"Yes, sir," Kilby said, while others nodded.

"Did anyone go and look for him?" Inspector Cartwright became aware that no one was looking at him
any longer, all eyes having become suddenly cast down.
"Didn't anyone go looking for him? Surely it would
have been quite a natural thing to do."

"I did, sir," Kilby said at the end of an oppressive
silence.

"What's your name?"

"Kilby, sir."

"Where did you go and look, Kilby?"

"The shed where the mower's kept, sir."

"Ah! That would explain why you urged Mr. Repping to look there, eh? And what did you discover?"

Kilby swallowed hard and then met Inspector Cartwright's gaze full on. "I saw his body, sir, when I looked through the keyhole. He was lying in a heap beside the mower. I knew it was him, sir, because I recognized his jacket."

"It must have given you a quite a shock, eh?"

"Yes, sir."

"But it didn't come as a total surprise?"

"Sir?"

"Seeing him dead on the shed floor?"

Even Kilby felt defenceless in the face of this deus ex machina.

"No, sir," he said in a faint whisper.

"Not a very popular master, I gather?"

"No, sir."

"Did anyone like him?" He glanced from boy to boy as he spoke.

"He was the most unpopular master in the whole of England, sir," Perry mi broke in.

Inspector Cartwright received this news with pursed lips and a thoughtful nod.

"It must be a relief to you to know he won't be teaching you any more." He paused. "Well, I think that's about all . . . unless anyone has a question to ask me."

Everyone looked toward Kilby, who appeared to be fighting some inner battle.

"Have you found the body yet, sir?" he blurted out at last.

Inspector Cartwright looked solemn. "Yes, it was down a crevice at the top of the cliffs. We'd never have discovered it if we hadn't been told."

"But who put it there, sir?"

"Whose body are we talking about?" Inspector Cartwright inquired in a tone of mock puzzlement.

"Mr. Cheeseman's, sir," half a dozen voices called out.

"Oh! Oh, his body's at the police station."

"Then whose body was it on the cliff, sir?" Kilby asked in a bewildered voice.

"Mrs. Cheeseman's."

"Is she dead, too?"

"Hers is the only body I know about."

"But I thought you said, sir, that Mr. Cheeseman . . ."

"Is at the police station, charged with the murder of his wife. We picked him up outside Dover last night. He and his lady friend were about to cross the Channel, but he was recognized when he went into a chemist's shop. It seems he'd had horrible griping pains in his stomach all day. But for that, he'd almost certainly have got away." Inspector Cartwright's eye had a strange glint as he went on: "As it is, he has told us everything, including how he placed an old bolster dressed in his jacket and trousers in the mower shed, which he removed as soon as he'd seen Kilby look through the keyhole. He reckoned that if he and his lady friend could disappear abroad and his wife's body was never found, the mystery would never be solved. The assumption would be that his wife had murdered *him* and then vanished. But those tummy pains were his undoing. And all because he underestimated your ability to make the porridge nastier than I'm sure it is." Inspector Cartwright stepped off the dais as if to go, then paused. "I'd like to offer you boys just two bits of advice. The first is not to take the law into your own hands and the second is, if you do, make sure your intended victim doesn't overhear your plans."

He reached the door and paused again. "But as things have turned out, you seem to have gained the best of both worlds. Got rid of a bully of a master and helped the police catch a murderer."

Morepork

NGAIO MARSH

On the morning before he died, Caley Bridgeman woke to the smell of canvas and the promise of a warm day. Bellbirds had begun to drop their two dawn notes into the cool air and a native wood pigeon flopped onto the ridgepole of his tent. He got up and went outside. Beech bush, emerging from the night, was threaded with mist. The voices of the nearby creek and the more distant Wainui River, in endless colloquy with stones and boulders, filled the intervals between bird song. Down beyond the river he glimpsed, through shadowy trees, the two Land-Rovers and the other tents: his wife's; his stepson's; David Wingfield's, the taxidermist's. And Solomon Gosse's. Gosse, with whom he had fallen out.

If it came to that, he had fallen out, more or less, with all of them, but he attached little importance to the circumstance. His wife he had long ago written off as an unintelligent woman. They had nothing in common. She was not interested in bird song.

"Tink. Ding," chimed the bellbirds.

Tonight, if all went well, they would be joined on tape with the little night owl—*Ninox novaeseelandiae,* the ruru, the morepork.

He looked across the gully to where, on the lip of a cliff, a black beech rose high against paling stars. His gear was stowed away at its foot, well hidden, ready to be installed, and now, two hours at least before the campers stirred, was the time to do it.

He slipped down between fern, scrub and thorny undergrowth to where he had laid a rough bridge above a very deep and narrow channel. Through this channel flowed a creek which joined the Wainui below the tents. At that point the campers had dammed it up to make a swimming pool. He had not cared to join in their enterprise.

The bridge had little more than a four-foot span. It consisted of two beech logs resting on the verges and overlaid by split branches nailed across them. Twenty feet below, the creek glinted and prattled. The others had jumped the gap and goaded him into doing it himself. If they tried, he thought sourly, to do it with twenty-odd pounds of gear on their backs, they'd sing a different song.

He arrived at the tree. Everything was in order, packed in green waterproof bags and stowed in a hollow under the roots.

When he climbed the tree to place his parabolic microphone, he found bird droppings, fresh from the night visit of the morepork.

He set to work.

At half-past eleven that morning. Bridgeman came down from an exploratory visit to a patch of beech forest at the edge of the Bald Hill. A tui sang the opening phrase of "Home to Our Mountains," finishing with a consequential splutter and a sound like that made by someone climbing through a wire fence. Close at hand, there was a sudden flutter and a minuscule shriek. Bridgeman moved with the habitual quiet of the bird watcher into a patch of scrub and pulled up short.

He was on the lip of a bank. Below him was the blond poll of David Wingfield.

"What have you done?" Bridgeman said.

The head moved slowly and tilted. They stared at each other. "What have you got in your hands?" Bridgeman said. "Open your hands."

The taxidermist's clever hands opened. A feathered

morsel lay in his palm. Legs like twigs stuck up their clenched feet. The head dangled. It was a rifleman, tiniest and friendliest of all New Zealand birds.

"Plenty more where this came from," said David Wingfield. "I wanted it to complete a group. No call to look like that."

"I'll report you."

"Balls."

"Think so? By God, you're wrong. I'll ruin you."

"Ah, stuff it!" Wingfield got to his feet, a giant of a man.

For a moment it looked as if Bridgeman would leap down on him.

"Cut it out," Wingfield said. "I could do you with one hand."

He took a small box from his pocket, put the strangled rifleman in it and closed the lid.

"Gidday," he said. He picked up his shotgun and walked away—slowly.

At noon the campers had lunch, cooked by Susan Bridgeman over the campfire. They had completed the dam, building it up with enormous turfs backed by boulders. Already the creek overflowed above its juncture with the Wainui. They had built up to the top of the banks on either side, because if snow in the back country should melt or torrential rain come over from the west coast, all the creeks and rivers would become torrents and burst through the foothills.

"Isn't he coming in for tucker?" Clive Grey asked his mother. He never used his stepfather's name if he could avoid it.

"I imagine not," she said. "He took enough to last a week."

"I saw him," Wingfield offered.

"Where?" Solomon Gosse asked.

"In the bush below the Bald Hill."

"Good patch for tuis. Was he putting out his honey pots?"

"I didn't ask," Wingfield said, and laughed shortly.

Gosse looked curiously at him. "Like that, was it?" he said softly.

"Very like that," Wingfield agreed, glancing at Susan. "I imagine he won't be visiting us today," he said. "Or tonight, of course."

"Good," said Bridgeman's stepson loudly.

"Don't talk like that, Clive," said his mother automatically.

"Why not?" he asked, and glowered at her.

Solomon Gosse pulled a deprecating grimace. "This is the hottest day we've had," he said. "Shan't we be pleased with our pool!"

"I wouldn't back the weather to last, though," Wingfield said.

Solomon speared a sausage and quizzed it thoughtfully. "I hope it lasts," he said.

It lasted for the rest of that day and through the following night up to eleven o'clock, when Susan Bridgeman and her lover left their secret meeting place in the bush and returned to the sleeping camp. Before they parted she said, "He wouldn't divorce me. Not if we yelled it from the mountaintop, he wouldn't."

"It doesn't matter now."

The night owl, ruru, called persistently from his station in the tall beech tree.

"*More-pork! More-pork!*"

Towards midnight came a soughing rumour through the bush. The campers woke in their sleeping bags and felt cold on their faces. They heard the tap of rain on canvas grow to a downpour. David Wingfield pulled on his gum boots and waterproof. He took a torch and went round the tents, adjusting guy ropes and making sure the drains were clear. He was a conscientious camper. His torchlight bobbed over Susan's tent and she called out, "Is that you? Is everything O.K.?"

"Good as gold," he said. "Go to sleep."

Solomon Gosse stuck his head out from under his

tent flap. "What a bloody bore," he shouted, and drew
it in again.

Clive Grey was the last to wake. He had suffered a
recurrent nightmare concerning his mother and his stepfather. It had been more explicit than usual. His body
leapt, his mouth was dry and he had what he thought of
as a "fit of the jimjams." Half a minute went by to the
sound of water—streaming, he thought, out of his
dream. Then he recognized it as the voice of the river,
swollen so loud that it might be flowing past his tent.

Towards daybreak the rain stopped. Water dripped
from the trees, clouds rolled away to the south and the
dawn chorus began. Soon after nine there came tenta-
tive glimpses of the sun. David Wingfield was first up.
He squelched about in gum boots and got a fire going.
Soon the incense of wood smoke rose through the trees
with the smell of fresh fried bacon.

After breakfast they went to look at the dam. Their
pool had swollen up to the top of both banks, but the
construction held. A half-grown sapling, torn from its
stand, swept downstream, turning and seeming to gesti-
culate. Beyond their confluence the Wainui, augmented
by the creek, thundered down its gorge. The campers
were obliged to shout.

"Good thing," Clive mouthed, "we don't want to get
out. Couldn't. Marooned. Aren't we?" He appealed to
Wingfield and pointed to the waters. Wingfield made a
dismissive gesture. "Not a hope," he signalled.

"How long?" Susan asked, peering into Wingfield's
face. He shrugged and held up three and then five fingers. "My God!" she was seen to say.

Solomon Gosse patted her arm. "Doesn't matter.
Plenty of grub," he shouted.

Susan looked at the dam where the sapling had
jammed. Its limbs quivered. It rolled, heaved, thrust up
a limb, dragged it under and thrust it up again.

It was a human arm with a splayed hand. Stiff as
iron, it swung from side to side and pointed at nothing
or everything.

Susan Bridgeman screamed. There she stood, with

her eyes and mouth open. "Caley!" she screamed. "It's Caley!"

Wingfield put his arm round her. He and Solomon Gosse stared at each other over her head.

Clive could be heard to say: "It *is* him, isn't it? That's his shirt, isn't it? He's drowned, isn't he?"

As if in affirmation, Caley Bridgeman's face, foaming and sightless, rose and sank and rose again.

Susan turned to Solomon as if to ask him if it was true. Her knees gave way and she slid to the ground. He knelt and raised her head and shoulders.

Clive made some sort of attempt to replace Solomon, but David Wingfield came across and used the authority of the physically fit. "Better out of this," he could be heard to say. "I'll take her."

He lifted Susan and carried her up to her tent.

Young Clive made an uncertain attempt to follow. Solomon Gosse took him by the arm and walked him away from the river into a clearing in the bush where they could make themselves heard, but when they got there found nothing to say. Clive, looking deadly sick, trembled like a wet dog.

At last Solomon said, "I can't b-believe this. It simply isn't true."

"I ought to go to her. To Mum. It ought to be me with her."

"David will cope."

"It ought to be me," Clive repeated, but made no move.

Presently he said, "It can't be left there."

"David will cope," Solomon repeated. It sounded like a slogan.

"David can't walk on the troubled waters," Clive returned on a note of hysteria. He began to laugh.

"Shut up, for God's sake."

"Sorry. I can't help it. It's so grotesque."

"Listen."

Voices could be heard, the snap of twigs broken underfoot and the thud of boots on soft ground. Into the clearing walked four men in single file. They had packs on their backs and guns under their arms and an air of fitting into their landscape. One was bearded, two clean-shaven, and the last had a couple of days' growth. When they saw Solomon and Clive they all stopped.

"Hullo, there! Good morning to you," said the leader. "We saw your tents." He had an English voice. His clothes, well-worn, had a distinctive look which they would have retained if they had been in rags.

Solomon and Clive made some sort of response. The man looked hard at them. "Hope you don't mind if we walk through your camp," he said. "We've been deer-stalking up at the head of Welshman's Creek but looked like getting drowned. So we've walked out."

Solomon said. "He's—we've both had a shock."

Clive slid to the ground and sat doubled up, his face on his arms.

The second man went to him. The first said, "If it's illness—I mean, this is Dr. Mark, if we can do anything."

Solomon said, "I'll tell you." And did.

They did not exclaim or overreact. The least talkative of them, the one with the incipient beard, seemed to be regarded by the others as some sort of authority and it turned out, subsequently, that he was their guide: Bob Johnson, a high-country man. When Solomon had finished, this Bob, with a slight jerk of his head, invited him to move away. The doctor had sat down beside Clive, but the others formed a sort of conclave round Solomon, out of Clive's hearing.

"What about it, Bob?" the Englishman said.

Solomon, too, appealed to the guide. "What's so appalling," he said, "is that it's there. Caught up. Pinned against the dam. The arm jerking to and fro. We don't know if we can get to it."

"Better take a look," said Bob Johnson.

"It's down there, through the b-bush. If you don't mind," said Solomon, "I'd—I'd be glad not to go b-back just yet."

"She'll be right," said Bob Johnson. "Stay where you are."

He walked off unostentatiously, a person of authority, followed by the Englishman and their bearded mate.
The Englishman's name, they were to learn, was Miles
Curtis-Vane. The other was called McHaffey. He was
the local schoolmaster in the nearest township down-
country and was of a superior and, it would emerge,
cantakerous disposition.

Dr. Mark came over to Solomon. "Your young
friend's pretty badly shocked," he said. "Were they re-
lated?"

"No. It's his stepfather. His mother's up at the camp.
She fainted."

"Alone?"

"Dave Wingfield's with her. He's the other member
of our lot."

"The boy wants to go to her."

"So do I, if she'll see me. I wonder—would you mind
taking charge? Professionally, I mean."

"If there's anything I can do. I think perhaps I
should join the others now. Will you take the boy up? If
his mother would like to see me, I'll come."

"Yes. All right. Yes, of course."

"Were they very close?" Dr. Mark asked. "He and
his stepfather?"

There was a longish pause. "Not very," Solomon
said. "It's more the shock. He's very devoted to his
mother. We all are. If you don't mind, I'll—"

"No, of course."

So Solomon went to Clive and they walked together
to the camp.

"I reckon," Bob Johnson said, after a hard stare at
the dam, "it can be done."

Curtis-Vane said, "*They* seem to have taken it for
granted it's impossible."

"They may not have the rope for it."

"We have."

"That's right."

"By Cripie," said Bob Johnson, "it'd give you the

willies, wouldn't it? That arm. Like a bloody sema-
phore."

"Well," said Dr. Mark, "what's the drill, then, Bob?
Do we make the offer?"

"Here's their other bloke," said Bob Johnson.

David Wingfield came down the bank sideways. He
acknowledged Curtis-Vane's introductions with guarded
nods.

"If we can be of any use," said Curtis-Vane, "just say
the word."

Wingfield said, "It's going to be tough." He had not
looked at the dam but he jerked his head in that direction.

"What's the depth?" Bob Johnson asked.

"Near enough five foot."

"We carry rope."

"That'll be good."

Some kind of reciprocity had been established. The
two men withdrew together.

"What would you reckon?" Wingfield asked. "How
many on the rope?"

"Five," Bob Johnson said, "if they're good. She's
coming down solid."

"Sol Gosse isn't all that fit. He's got a crook knee."

"The bloke with the stammer?"

"That's right."

"What about the young chap?"

"All right normally, but he's—you know—shaken
up."

"Yeah," said Bob. "Our mob's O.K."

"Including the pom?"

"He's all right. Very experienced."

"With me, we'd be five," Wingfield said.

"For you to say."

"She'll be right, then."

"One more thing," said Bob. "What's the action
when we get him out? What do we do with him?"

They debated this. It was decided, subject to Solomon Gosse's and Clive's agreement, that the body
should be carried to a clearing near the big beech and

left there in a ground sheet from his tent. It would be a decent distance from the camp.

"We could build a bit of a windbreak round it," Bob said.

"Sure."

"That's his tent, is it? Other side of the creek?"

"Yeah. Beyond the bridge."

"I didn't see any bridge."

"You must have," said Wingfield, "if you came that way. "It's where the creek runs through a twenty-foot-deep gutter. Couldn't miss it."

"Got swept away, it might have."

"Has the creek flooded its banks, then? Up there?"

"No. No, that's right. It couldn't have carried away. What sort of bridge is it?"

Wingfield described the bridge. "Light but solid," he said. "He made a job of it."

"Funny," said Bob.

"Yeah. I'll go up and collect the ground sheet from his tent. And take a look."

"We'd better get this job over, hadn't we? What about the wife?"

"Sol Gosse and the boy are with her. She's O.K."

"Not likely to come out?"

"Not a chance."

"Fair enough," said Bob.

So Wingfield walked up to Caley Bridgeman's tent to collect his ground sheet.

When he returned, the others had taken off their packs and laid out a coil of climbers' rope. They gathered round Bob, who gave the instructions. Presently the line of five men was ready to move out into the sliding flood above the dam.

Solomon Gosse appeared. Bob suggested that he take the end of the rope, turn it round a tree truck and stand by to pay it out or take it up as needed.

And in this way and with great difficulty Caley Bridgeman's body was brought ashore, where Dr. Mark examined it. It was much battered. They wrapped it in the ground sheet and tied it round with twine. Solomon

Gosse stood guard over it while the others changed into dry clothes.

The morning was well advanced and sunny when they carried Bridgeman through the bush to the foot of the bank below that tree which was visited nightly by a morepork. Then they cut manuka scrub.

It was now that Bob Johnson, chopping through a stand of brushwood, came upon the wire, an insulated line, newly laid, running underneath the manuka and well hidden. They traced its course: up the bank under hanging creeper to the tree, up the tree to the tape recorder. They could see the parabolic microphone much farther up.

Wingfield said, "So that's what he was up to."

Solomon Gosse didn't answer at once, and when he did, spoke more to himself than to Wingfield. "What a weird bloke he was," he said.

"Recording bird song, was he?" asked Dr. Mark.

"That's right."

"A hobby?" said Curtis-Vane.

"Passion, more like. He's got quite a reputation for it."

Bob Johnson said, "Will we dismantle it?"

"I think perhaps we should," said Wingfield. "It was up there through the storm. It's a very high-class job— cost the earth. We could dry it off."

So they climbed the tree, in single file, dismantled the microphone and recorder and handed them down from one to another. Dr. Mark, who seemed to know, said he did not think much damage had been done.

And then they laid a rough barrier of brushwood over the body and came away. When they returned to camp, Wingfield produced a bottle of whisky and enamel mugs. They moved down to the Land-Rovers and sat on their heels, letting the whisky glow through them.

There had been no sign of Clive or his mother.

Curtis-Vane asked if there was any guessing how long it would take for the rivers to go down and the New Zealanders said, "No way." It could be up for days. A week, even.

"And there's no way out?" Curtis-Vane asked. "Not if you followed down the Wainui on this side, till it empties into the Rangitata?"

"The going's too tough. Even for one of these jobs." Bob indicated the Land-Rovers. "You'd never make it."

There was a long pause.

"Unpleasant," said Curtis-Vane. "Especially for Mrs. Bridgeman."

Another pause. "It is, indeed," said Solomon Gosse.

"Well," said McHaffey, seeming to relish the idea. "If it does last hot, it won't be very nice."

"Cut it out, Mac," said Bob.

"Well, you know what I mean."

Curtis-Vane said, "I've no idea of the required procedure in New Zealand for accidents of this sort."

"Same as in England, I believe," said Solomon. "Report to the police as soon as possible."

"Inquest?"

"That's right."

"Yes. You're one of us, aren't you? A barrister?" asked Curtis-Vane.

"And solicitor. We're both in this country."

"Yes, I know."

A shadow fell across the group. Young Clive had come down from the camp.

"How is she?" Wingfield and Gosse said together.

"O.K.," said Clive. "She wants to be left. She wants me to thank you," he said awkwardly, and glanced at Curtis-Vane, "for helping."

"Not a bit. We were glad to do what we could."

Another pause.

"There's a matter," Bob Johnson said, "that I reckon ought to be considered."

He stood up.

Neither he nor Wingfield had spoken beyond the obligatory mutter over the first drink. Now there was in his manner something that caught them up in a stillness. He did not look at any of them but straight in front of him and at nothing.

"After we'd finished up there I went over," he said,

"to the place where the bridge had been. The bridge that you"—he indicated Wingfield—"talked about. It's down below, jammed between rocks, half out of the stream."

He waited. Wingfield said, "I saw it. When I collected the gear." And he, too, got to his feet.

"Did you notice the banks? Where the ends of the bridge had rested?"

"Yes."

Solomon Gosse scrambled up awkwardly. "Look here," he said. "What is all this?"

"They'd overlaid the bank by a good two feet at either end. They've left deep ruts," said Bob.

Dr. Mark said, "What about it, Bob? What are you trying to tell us?"

For the first time Bob looked directly at Wingfield.

"Yes," Wingfield said. "I noticed."

"Noticed *what*, for God's sake!" Dr. Mark demanded. He had been sitting by Solomon, but now moved over to Bob Johnson. "Come on, Bob," he said. "What's on your mind?"

"It'd been shifted. Pushed or hauled," said Bob. "So that the end on this bank of the creek rested on the extreme edge. It's carried away taking some of the bank with it and scraping down the face of the gulch. You can't miss it."

Clive broke the long silence. "You mean—he stepped on the bridge and fell with it into the gorge? And was washed down by the flood? Is that what you mean?"

"That's what it looks like," said Bob Johnson.

Not deliberately, but as if by some kind of instinctive compulsion, the men had moved into their original groups. The campers: Wingfield, Gosse and Clive; the deer-stalkers: Bob, Curtis-Vane, Dr. Mark and McHaffey.

Clive suddenly shouted at Wingfield, "What are you getting at! You're suggesting there's something crook about this? What the hell do you mean?"

"Shut up, Clive," said Solomon mildly.

"I won't bloody shut up. If there's something wrong I've a right to know what it is. She's my mother and he was—" He caught himself. "If there's something funny about this," he said, "we've a right to know. *Is* there something funny?" he demanded. "Come on. Is there?"

Wingfield said, "O.K. You've heard what's been suggested. If the bridge *was* deliberately moved—manhandled—the police will want to know who did it and why. And I'd have thought," added Wingfield, "you'd want to know yourself."

Clive glared at him. His face reddened and his mouth trembled. He broke out again: "Want to know! Haven't I said I want to know! What the hell are you trying to get at!"

Dr. Mark said, "The truth, presumably."

"Exactly," said Wingfield.

"Ah, stuff it," said Clive. "Like your bloody birds," he added, and gave a snort of miserable laughter.

"What can you mean?" Curtis-Vane wondered.

"I'm a taxidermist," said Wingfield.

"It was a flash of wit," said Dr. Mark.

"I see."

"You all think you're bloody clever," Clive began at the top of his voice, and stopped short. His mother had come through the trees and into the clearing.

She was lovely enough, always, to make an impressive entrance and would have been in sackcloth and ashes if she had taken it into her head to wear them. Now, in her camper's gear with a scarf round her head, she might have been ready for some lucky press photographer.

"Clive darling," she said, "what's the matter? I heard you shouting." Without waiting for his answer, she looked at the deer-stalkers, seemed to settle for Curtis-Vane, and offered her hand. "You've been very kind," she said. "All of you."

"We're all very sorry," he said.

"There's something more, isn't there? What is it?"

Her own men were tongue-tied. Clive, still fuming, merely glowered. Wingfield looked uncomfortable and

Solomon Gosse seemed to hover on the edge of utterance and then draw back.

"Please tell me," she said, and turned to Dr. Mark. "Are you the doctor?" she asked.

Somehow, among them, they did tell her. She turned very white but was perfectly composed.

"I see," she said. "You think one of us laid a trap for my husband. That's it, isn't it?"

Curtis-Vane said, "Not exactly that."

"No?"

"No. It's just that Bob Johnson here and Wingfield do think there's been some interference."

"That sounds like another way of saying the same thing."

Solomon Gosse said. "Sue, if it has happened—"

"And it has," said Wingfield.

"—it may well have b-been some gang of yobs. They do get out into the hills, you know. Shooting the b-birds. Wounding deer. Vandals."

"That's right," said Bob Johnson.

"Yes," she said, grasping at it. "Yes, of course. It may be that."

"The point is," said Bob, "whether something ought to be done about it."

"Like?"

"Reporting it, Mrs. Bridgeman."

"Who to?" Nobody answered. "Report it where?"

"To the police," said Bob Johnson flatly.

"Oh no! *No!*"

"It needn't worry you, Mrs. Bridgeman. This is a national park. A reserve. We want to crack down on these characters."

Dr. Mark said, "Did any of you see or hear anybody about the place?" Nobody answered.

"They'd keep clear of the tents," said Clive at last. "Those blokes would."

"You know," Curtis-Vane said, "I don't think this is any of our business. I think we'd better take ourselves off."

"No!" Susan Bridgeman said. "I want to know if you

believe this about vandals." She looked at the deer-stalkers. "Or will you go away thinking one of us laid a trap for my husband? Might one of you go to the police and say so? Does it mean that?" She turned on Dr. Mark. "Does it?"

Solomon said, "Susan, my dear, *no,*" and took her arm.

"I want an answer."

Dr. Mark looked at his hands. "I can only speak for myself," he said. "I would need to have something much more positive before coming to any decision."

"And if you go away, what will you all do? I can tell you. Talk and talk and talk." She turned on her own men. "And so, I suppose, will we. Or won't we? And if we're penned up here for days and days and he's up there, wherever you've put him, not buried, not—"

She clenched her hands and jerked to and fro, beating the ground with her foot like a performer in a rock group. Her face crumpled. She turned blindly to Clive.

"I *won't,*" she said. "I *won't* break down. Why should I? I won't."

He put his arms round her. "Don't you, Mum," he muttered. "You'll be all right. It's going to be all right."

Curtis-Vane said, "How about it?" and the deer-stalkers began to collect their gear.

"No!" said David Wingfield loudly. "No! I reckon we've got to thrash it out and you lot had better hear it."

"We'll only b-bitch it all up and it'll get out of hand," Solomon objected.

"No, it won't," Clive shouted. "Dave's right. Get it sorted out like they would at an inquest. Yeah! That's right. Make it an inquest. We've got a couple of lawyers, haven't we? They can keep it in order, can't they? Well, can't they?"

Solomon and Curtis-Vane exchanged glances. "I really don't think—" Curtis-Vane began, when unexpectedly McHaffey cut in.

"I'm in favour," he said importantly. "We'll be called on to give an account of the recovery of the body and that could lead to quite a lot of questions. How I look at it."

"Use your loaf, Mac," said Bob. "All you have to say is what you know. Facts. All the same," he said, "if it'll help to clear up the picture, I'm not against the suggestion. What about you, Doc?"

"At the inquest I'll be asked to speak as to"—Dr. Mark glanced at Susan—"as to the medical findings. I've no objection to giving them now, but I can't think that it can help in any way."

"Well," said Bob Johnson, "it looks like there's no objections. There's going to be a hell of a lot of talk and it might as well be kept in order." He looked round. "*Are* there any objections?" he asked. "Mrs. Bridgeman?"

She had got herself under control. She lifted her chin, squared her shoulders and said, "None."

"Fair enough," said Bob. "All right. I propose we appoint Mr. Curtis-Vane as—I don't know whether chairman's the right thing, but—well—"

"How about coroner?" Solomon suggested, and it would have been hard to say whether he spoke ironically or not.

"Well, C.-V.," said Dr. Mark, "what do you say about it?"

"I don't know what to say, and that's the truth. I—it's an extraordinary suggestion," said Curtis-Vane, and rubbed his head. "Your findings, if indeed you arrive at any, would, of course, have no relevance in any legal proceedings that might follow."

"Precisely," said Solomon.

"We appreciate that," said Bob.

McHaffey had gone into a sulk and said nothing.

"I second the proposal," said Wingfield.

"Any further objections?" asked Bob.

None, it appeared.

"Good. It's over to Mr. Curtis-Vane."

"My dear Bob," said Curtis-Vane, "what's over to me, for pity's sake?"

"Set up the program. How we function, like."

Curtis-Vane and Solomon Gosse stared at each other. "Rather you than me," said Solomon dryly.

"I suppose," Curtis-Vane said dubiously, "if it meets with general approval, we could consult about procedure?"

"Fair go," said Bob and Wingfield together, and Dr. Mark said, "By all means. Leave it to the legal minds."

McHaffey raised his eyebrows and continued to huff.

It was agreed that they should break up: the deer-stalkers would move downstream to a sheltered glade, where they would get their own food and spend the night in pup tents; Susan Bridgeman and her three would return to camp. They would all meet again, in the campers' large communal tent, after an early meal.

When they had withdrawn, Curtis-Vane said, "That young man—the son—is behaving very oddly."

Dr. Mark said, "Oedipus complex, if ever I saw it. Or Hamlet, which is much the same thing."

There was a trestle table in the tent and on either side of it the campers had knocked together two greenwood benches of great discomfort. These were made more tolerable by the introduction of bush mattresses—scrim ticking filled with brushwood and dry fern.

An acetylene lamp had been placed in readiness halfway down the table, but at the time the company assembled there was still enough daylight to serve.

At the head of the table was a folding camp stool for Curtis-Vane, and at the foot, a canvas chair for Susan Bridgeman. Without any discussion, the rest seated themselves in their groups: Wingfield, Clive and Solomon on one side; Bob Johnson, Dr. Mark and McHaffey on the other.

There was no pretence at conversation. They waited for Curtis-Vane.

He said, "Yes, well. Gosse and I have talked this over. It seemed to us that the first thing we must do is to define the purpose of the discussion. We have arrived at this conclusion: We hope to determine whether Mr.

Caley Bridgeman's death was brought about by accident or by malpractice. To this end we propose to examine the circumstances preceding his death. In order to keep the proceedings as orderly as possible, Gosse suggests that I lead the inquiry. He also feels that as a member of the camping party, he himself cannot, with propriety, act with me. We both think that statements should be given without interruption and that questions arising out of them should be put with the same decorum. Are there any objections?" He waited. "No?" he said. "Then I'll proceed."

He took a pad of writing paper from his pocket, laid a pen beside it and put on his spectacles. It was remarkable how vividly he had established a courtroom atmosphere. One almost saw a wig on his neatly groomed head.

"I would suggest," he said, "that the members of my own party"—he turned to his left—"may be said to enact, however informally, the function of a coroner's jury."

Dr. Mark pulled a deprecating grimace, Bob Johnson looked wooden and McHaffey self-important.

"And I, if you like, an ersatz coroner," Curtis-Vane concluded. "In which capacity I put my first question. When was Mr. Bridgeman last seen by his fellow campers? Mrs. Bridgeman? Would you tell us?"

"I'm not sure, exactly," she said. "The day he moved to his tent—that was three days ago—I saw him leave the camp. It was in the norning."

"Thank you. Why did he make this move?"

"To record native bird song. He said it was too noisy down here."

"Ah, yes. And was it after he moved that he rigged the recording gear in the tree?"

She stared at him. "Which tree?" she said at last.

Solomon Gosse said, "Across the creek from his tent, Sue. The big beech tree."

"Oh. I didn't know," she said faintly.

Wingfield cut in. "Can I say something? Bridgeman was very cagey about recording. Because of people getting curious and butting in. It'd got to be a bit of an obsession."

"Ah, yes. Mrs. Bridgeman, are you sure you're up to this? I'm afraid—"

"Perfectly sure," she said loudly. She was ashen white.

Curtis-Vane glanced at Dr. Mark. "If you're quite sure. Shall we go on, then?" he said. "Mr. Gosse?"

Solomon said he, too, had watched Bridgeman take his final load away from the camp and had not seen him again. Clive, in turn, gave a similar account.

Curtis-Vane asked, "Did he give any indication of his plans?"

"Not to me," said Gosse. "I wasn't in his good b-books, I'm afraid."

"No?"

"No. He'd left some of his gear on the ground and I stumbled over it. I've got a dicky knee. I didn't do any harm, b-but he wasn't amused."

David Wingfield said, "He was like that. It didn't amount to anything."

"What about you, Mr. Wingfield? You saw him leave, did you?"

"Yes. Without comment."

Curtis-Vane was writing. "So you are all agreed that this was the last time any of you saw him?"

Clive said, "Here! Hold on. You saw him again, Dave. You know. Yesterday."

"That's right," Solomon agreed. "You told us at lunch, Dave."

"So I did. I'd forgotten. I ran across him—or rather he ran across me—below the Bald Hill."

"What were you doing up there?" Curtis-Vane asked pleasantly.

"My own brand of bird-watching. As I told you, I'm a taxidermist."

"And did you have any talk with him?"

"Not to mention. It didn't amount to anything."

His friends shifted slightly on their uneasy bench.

"Any questions?" asked Curtis-Vane.

None. They discussed the bridge. It had been built some three weeks before and was light but strong. It was agreed among the men that it had been shifted and that it would be just possible for one man to lever or push it into the lethal position that was indicated by the state of the ground. Bob Johnson added that he thought the bank might have been dug back underneath the bridge. At this point McHaffey was aroused. He said loftily, "I am not prepared to give an opinion. I should require a closer inspection. But there's a point that has been overlooked, Mr. Chairman," he added with considerable relish. "Has anything been done about footprints?"

They gazed at him.

"About footprints?" Curtis-Vane wondered. "There's scarcely been time, has there?"

"I'm not conversant with the correct procedure," McHaffey haughtily acknowledged. "I should have to look it up. But I do know they come into it early on or they go off colour. It requires plaster of Paris."

Dr. Mark coughed. Curtis-Vane's hand trembled. He blew his nose. Gosse and Wingfield gazed resignedly at McHaffey. Bob Johnson turned upon him. "Cut it out, Mac," he said wearily, and cast up his eyes.

Curtis-Vane said insecurely, "I'm afraid plaster of Paris is not at the moment available. Mr. Wingfield, on your return to camp, did you cross by the bridge?"

"I didn't use the bridge. You can take it on a jump. He built it because of carrying his gear to and fro. It was in place."

"Anybody else see it later in the day?"

"I did," said Clive loudly. As usual, his manner was hostile and he seemed to be on the edge of some sort of demonstration. He looked miserable. He said that yesterday morning he had gone for a walk through the bush and up the creek without crossing it. The bridge had been in position. He had returned at midday, passing through a patch of bush close to the giant beech. He had not noticed the recording gear in the tree.

"I looked down at the ground," he said, and stared at his mother, "not up."

This was said in such an odd manner that it seemed to invite comment. Curtis-Vane asked casually, as a barrister might at a tricky point of cross-examination: "Was there something remarkable about the ground?"

Silence. Curtis-Vane looked up. Clive's hand was in his pocket. He withdrew it. The gesture was reminiscent of a conjurer's: a square of magenta-and-green silk had been produced.

"Only this," Clive said, as if the words choked him. "On the ground. In the bush behind the tree."

His mother's hand had moved, but she checked it and an uneven blush flooded her face. "Is *that* where it was!" she said. "It must have caught in the bushes when I walked up there the other day. Thank you, Clive."

He opened his hand and the scarf dropped on the table. "It was on the ground," he said, "on a bed of cut fern."

"It would be right, then," Curtis-Vane asked, "to say that yesterday morning when Mr. Wingfield met Mr. Bridgeman below the Bald Hill, you were taking your walk through the bush?"

"Yes," said Clive.

"How d'you know that?" Wingfield demanded.

"I heard you. I was quite close."

"Rot."

"Well—not you so much as him. Shouting. He said he'd ruin you," said Clive.

Solomon Gosse intervened. "May I speak? Only to say that it's important for you all to know that B-B-Bridgeman habitually b-behaved in a most intemperate manner. He would fly into a rage over a chipped saucer."

"Thank you," asid Wingfield.

Curtis-Vane said, "Why was he cross with you, Mr. Wingfield?"

"He took exception to my work."

"Taxidermy?" asked Dr. Mark.

"Yes. The bird aspect."

"I may be wrong," McHaffey said, and clearly considered it unlikely, "but I thought we'd met to determine when the deceased was last seen alive."

"And you are perfectly right," Curtis-Vane assured him. "I'll put the question: Did any of you see Mr. Bridgeman after noon yesterday?" He waited and had no reply. "Then I've a suggestion to make. If he was alive last evening there's a chance of proving it. You said when we found the apparatus in the tree that he was determined to record the call of the morepork. Is that right?"

"Yes," said Solomon. "It comes to that tree every night."

"If, then, there is a recording of the morepork, he had switched the recorder on. If there is no recording, of course nothing is proved. It might simply mean that for some reason he didn't make one. Can any of you remember if the morepork called last night? And when?"

"I do. I heard it. Before the storm blew up," said Clive. "I was reading in bed by torchlight. It was about ten o'clock. It went on for some time and another one, further away, answered it."

"In your opinion," Curtis-Vane asked the deerstalkers, "should we hear the recording—if there is one?"

Susan Bridgeman said, "I would rather it wasn't played."

"But why?"

"It—it would be—painful. He always announced his recordings. He gave the date and place and the scientific name. He did that before he set the thing up. To hear his voice—I—I couldn't bear it."

"You needn't listen," said her son brutally.

Solomon Gosse said, "If Susan feels like that about it, I don't think we should play it."

Wingfield said, "But I don't see—" and stopped

short. "All right, then," he said. "You needn't listen, Sue. You can go along to your tent, can't you?" And to Curtis-Vane: "I'll get the recorder."

McHaffey said, "Point of order, Mr. Chairman. The equipment should be handled by a neutral agent."

"Oh, for God's sake!" Wingfield exclaimed.

"I reckon he's right, though," said Bob Johnson.

Curtis-Vane asked Susan Bridgeman, very formally, if she would prefer to leave them.

"No. I don't know. If you must do it—" she said, and made no move.

"I don't think we've any right to play it if you don't want us to," Solomon said.

"That," said McHaffey pleasurably, "is a legal point. I should have to—"

"Mr. McHaffey," said Curtis-Vane, "there's nothing 'legal' about these proceedings. They are completely informal. If Mrs. Bridgeman does not wish us to play the record, we shall, of course, not play it."

"Excuse me, Mr. Chairman," said McHaffey, in high dudgeon. "That is your ruling. We shall draw our own conclusions. Personally, I consider Mrs. Bridgeman's attitude surprising. However—"

"Oh!" she burst out. "Play it, play it, play it. Who cares! I don't. Play it."

So Bob Johnson fetched the tape recorder. He put it on the table. "It may have got damaged in the storm," he said. "But it looks O.K. He'd rigged a bit of a waterproof shelter over it. Anyone familiar with the type?"

Dr. Mark said, "It's a superb model. With that parabolic mike, it'd pick up a whisper at ten yards. More than I could ever afford, but I think I understand it."

"Over to you, then, Doc."

It was remarkable how the tension following Susan Bridgeman's behaviour was relaxed by the male homage paid to a complicated mechanism. Even Clive, in his private fury, whatever it was, watched the opening up of the recorder. Wingfield leaned over the table to get a better view. Only Solomon remembered the woman and went to sit beside her. She paid no attention.

"The tape's run out," said Dr. Mark. "That looks promising. One moment; I'll rewind it."

There broke out the manic gibber of a reversed tape played at speed. This was followed by intervals punctuated with sharp dots of sound and another outburst of gibberish.

"Now," said Dr. Mark.

And Caley Bridgeman's voice, loud and pedantic, filled the tent.

"Ninox novaeseelandiae. Ruru. Commonly known as Morepork, Tenth January, 1977. Ten-twelve P.M. Beech bush. Parson's Nose Range. Southern Alps. Regarded by the Maori people as a harbinger of death."

A pause. The tape slipped quietly from one spool to the other.

"More-pork!"

Startling and clear as if the owl called from the ridgepole, the second note a minor step up from the first. Then a distant answer. The call and answer were repeated at irregular intervals and then ceased. The listeners waited for perhaps half a minute and then stirred.

"Very successful," said Dr. Mark. "Lovely sound."

"But are you sure? Darling, you swear you're sure?"

It was Susan Bridgeman. They turned, startled, to look at her. She had got to her feet. Her teeth were closed over the knuckles of her right hand. "No!" she whispered. "No, *no*."

Solomon Gosse lunged across the table, but the tape was out of his reach and his own voice mocked him.

"Of course I'm sure, my darling. It's foolproof. He'll go down with the b-b-b-bridge."

Who Killed the Cat?

PETER DICKINSON

In the slow dusk typical of the planet, David carried the body back towards the camp. He was thinking not about its death, but about its name. Cat. Except for being roughly the right size, it was nothing like a cat—a plump body covered with coarse gingery hair too sparse to conceal the folds and dewlaps of indigo flesh which sagged in a variety of curves according to the attitude the creature chose to lounge in. It was a not-quite-biped, with long forelimbs, three-fingered, and short hind limbs. It had no visible neck, but a hackle of black fur ran from its shoulders over the almost perfect sphere of its skull, stopping abruptly at the line which would have joined the centres of its round yellow eyes, whose double lids closed inward from the sides. Its mouth was round, too. It had no nose and no sense of smell, which made it one of the rare exceptions to the galactic norm of five senses for all higher creatures. (Not all had the same five, of course: the crew of David's ship disposed of nine among them.) But then Cat was hardly a crew member; only a pet or mascot, really. David had never heard of a ship that didn't carry a Cat—that was odd, because he had never heard, either, of a Cat doing anything useful for a crew, and ships didn't normally lug waste weight round the galaxy, even the odd four kilos of Cat's body. It wasn't a normal kind of superstition, either, half mocked and half revered. You didn't blame the Cat for a luckless voyage. You just took it along with you, and barely noticed it. By the time he reached

208

the camp, David was beginning to think that he should have noticed these oddities before. After all, it was his function to notice and remember facts and then to fit them into patterns.

He found a Bandicoot by the fire, curled asleep like an annelid fossil, but twitching violently with its dreams. Hippo was by the ship, rubbing her back against a support strut, like a cow scratching at a post.

"Hey, careful!" said David. "That strut's designed for most shocks, but not for that."

"Ooh, isn't it?" said Hippo vaguely. "Sorry. I forgot. I'm itchy."

She trundled towards the fire and stood gazing pathetically at David with her large-fringed eyes, pinker than ever in the light of the flames. Hippo was better named than Cat. Coming from a large planet which was mostly glutinous swamp, her species had evolved to a shape something like a terrestrial hippopotamus, only larger. Her head was different, with its big brain case and short prehensile trunk, but her eyes lay on its upper surface, so that she tended to lower her head, as if shy, when talking to one. She was a lot of weight to carry around, but less than her equivalent in tractors and carrying machines; and she could seal off her huge lungs and work in vacuum conditions, or in noxious gases, for several hours at a time. Hippos came in a wide variety of colours. This one was pale yellow.

"Do you think I'm pregnant, Man?" she said. "That would be most inconvenient."

The lowered head made her look as though she should have been blushing as she spoke. David snorted with suppressed laughter.

"I don't think it's likely, darling," he said. "I know you go in for delayed implantation, but it must be a couple of years since you last went to a dance, isn't it?"

"But it would be inconvenient, all the same?"

"Understatement of the century."

Hippos were the kindest, gentlest, most lovable creatures David knew. This made their life cycle seem even more horrifying than it was. At certain seasons on their native planet they would meet for a "dance," a massive sexual thresh-about in the sludge, with all the males impregnating all the females, if possible. Then nothing happened till the wind was right and the weather was right, when the females would go through their incredibly brief pregnancy, which would end with their backs erupting into a series of vents and releasing a cloud of seedlike objects, each consisting of a hard little nut at the core which contained the foetus and a fluffy ball of sticky filaments surrounding it, the whole thing light enough to float on the wind like thistledown. These "seeds" seemed to have some instinct that drew them towards living flesh; those that failed to find any perished, but those that landed on a warm-blooded animal stuck there and burrowed in, completing their foetal development inside the host, supplying themselves with all their physical and chemical needs from the host's organs. The host did not survive the process. The variety of possible hosts accounted for the different colours of Hippos.

David thought it extremely unlikely that this one was pregnant. For some reason, he couldn't at the moment recall the maximum known period between fertilization and birth, but it couldn't possibly be two years. Surely not. But just supposing . . . The idea of surveying a planet in which Hippo spores might still be drifting on the wind made him shudder. And Hippo herself wouldn't be much use till her back had healed. . . . He decided to change the subject.

"I'm afraid Cat's dead," he said.

"Oh, dear, oh, dear," said Hippo. "Where did you find him?"

"Out among the rocks over there. He must have been scrambling about and fallen, or something."

"Are you sure he's dead? Couldn't Doc do anything?"

"I doubt it. He feels very dead to me."

"Do go and fetch Doc, Man. Please."

"All right."

Doc was in a bad mood. As David lifted his bucket off its gimbals, he put a hooter out of the water and said, "I thought you told me this wasn't an earthquake planet."

"Nor it is."

"Whole ship's been jumping around like a— Hi! Careful! You're going to spill me, you dry slob."

David ignored him, but carried the bucket rapidly through the shuddering ship till he reached the entry port.

"Hippo!" he yelled. "Stop that! You'll have the ship over!"

Apologetically she moved away from the strut.

"Oh, I *am* sorry, Man," she lowed. "The Bandy should have told me."

"Didn't notice," squeaked the Bandicoot, awake now. "Why should I?"

"Where are the others, Bandy?" called David.

"Coming, coming," shrilled the Bandicoot.

Bandicoots were a four-sex species, deriving from a planet so harsh that it took many square miles to support a single specimen. They had evolved great telepathic powers in order to achieve occasional meetings of all four sexes, and this made them an ideal communications network on the many planets where mechanical systems were swamped by local radio stars. David had no idea why they were called Bandicoots—they looked more like armadillos on stilts—and even after years of companionship he couldn't tell one from another. They could, of course, because the network functioned at full strength only when all four sexes took part. Their normal voices were far above David's hearing range; the twittering he could just hear was for them the deepest of basses.

"Here's your patient, Doc," he said, settling the bucket by Cat's body.

Doc extended a pseudopod, shimmering orange with the firelight and green with its own luminescence, and made it flow up Cat's spine. His hooter emerged from the water.

"Blunt instrument," he said.

"Sure it wasn't a fall?" said David.

"Course I am, you idiot. It takes more than a fall to kill a Cat. You have to know exactly how and where to hit. Somebody did."

"Somebody?" said Hippo. "I thought there wasn't anybody on this planet. Skunk said so."

"How long ago, Doc?" said David. "Sure he's dead?"

"I'm still looking. Hm."

David had never much cared for Doc's bedside manner, but had always trusted him totally, as all the crew had to trust one another. Now he wondered how, that time he was infested with green-fever larvae out round Delta Orion, he could have lain so calmly and let Doc extend his filaments all through his body, locating and destroying the little wrigglers and modifying David's autoimmune system to produce antibodies against the bacteria they had carried. Doc was a sea anemone. The pseudopod he was using to explore Cat's body was a specialized section of his digestive organs, and the filament tips were capable of recognizing at a touch the identity of all the microscopic particles which he needed for the endless process of renewing every cell in his body once a week. Almost all Doc's life was taken up with the process of self-renewal, but he said it was worth the trouble because it made him immortal. It also made him a good doctor, when he could spare the time.

"Tsk, tsk," he said. "Yes, dead as nails, whatever they are. About twenty minutes ago."

"That's not long," said Hippo. "Can't you patch him up?"

"I'd have a go if it was you, darling," said Doc. "It's not worth the effort for a Cat."

"But you spent so much time looking after it," said Hippo pleadingly.

"It was a lousy hypochondriac," said Doc. "I've got better things to do."

"Coming, coming," shrilled the Bandicoot.

"Hippo, get away from that strut," said David. "Find a tree or something."

"Trees on this planet are so feeble," said Hippo. "I've used up all that lot."

Through the remains of dusk David could see that the grove of primitive palms by which they had set up camp had considerably altered in outline. He remembered hearing a certain amount of splintering and crashing as he was walking back to camp.

"You'd better get Doc to have a look at you," he said. "Doc, poor Hippo's got an itchy back."

"Never get through that ugly thick hide," mumbled Doc. "Got better things to do."

"I know it's nonsense, but I can't help thinking I'm pregnant," said Hippo.

"Get yourself an obstet . . . an obstet . . ." said Doc as he withdrew all but the limb of his pseudopod beneath the surface.

"Doc!" said David. "You aren't eating Cat!"

"Oh, no!" said Hippo, with all the revulsion, normally suppressed in her case, of herbivores for meateaters.

"Doc!" shouted David.

The hooter came an inch out of the water.

"Lot of good stuff in there," said Doc, slurring the syllables until he was barely comprehensible. "No point wasting it. All these months living on chemical soup."

"What about the Hippocratic oath!" said David.

"Coming, coming!" shrieked the Bandicoot, rising and jiggling like a sandhopper on its spindly legs. Its cry was answered by another from the sky, and a moment later, with the usual blur and buzz of wings, Bird settled at the edge of the ring of darkness. The second Bandicoot dropped from her back and jigged across to join the first.

"Bandy said to skim home," said Bird in the metallic voice produced by moving one wing case to make a flow of air and then modifying the flow with the sensitive leading edge of the wing itself.

"What's up, Man?" she asked. "The Bandy told you about the wreck?"

"No. And I didn't say anything about bringing you home. The last my Bandy told me was about a seam of Sperrylite you thought you'd spotted. What kind of a wreck? How old?"

Bird raised a wing case and let it fall back, producing a sharp explosion like a mining blast. This was her form of swearing.

"I'll chop him up and feed him to my husband," she rasped.

She had met her "husband" in the larval stage, when they were both about three inches long, and after a brief, blind courtship had incorporated him in her body, where he now lay, like an extra gland, somewhere near the back of her four-foot thorax. Doc had once paid him a visit, out of curiosity, and said that there was still an intelligence there, of a sort, but that it spent all its time dreaming. He guessed that the dreams were non-representational, but had never been able to interest Skunk or the Badicoots in finding out. Bird was not merely a flying scout. She had evolved from a migratory species whose guidance system depended on their ability to sense the magnetic field of their planet with great accuracy; so now she was able, skimming on her gauzy wings above the surface of a strange planet, to map the irregularities where different metallic ores showed up. And in deep space she was like an old sailor with a weather eye, able to sense long before it registered on the instruments the coming of one of the particle storms that could rush like a cyclone out of the apparently blank spaces between the stars.

"Yup; space wreck," she said. "More than a month old, less than a year. Real mess. Didn't go in, but my Bandy said he couldn't feel anybody thinking down there. I was just going to skim in close when he told me to hurry home. I was coming, anyway, but what made him do that?"

"Nothing, except Cat's dead."

"Somebody killed him," said Hippo.

"With a blunt instrument," said David.

Bird made a contemptuous rustle with her wing cases, and before the sound had ended Mole came snouting out of the earth beyond the fire, shaking soil from his pelt like a dog shaking off water. As the flurry of pellets pattered down, the third Bandicoot scrambled out of the capsule which Mole trailed behind him on his subterranean journeys, and skittered off to join the other two. Now all three were hopping like hailstones on paving, and shrilling at each other in and out of the limits of David's hearing range.

"What's up?" growled Mole.

"Cat's dead and I'm pregnant," said Hippo.

"I don't know why I bother," said Mole. "Soon as this trip's over I'm paying off and going home."

He would have trouble finding it, thought David. Home for Mole was somewhere in the Ophiucus area, a planet—or rather an ex-planet—which had become detached from its sun and all of whose life forms had evolved in a belt between the surface permafrost and the central fires.

"Home?" said Bird. "Yup. Good thinking. Count me in on payday."

She clicked and tocked in a thoughtful way. Doc put his hooter up, sighed, "Ho-o-o-o-ome," and plopped back under.

Home. Why not? Earth. Clothed, soft-skinned bipeds. David was a rich man, in theory, by now. He could afford to retire, buy four or five young wives and a mother-in-law, and a nice little island. . . .

The Whizzers cut the reverie short by slithering into the camp, bringing the last of the Bandicoots. At once all thought and talk were impossible in the frenzy of jigging and shrilling, until Bird turned on the four of them and drove them, with a series of fierce explosions, round to the far side of the ship. Meanwhile, Skunk crawled down from the Whizzer he had been riding. The Whizzers were legless reptiles from a planet of crushing gravity. They were about seven feet long and three feet wide, but less than a foot high, and on planets less massive than their own they could carry reasonable weights over almost any surface at speeds of up to sixty miles an hour. They flowed. David seldom got the chance to ride one, because his function was to stay at base and coordinate information with his own stored knowledge; but sometimes, when he needed to see something with his own eyes, a Whizzer had taken him and he had found the ride as much fun as surfboarding. Despite being hermaphrodites, Whizzers paired for life. They were deeply religious.

Skunk was also a hermaphrodite and legless, but otherwise nothing like a Whizzer—slow, sightless, a nude blob, corrugated with scent glands. He could synthesize and aim a jet of any odour he wished. He could stun even Hippo with a stink, provided her nostril was unsealed. On the anniversary of David's first joining the crew, Skunk had presented him with a smell which was all the pleasures of his life, remembered and forgotten, linked into ten minutes of ecstasy. Skunk knew what odours to produce because he was a telepath, not in the style of the Bandicoots, but able to sense the minutest variations of emotion; thus he could attract or repel, numb or excite, at will. David had seen him organize the slaves of a fully functioning mine in Altair to load the ship with jade while their trance-held guards watched, impotent. That had been a rich trip, if risky. Pity they'd had to trade the loot for fuel at a way station. . . . Skunk had almost total power except over creatures such as Cats, which had no sense of smell. He could be any colour he chose. He could feel danger long before David could analyze it. Surface scouting on a new planet was always done by a team of two Whizzers, one Bandicoot and a Skunk.

"The Bandicoot said we were to return," hissed one of the Whizzers. "What new providence has the Lord effected?"

"I don't know," said David. "I think that the Bandicoots just wanted to get together."

"Listen to them," said Mole.

"Disgusting," said the Whizzers.

"A very untidy relationship," said Bird smugly.

"Dear little things," said Hippo.

"Hippo, get away from that strut," said David.

"Sorry," said Hippo. "You know, I really am pregnant."

"You and who else?" said Bird. "You aren't the only female in these parts, remember. There's me, too, and several halves and quarters."

"But it's important," said Hippo.

"It's hysterical," snapped Bird. "Get Doc to check. He'll tell you."

"Doc's drunk," said David. "He's found some substances in Cat's body. . . . But if Hippo does give birth, it means she'll produce a cloud of seeds which float about until they stick to a living body—then they burrow in and eat it out from the inside."

"Charming," said Bird. "What happens if they land on another Hippo?"

"Why do you think they've evolved that hide, and the ability to seal off?" said David.

"Well, we'll just have to copy her," said Bird. "Get inside the ship, seal off, and wait till the happy event is over."

"But you can't do that," said Hippo. "What about my babies? What will they eat?"

"Oh, they'll find something," said Bird.

"But was it not revealed to Brother/Sister Skunk that the Lord has not yet seen fit to bring forth warm-blooded creatures upon this planet?" said one Whizzer.

"Infinite is His mercy. Strange are His ways," said the other.

David started trying to work out whether Hippo could bust her way into the ship. His analysis wouldn't cohere. He didn't know how much extra strength to allow for the desperation of maternal feelings, and all the other constants seemed to be slithering around. Then, in the middle of this mess, a wholly irrelevant point struck him. He ought to have seen it before.

"That means one of us killed Cat," he said.

There was a sudden silence, apart from the climax of

shrilling beyond the ship. Strange are His ways, thought David.

"Yes. Man," said Skunk in his laboriously produced groan. "Something. Odd. Cat. Dead. Must. Know. How. Why."

"Sorry, I can't help," said David. "I don't know."

"Come off it," snapped Bird. "You've got to know. That's what you're here for, to classify and analyze information. That's why we bother to cart you around with us—it's your function."

"I'm afraid I'm not functioning very well today," said David.

"Feeling all right?'" hooted Doc. "Like me to have a squint inside you?"

"Not on your life," said David. "I'm fine. Only—"

"Only you're not kissing well going to bother," said Bird.

"Sister Bird," hissed the Whizzers. "You must modify your language or we desert."

There was a moment of shock. Nobody ever deserted. Nobody ever even joked about it. By the same token, Bird always remembered not to swear in front of the Whizzers.

"Yet the Lord has revealed to Brother/Sister Skunk that the duty has fallen on us to discover how and why Brother Cat was called to his Maker," said one Whizzer.

"Blessed is His name," said the other.

"All right," said Mole, "let's go along with that. We can all analyze a bit, I suppose. We don't have Men around at home, do we? Doc, sober up and pay attention. Bird, go and see if the Bandies have finished whatever it is they do. . . ."

David withdrew into himself. He was not Man, he was David. He felt enormous reluctance to take part in analytic processes. It didn't matter who had killed Cat, or why, and the others were only discussing it because Skunk said it was important: they were accepting Skunk's dictum out of habit, because they were used to the idea of Skunk being right about that sort of thing, just as they were used to the idea of Bird being right about the threat of a particle storm. Those were part of their functions. It didn't mean that Skunk was in command—no one was, or they all were. They collected information through their nine senses, relayed it if necessary through the Bandicoots, and David collated it with what he knew and interpreted the resulting probabilities. Then, always till now, it had become clear what they should do next and there had been no point on taking a vote, or even discussing the issue. They were a crew, a unit like a beehive or a termite nest. They had lost their previous Hippo because they'd landed on a quaking planet and the only way to take off from its jellylike surface was for that Hippo (a young one, male, mauve) to hold the ship upright from the outside while they blasted clear. At the time it had seemed sad, but not strange, to leave poor Hippo roasted there, and Hippo had seemed to think so, too. The Whizzers had sung a hymn as they'd blasted off, he remembered. But now . . .

Now he sat in the ring of creatures round the campfire and felt no oneness with them. They were aliens. They squeaked and boomed and lowed and rasped in words he could scarcely understand, though they were all speaking standard English. The fire reflected itself from the facets of Bird's eyes; her mandibles clashed like punctuation marks in the flapping talk from her wing cases. Doc had withdrawn his pseudopod from Cat's drained body and the surface of his water was frothy with the by-products of his feast. The Bandicoots had joined the circle and were engrossed in the talk, all four heads jerking this way and that as if joined by a crank rod. The Whizzers lay half folded together, like a pair of clasped hands. Mole had absent-mindedly dug himself down and was listening with his elbows at ground level and his snout resting on his little pink palms with their iron-coloured claws. Skunk, too, had forgotten himself enough to be producing vague whiffs and stinks, as if trying to supplement the difficult business of speech with the communication system he used among his own kind.

I belong on earth, thought David. What am I doing here? Being part of a crew, that's what. But what is the crew doing here? Prospecting, with a bit of piracy when the chance offers, that's what. But why? Why any longer? He was rich—they all were, enormously rich in the currency of their home planets. Or were they? All those claims. Were they valid? Had anyone exploited them? That jade, hijacked in Altair—a share of that would have been enough to buy David twenty wives and islands for all of them, but without argument they had traded it for less than a thousandth of its value in fuel. To what end? More exploration, more claims . . .

David knew all this quite well. It was part of his memory—of all their memories—and there had seemed to be quite good reasons for it at the time. None of them had been the real reason, the need to stay together as a crew. . . . And now the knowledge and the memory were strange, as strange as the ring of aliens who had fallen silent and were staring at him—those that had eyes to stare with.

"Man," groaned Skunk. "Why. You. Kill. Cat?"

David barely understood the blurred syllables.

"Me?" he said. "Oh, rubbish. And my name's David."

"Come off it," clattered Bird. "It's got to be you. Doc was in his bucket, with no transport. Hippo was with the base camp Bandy."

"The base camp Bandy was asleep," said David. "Hippo could have done it."

"Do you really think so?" said Hippo.

"No. Go on, Bird."

"The rest of us were scouting, none alone. You were alone. You left the camp. Why?"

"I wanted to go over to the rocks. I can't remember why."

"Not functioning again?"

"I suppose so."

"Two possibilities suggest themselves. Either you are

suffering brain damage, which would account for your failure to function, and your killing Cat, and your not remembering that you had done so or why you went to the rocks. Or you are functioning, killed Cat for your own reasons and are concealing this by pretending not to function."

"That's easy to check," said David. "Ask the Bandies. Am I functioning, Bandies?"

The eight eyes swivelled towards him on short stalks.

"Yesyesyesyes," shrilled the Bandicoots. "Man's functioning fine."

It was true. The hesitation, the slither, the blur of thought of the last two hours had been sucked away like mist sucked off autumn meadows by the sun, leaving the normal clarity of instant connections, of each detail of knowledge and experience available at the merest whisper of a wish. Except that in this shadowless illumination David could see for the first time that the state was not normal. It was what he was used to, yes; but for a member of the genus *Homo sapiens* it was abnormal. The sapience had been distorted into grotesque growth, like the udder of a dairy cow.

"O.K., I'm functioning now," he said. "But was I functioning when you got back to camp, Bandies?"

"Don't remember," they said. "Busybusybusy."

"Are we sure it matters?" said Hippo. "We've only lost a Cat, and look, we've got another one."

David saw their heads turn, but himself, caught in the rapture of returned illumination, barely glanced at the newcomer crouching at the fringe of the circle of fire-light. A large Cat, almost twice the size of the old one, sidled towards Doc's bucket, trailing one hind leg. It had a fresh wound in its shoulder. As Doc's glimmering pseudopod rose and attached itself to the wound, David placed these new facts in their exact locations on the harsh-lit landscape of his knowledge.

"Yes, it matters," he said. "Skunk was right. It matters immensely to all of us. Look at me. Did I kill Cat?"

He willed their attentions away from the wounded Cat and onto him.

"All right," he said. "You be the jury. You decide. You aren't my peers, any of you, because we're all so different, but we've got one thing in common which is more important than any difference. Now listen. Think. There isn't much time. What's happened since sunset? Up to then we were all functioning normally. The survey parties were out. The reports were coming in, everything as usual. Then, just as it began to get dark, Bird found a wreck, and her Bandy didn't report it. Instead, all three Bandies told their parties to come home. About the same time, I got an urge to visit the rocks, where I found Cat's body. I got back and found Hippo scratching herself on a support strut and saying that she was pregnant. If that was true, it meant that she had delayed implantation for an incredible length of time. Next, Doc started eating Cat, instead of trying to restore him to life; he also complained about his hypochondria. Hippo was shocked, though she normally manages not to worry about the carnivores in the crew. As soon as Mole got back, he started saying he wanted to go home, and Bird and Doc said the same, and the Bandicoots went into their mating behaviour, which they've never done before when we've been landed, though it's only natural that they should—the presence of a four is immensely stimulating to Bandies—and Bird swore in front of the Whizzers and the Whizzers complained, and I realized I'd stopped functioning. . . . How are you feeling, Hippo?"

"How kind of you to ask," said Hippo, incapable of irony. "Yes, I'm afraid I may have been a wee bit careless and let myself get . . . you know what. I think I'll probably pop later tonight, but if you all get aboard and close the ports and I go downwind, you'll be quite safe. My poor darlings will just have to take their chance."

"Remember what she was saying twenty minutes ago?" said David.

"The Lord has changed her heart," said a Whizzer.

"Infinite is His mercy," said the other one.

"Do you still want to go home, Bird?" said David.

"Come off it. I notice you don't ask old Mole. Just

because I'm female you pick on me for a moment of nostalgia, as if I was a brainless ninny all the time."

"But you're back to normal now? You, too, Mole? And the Bandies? And me. But it isn't normal. We're all behaving in ways which are unnatural for our species. We're suppressing some parts of our behaviour and exaggerating other parts. It isn't normal for me to act like a fault-free computer. My brain has computerlike abilities, but in order to function as a crew member I've had to adapt them. It isn't normal for Bandies not to mate whenever four of them meet, but they've suppressed that side of their behaviour. It's the same with all of us. Now think of the order of events. Cat dies. We stop being a crew and become individuals. A new Cat turns up, and we start being something like a crew again; only this new Cat is badly wounded and not paying proper attention, which is why we have still got a little time left."

David glanced towards the bucket. The water level, which had at first perceptibly sunk, was steady now. As soon as it started to rise, it would mean that Doc was beginning to withdraw his substance from the Cat's body.

"Listen," he said. "Do you remember that load of jade we hijacked round Altair? We could all have retired on that, but we didn't. Instead, we got rid of it at the first opportunity, for a ludicrous price. Why? Because it would have broken us up as a crew, and we've got to stay as a crew, not for our own sake but for Cat's. The Cat is a parasitic species. I don't know anything about natural Cat behaviour—which is interesting, considering that I've got all your details stored away—but my bet is that on their own planet Cats are parasitic on lower animals. When the first explorers reached their planet they simply adapted them into the system, and now the function of a space crew is to provide a safe environment for a Cat."

"It wasn't safe for our Cat," said Mole.

"It was almost safe. Between us we could control any normal dangers, except one. You missed a point in your analysis, you know. Doc said that if you're going to kill a Cat you have to know exactly where to hit. The only crew members who might have known were Doc and myself. Doc couldn't have got to the rocks, and I've already told you I don't know much about Cats, because our Cat never allowed me to. But there's one other creature who would have known, one creature whom neither Skunk nor the Bandies would have detected when they were feeling for traces of higher life on this planet. That's another Cat. A Cat which survived the space wreck. A Cat large enough to ambush and kill our Cat despite a broken leg. Our Cat must have fought and wounded it in the shoulder; our Cat must also somehow have mentally sent for me as the fight began, which was why I went out to the rocks, but I was too late. . . ."

David glanced at the bucket again. The water level had risen halfway to its normal level and the strange Cat was stirring.

"We've got to be quick," he said. "There's no time left. In a moment this new Cat will take us over. But we don't have to give in. Cats don't have total control. This one had to hang around and wait for the Bandies to finish their mating pattern, because that was an urge too powerful to be interrupted once it had begun. I don't think Cats are very intelligent—they don't have to be, because we do their thinking for them. But now we are aware what they do to us, I believe that we've got the will power and intelligence to resist the control, long enough to get clear. We can go home, find out if any of our claims are valid, and if they are we can retire. Surely we can cooperate that long, without being forced to by a Cat. You've got to make up your minds. Now, at once. That is part of the analysis. What's your verdict?"

The new Cat quivered, shook itself and stood up by the bucket. Fresh scar tissue showed on its shoulder—so Doc had done a rush job. The Cat took a pace towards the fire. If only it had had a sense of smell,

Skunk could have controlled it. But it hadn't. That, too, was part of the analysis.

"Quick. What's your verdict?" hissed David.

He felt the pressure of their attentions focused on him.

"Guilty," groaned Skunk. "Man. Guilty. Of. Mutiny."

David was only for an instant conscious of the blast of odour that laid him out.

He woke sometime after midnight. The embers were dim, but gave just enough light for him to see that the ship's port was closed. Hippo was crashing around in the remains of the ruined grove. David rose, intending to go and say goodbye, but his legs walked him away from her—just as, a few hours back, they had walked him for no good reason towards the rocks. He was ceasing to function, but his normal intelligence was sound enough to tell him that he could never rejoin the crew, any crew, because his knowledge of the behaviour of Cats would henceforth be part of his memory and thus part of his function. He would not be able to perform his tasks without being aware of why he was doing so.

As the harsh clarity of thought faded into softer textures, full of vaguenesses and shadows, David became conscious of the planet around him, of the sweetness of its air, of the rustle of primitive leathery leaves, of the ticking insect life that might one day evolve towards a creature like Bird. He had known all these things, of course, soon after the ship had landed, but known them merely as facts—the chemical composition of the air, the level of evolution of plant and insect—and not as sensations, accepted and relished through channels other than those of the intellect.

Behind him the sound of splintering timber ceased. From vast lungs came a strange whinnying noise, dying into a long sigh. David realized he had been walking downwind from Hippo. His legs continued to do so. Breeze at, say, six kph—at any rate, a little faster than he had been walking. He had about a kilometer start, so the seed cloud should reach him in . . . His mind refused to tackle even that simple sum, because it kept slithering off into irrelevancies, such as the sudden thought that Cats had five senses after all; and that they were more intelligent than he had guessed; and, to judge by their revenges, more catlike.

Waiting for
Mr. McGregor

JULIAN SYMONS

PRELUDE

Even in these egalitarian English days nannies are still
to be seen in Kensington Gardens, pushing ahead of
them the four-wheeled vehicles that house the children
of the rich. On a windy day in April a dozen perambu-
lators were moving slowly in the direction of the Round
Pond, most of them in pairs. The nannies all wore uni-
forms. Their charges were visible only as well-wrapped
bundles, some of them waving gloved fists into the air.

The parade was watched by more people than usual.
A blond young man sat on a bench reading a newspaper. A pretty girl at the other end of the bench looked
idly into vacancy. A rough-looking character pushed a
broom along a path in a desultory way. The next bench
held a man in black jacket, striped trousers and bowler
hat reading the *Financial Times,* a man of nondescript
appearance with his mouth slightly open and a tramp-
like figure who was feeding pigeons with crumbs from a
paper bag. Twenty yards away, another young man
leaned against a lamppost.

A pram with a crest on its side approached the bench
where the blond young man sat. The nanny wore a neat
cap and a blue-striped uniform. Her baby could be seen
moving about and a wail came from it, but its face was
hidden by the pram hood. The pram approached the
bench where the man in the black jacket sat.

The blond young man dropped his newspaper. The

group moved into action. The young man and the girl, the three people at the next bench, the man beside the lamppost and the man pushing the broom took from their pockets masks which they fitted over their faces. The masks were of animals. The blond young man was a rabbit, the girl a pig, the others a squirrel, a rat, another pig, a cat and a frog.

The masks were fitted in a moment, and the animal seven converged upon the pram with the crest on its side. Half a dozen people nearby stood and gaped, and so did other nannies. Were they all rehearsing a scene for a film, with cameras hidden in the bushes? In any case, English reticence forbade interference, and they merely watched or turned away their heads. The nanny beside the pram uttered a well-bred muted scream and fled. The child in the pram cried lustily.

The blond young man was the first beside the pram, with the girl just after him. He pushed down the hood, pulled back the covers, and recoiled at what he saw. The roaring baby in the pram was of the right age and looked of the right sex. There was just one thing wrong about the baby. It was coal black.

The young man looked at the baby disbelievingly for a moment, then shouted at the rest of them: "It's a plant. Get away, fast."

The words came distorted through the mask, but their sense was clear enough, and they followed accepted procedure, scattering in three directions and tearing off the masks as they went. Pickup cars were waiting for them at different spots in the Bayswater Road, and they reached them without misadventure except for the tramp, who found himself confronted by an elderly man brandishing an umbrella.

"I saw what you were doing, sir. You were frightening that poor—"

The tramp swung a loaded cosh against the side of his head. The elderly man collapsed.

The baby went on roaring. The nanny came back to him. When he saw her he stopped roaring and began to chuckle.

Somebody blew a police whistle, much too late. The cars all got away without trouble.

"What happened?" asked the driver of the car containing the blond young man and the pretty girl.

"It was a plant," he said angrily. "A bloody plant."

TRIAL AND VERDICT

Hilary Engels Mannering liked to say that his life had been ordered by his name. With a name like Hilary Mannering, how could one fail to be deeply aesthetic in nature? (How the syllables positively flowed off the tongue!) And Engels, the name insisted on by his mother because she had been reading Engels's account of conditions among the Manchester poor a day or two before his birth—if one was named Engels, wasn't one almost in duty bound to have revolutionary feelings? Others attributed the pattern of Hilary's adult life to his closeness to his mother and alienation from his father. Others said that an only child of such parents was bound to be odd. Others still talked about Charlie Ramsden.

Johnny Mannering, Hilary's father, was a cheerful extrovert, a wine merchant who played tennis well enough to get through the preliminary rounds at Wimbledon more than once, had a broken nose and a broken collarbone to show for his courage at rugby, and when rugby and tennis days were over became a scratch golfer. To say that Johnny was disappointed in his son would be an understatement. He tried to teach the boy how to hold a cricket bat, gave Hilary a tennis racquet for his tenth birthday and patted the ball over the net to him endlessly. Endlessly and uselessly. "What I can't stand is that he doesn't even try," Johnny said to his wife, Melissa. "When the ball hit him on the leg today—a tennis ball, mind you—he started snivelling. He's what you've made him, a snivelling little milksop."

Melissa took no notice of such remarks, and indeed hardly seemed to hear them. She had a kind of statuesque blank beauty which concealed a deep dissatisfaction with the comfortable life that moved between a manor house in Sussex and a large apartment in Kensington. She should have been—what should she have been? A rash romantic poet, a heroine of some lost revolution, an explorer in Africa, anything but what she was, the wife of a wealthy sporting English wine merchant. She gave to Hilary many moments of passionate affection to which he passionately responded, and days or even months of neglect.

In the nursery years which many psychologists think the most important of our lives, Hilary was cared for by bib-bosomed Anna, who washed and bathed him, wiped his bottom when he was dirty, and read to him endlessly the stories of Beatrix Potter. Peter Rabbit, Squirrel Nutkin and Samuel Whiskers, Pigling Bland and Jeremy Fisher, became figures more real to the small boy than his own parents. And brooding over all these nursery characters, rather as Hilary's father brooded with angry discontent over his unsatisfactory household, was the farmer Mr. McGregor, who had put Peter Rabbit's father into a pie, and whose great foot could be seen in one illustration about to come down on Peter. Anna read and Hilary shivered, finding in the figure of the farmer an image of his own frightening father.

Childhood does not last forever, but there are those who cling to childish things rather than putting them away. Hilary went up to Oxford—which to Johnny Mannering was still the only possible university—in the early sixties, just before the days of the Beatles and permissiveness. There he displayed the collected works of Beatrix Potter on his shelves beside books more fashionable for an undergraduate. "But, my dear, these are the existential masterpieces of the century," he said in his pleasant, although thin and slightly fluting, voice. "The passions, the deceits, the *poignancy* of it all; really, Proust and Joyce are nothing to it." Beatrix Potter gave him the only celebrity he achieved at Oxford. He joined two or three radical groups and left them within a few weeks, did a little acting but could not remember his lines, had three poems published in a small magazine.

He had just one friend, a broad-shouldered, blond, puzzled-looking rugger blue named Charlie Ramsden, who had been at Hilary's public school, and had always regarded him as a genius. This view was not changed when Hilary took as poor a degree as his own, something they both attributed to the malice of the examiners. Hilary, on his side, treated Charlie with the affectionate superiority one might give to a favourite dog. "You must meet Charlie," he would say to new acquaintances. "He's terribly good at *rugby football*." Charlie would smile ruefully, rub his nose and say, " 'Fraid I am." They were really, as the acquaintances remarked with astonishment, almost inseparable. Not long after he came down, Hilary suprised his friends, not to mention his parents, by marrying a girl he had met in his last year at Oxford. Joyce was the daughter of an old and enormously rich family, and the wedding got a good deal of attention from gossip writers. Charlie Ramsden was best man.

The marriage was six months old when Johnny Mannering, driving home with Melissa after a party, skidded on an icy road and went over the central barrier into the lane of oncoming traffic, where his car was hit head on by a lorry. Both Johnny and Melissa were killed immediately. At the age of twenty-five Hilary found himself the distinctly rich owner of the family business. Within another six months his marriage had ended. Hilary never told anybody what was in the note that Joyce left upon the drawing room mantelpiece of their house in Belgravia, beyond saying that she had done the boringly conventional thing as usual. There was no doubt, however, that she had gone away with a man, and his identity did cause surprise. The man was Charlie Ramsden.

Hilary divorced Joyce, she married Charlie, and they settled in South Africa, where he became a farmer. Those closest to Hilary (but nobody was very close to him) said that he recovered from the loss of Joyce, but that he never forgave Charlie Ramsden. He never mentioned either of them again. In the years that followed, he gathered the biggest collection of Beatrix Potter manuscripts, first editions and association copies in the world, put up money for a radical magazine, with which he became bored after a couple of issues, and for two plays, both of which were flops. He travelled abroad a good deal, sometimes in the company of young actors who appeared in the plays. In Amsterdam, on one of these trips, he met Klaus Dongen.

Klaus was half Dutch, half German, a revolutionary terrorist who believed that destruction of all existing national states must precede the advent of a free society. His group, the NLG or Netherlands Liberation Group, claimed credit for half a dozen assassinations, including one of a prominent Dutch politician, for a bomb that blew up in a crowded restaurant, and another in a shopping precinct that killed twenty people and injured twice that number. Klaus was not interested in Hilary's ideas but in his money. Hilary was not interested in Klaus so much as in his NLG associates, who seemed to him as fascinatingly dangerous as panthers, perfect associates for somebody named Hilary Engels Mannering. It was through Klaus that Hilary got in touch with young men and women of similar beliefs in Britain. He did not take them on trust. Each of them was required to perform an illegal act—arson, theft, violent robbery—before acceptance into the BPB. What did BPB stand for? The Beatrix Potter Brigade.

It was of course Hilary who had chosen the ludicrous name, and he had gone further, giving members of the group names of characters in the stories and insisting that they should wear appropriate masks when carrying out group exploits. Among their achievements were a bomb planted in a cabinet minister's house (it exploded, but unfortunately everybody was out), a fire bomb that had burned down most of a large London hotel, and a wages theft from London Airport. Hilary himself stayed in the background, interviewing possible new recruits and setting them tests which some refused to undertake. He would then explain that he was a theatrical producer who had been testing their reactions (which was true enough in a way), and pay them off with a ten-pound note. The enterprise had the elements of theatricality and childishness that he loved, and for three years now it had completely absorbed him.

On the afternoon of the unsuccessful attempt in Kensington Gardens, the members of the group gathered in an extension of Mannering's wine cellars that ran below the Thames near London Bridge. They entered by a door in an alley, which led to a passage and a storeroom. In the storeroom a perfectly camouflaged door led to a single large, windowless room. There were wine racks along two walls, with dusty bottles in them. On the other walls were prints of Beatrix Potter characters—the cat Simpkin buying food for the tailor of Gloucester, Mrs. Tiggy-Winkle the hedgehog in her kitchen, Pigling Bland on the way to market, and of course Peter Rabbit, who was shown escaping from Farmer McGregor's attempt to catch him with a sieve. The ceiling was low and the lighting came from lamps invisibly sunk into it, so that the effect was one of mysterious gloom. There was only one visible door, which was said to lead directly to the Thames.

"It's romantic," Klaus Dongen had said when he saw it. "And ridiculous."

"And safe," Hilary had replied.

There were ten of them besides Hilary, and he waited until they all arrived, refusing to listen when both Peter Rabbit and Simpkin tried to tell him what had happened. Hilary was now in his late thirties, a tall, thin man with a sharp nose and a mouth perpetually turned down at the corners as though he had just tasted something bitter. He was older than the rest of them, and although his fluting voice had something absurd about it, he seemed in some indefinable way dangerous. His restlessness, his jerky movements, the sudden grimaces intended as laughs, all gave the impression that he was inhabited by some violent spirit which he was only just able to keep under control.

"Now that we are all here," he said at last, "I should

like a report on what happened. Peter, you were in charge of the operation."

The thick-set blond young man said, "It was a plant; they must have been onto it the whole time. It's a bloody miracle we all got away."

Hilary sighed gently. "That is hardly the way to present a report, Peter——"

"My name's not Peter. I'm sick of playing kids' games." There was a murmur of agreement. "If you'd set this up properly——"

"Is that the way it goes? You're blaming me, yet you are incapable even of presenting a report on what went wrong."

"How can you present a report on a disaster?" He stared down at the table as though he were a discontented schoolboy, and he looked remarkably like Charlie Ramsden.

Hilary pinched out the end of a Russian cigarette, used a long, narrow lighter and puffed blue smoke. "Since you are unable or unwilling to present a report, I must do so myself."

"You weren't there," said the tramp who had been feeding pigeons.

"Really, Squirrel Nutkin? Would you like me to describe the man you hit when you got away?" The tramp looked at him unbelievingly. "I was on the seventh floor of a building almost opposite, watching through binoculars."

"But not present," somebody said.

"Not present, as you say. The directing mind should be separate from the executive hand. But let us examine the affair from the beginning. It was suggested by a foreign colleague that we should take the son of the Duke of Milchester and hold him for ransom. The sum asked would be a quarter of a million pounds, which the Duke could comfortably have paid by selling a couple of pictures. Now let me tell you the object of this—to use a piece of deplorable American slang—snatch. Why do we want the money? It is to give financial backing for a project to be undertaken from overseas by a very, *very* famous person. Can you guess?"

"The Wolf." The pretty girl who had sat on the bench with the blond young man breathed the words reverently. And reverence was in order. The Wolf was the most famous terrorist in the world, a man who killed with impersonal detachment, and had never been known to refuse a job if the fee was big enough.

"Well done, Pigwig." Hilary smiled, but even his smile was acid. "But it is not wise to use that name. I shall call him Mr. McGregor, the ruler of all the little Flopsy Bunnies and squirrels and mice and pigs. And do you know Mr. McGregor's target, his projected target?"

"One of the newspaper owners," Squirrel Nutkin suggested.

"A politician? The Chancellor, the Prime Minister?" That was Pigwig.

Hilary shook his head. "Look higher."

"You don't mean—"

"Oh, but I do. Mr. McGregor will be aiming at— what shall I call it—the highest in the land."

There was a gasp around the table. Again Hilary gave them his acid smile. Then the blond young man said, "But it all went wrong; we couldn't even get the kidnapping right. Why should the Wolf think we can set up an almost impossible job when we've fallen down on this one?"

"The Wolf—Mr. McGregor—sets up his own jobs, as you call them. We should be his paymaster, nothing more. But as you say, this exercise went wrong. We had not one but two dress rehearsals, and you knew exactly what the nanny looked like. So what happened?"

"The baby wasn't the Duke's. It was pitch black."

"That's right. I looked into the pram, I saw it." Pigwig nodded agreement.

"They knew what we were doing and substituted the baby. And you can see what that means." The thrust of his jaw, the jutting of his chin, were really very reminiscent of Charlie Ramsden.

Hilary rose, walked quickly and silently over to a cupboard above the wine racks and opened it to reveal glasses and, in a refrigerated section, several bottles of champagne. This was a ritual. When they assembled at the cellars there would always be champagne in the cupboard, and it was always Moët & Chandon of a good year. Pigwig, one of the group's newer members, had thought of saying that she would prefer whisky, but had decided against it.

The corks came out, the champagne was poured. Hilary raised his glass.

"I drink to Mr. McGregor. And to the success of his mission. When he comes."

"But he won't be coming now, will he? As you said, he only works for cash." That was the man in the black jacket and striped trousers, an unnoticeable sandy fellow with a toothbrush moustache.

"Very true, Simpkin. But in the meantime we have a problem. The conclusion from what happened is simple and unmistakable."

"Somebody grassed." It was the only other woman round the table who spoke. She was in her late twenties, had a knife scar on her cheek and a heavy, ruthless face. It had been a touch of irony on Hilary's part to name her after the genial hedgehog Mrs. Tiggy-Winkle.

"Again I deplore the use of slang, but it expresses a truth. Traitor, Judas, grass—it does not matter what name we use. The fact is that one of us must have told the authorities. Or told somebody else, who gave us away. Did any of you tell a friend, a lover, a wife, a husband?" Nobody spoke. "Just so. It is as I feared."

"There's one queer thing," Simpkin said. "If the counter-espionage boys were tipped off, why weren't they all over the place, why let us get away? Isn't it possible that it was a genuine change of plan, and we were just unlucky?"

"With a *black* baby, Simpkin? I should like to think that was true, but a black baby! Somebody was playing a joke on us."

"I know who it was," Peter Rabbit said. He pointed across the table at Simpkin. "You."

"And how does Peter Rabbit make that out?" There was an undercurrent of mockery in Hilary's voice, but he did not fail to notice that Simpkin was left sitting at one end of the table, the others drawing away as though he had an infectious disease. Simpkin himself seemed unaffected. He drained the glass in front of him, and refilled it from one of the bottles on the table.

"I'll tell you how I know," Peter Rabbit began in a low, furious voice. Hilary stopped him. His eyes were bright with pleasure.

"We must do this according to law. There was no trial in any Beatrix Potter story—"

"Sod the Beatrix Potter stories," said the man who had been leaning against the lamppost, a youth whose spottiness was partly hidden by his thick beard.

"Now then, Samuel Whiskers, no bad language *if* you please," Hilary said indulgently.

The young man who had been pushing a broom spoke. He was another recent recruit, a broad-shouldered figure with a round ruddy face and a snoutish, vertical-nostrilled nose which had led Hilary to christen him Pigling Bland. Like all of them except Peter Rabbit and Hilary himself, he spoke in the mid-Atlantic accent that denies the existence of English class distinctions.

"He's right. We don't want any playing about. If there's a grass, we've got to know who it is."

"Precisely, Pigling. But let us do it by considering evidence rather than simple accusation. Simpkin, you are the accused; you may remain where you are. Peter Rabbit, you will be prosecutor; you should go to the other side of the table. The rest of you will serve as the jury and should group yourselves at the end. Thank you. I will serve as judge, summing up the evidence, although the verdict will be yours. I think I should sit away from you. Over here, perhaps." He placed his chair beside the door. "If you wish, Simpkin, you may ask one of the jury to defend you."

"I'll defend myself," Simpkin said. Of all the people in the room, he seemed the least moved.

"Very well. Prosecuting counsel, begin."

The blond young man did not look at Hilary. "I should like to say that this is a stupid way—"

Hilary tapped on the arm of his chair with the lighter he was using for another cigarette. "Out of order. Produce your evidence."

"All right. Simpkin joined the group four months ago. Since then he's been concerned in three jobs. The first was leaving a bomb in an Underground train. He did that himself. At least he says so, but the bomb never went off. Did he ever leave it?"

Simpkin intervened. "Can I answer that?"

"Not now. You'll have your turn." Hilary's eyes had been closed, and now he shut them again. With eyes closed, Peter Rabbit's voice sounded exactly like Charlie Ramsden's.

"Two. Simpkin was one of the people who planned to get a comrade out of Brixton Prison. Almost at the last minute the comrade was moved to Parkhurst. Coincidence? Perhaps. Three. A couple of weeks ago, we should have had an open-and-shut job, getting documents out of a ministry file. They'd have been very useful to us. You, Jeremy Fisher"—he nodded at a man who had been driving one of the getaway cars—"I don't know your name, so I have to call you that—you set it up; you had a friend on the inside. Simpkin is supposed to know the ministry layout, which is why he was involved so closely. The job went through all right, but the papers weren't in the file.

"And four, the job today. You were the grass."

He stopped. Hilary opened his eyes. "Is that all?"

"No. But I'd like to hear what he has to say."

Simpkin's features were watchful; he really did look a little like the cat he was supposed to represent. "No need to say much. One, I left the bomb. The mechanism was faulty; it was reported in the press."

"Of course. You fixed a cover story."

Simpkin shrugged. "Number two was a coincidence, must have been. Number three, maybe the papers had been taken out months earlier. Anyway, why pick on me; why not Jeremy Fisher?"

"He wasn't in on the other jobs. You were."

"So were you." Simpkin permitted himself a brief cat-like smile. "And if you remember, I was against this snatch. I thought it was too risky."

"I'm an old member, not a new one. We've made mistakes before, but it's since you joined us that things have been going wrong persistently. And of course you'd be against the snatch; that was another bit of cover."

Hilary moved in his chair. "You said there was something more."

"Yes. Some of you know that I have—that I see people—"

"We know about your social position," Mrs. Tiggy-Winkle said in her harsh voice. "We know you meet the best people. I've seen your name in the papers."

"All right," Peter Rabbit said. "Through my position I've been able to get a good deal of information. You know that," he said to Hilary, who nodded and smiled his acid smile. "Last Wednesday I had dinner at Horton's, which is a small luncheon and dining club with a very restricted membership. Top people in the services and the ministries, a few members of the government and so on."

"Top people, period," Mrs. Tiggy-Winkle said. "Nice company you keep."

The young man ignored her. "Horton's has a couple of rooms where you can take people for dinner if you've got something extremely private to discuss. On this night—it was fairly late, very few people in the club— three people came out of one of these rooms. One was Giles Ravelin, who's an assistant head in MI6. He's a member of Horton's, and the two others must have been his guests. One was Sir Llewellyn Scott, who acts as a sort of link man between the police and the counterespionage agencies. And the third was Simpkin." He paused. "I want him to explain how he came to be there. If he can."

It was for such moments as these that Hilary lived, moments of excitement outside the routine of life. Revolutionary intrigue he had found for the most part boring, a matter of dull little men discussing how to obtain power over other dull little men. But the possible visit of the Wolf, the fun of calling him Mr. McGregor, the tension in this long, low windowless room with its hidden light that made every face look ghostly pale—oh, these were the moments that made life worth living, whatever their outcome. How would Simpkin react to Charlie Ramsden—no, to Peter Rabbit? What would he say?

The silence was total. All of them were staring at Simpkin, waiting for Simpkin. At last he gave a faint, catlike cough. "What was the light like?"

"The *light?*" Then he realized the question's purpose. "A good deal better than it is here. Good enough to recognize you."

"How near were you to this man?"

"I was four feet away or less, sitting in an alcove. You didn't see me, or I don't think so, because I was partly hidden. But I had a good view of you."

"You saw the man for how long? Two seconds?"

"Long enough. It was you. I'll ask you again. What were you doing there; who do you work for?"

From the rest of them, those appointed as a jury, there came a murmur, an angry dangerous sound. "Answer him," Samuel Whiskers said. "If you don't, we'll know what to think."

"I can't answer," Simpkin said flatly. "I wasn't there." There was a moment's pause while they digested this. "I was never inside that place in my life, never heard of it. I gave him a chance to say he was mistaken, but he didn't take it. He's lying."

The two men looked at each other across the table. "You bloody Judas, you won't get out of it like that," Peter Rabbit said.

Hilary steepled his fingers and offered a judge's comment. "It comes to this, then: that we have an accusation but no proof."

"You said it was last Wednesday. What time did this meeting take place?" the pretty girl known as Pigwig asked.

"Between ten and ten-thirty at night."

"You're sure it was Wednesday, certain that was the day?"

As Peter Rabbit said he was sure, Simpkin seemed suddenly to wake from a brown study and showed his first sign of emotion, almost shouting at her to keep out of this, it wasn't her affair. She disregarded him.

"Last Wednesday, Bill—"

"You are not to use personal names," Hilary cried. "Pseudonyms *must* be preserved."

"What stupid game are you playing; who do you think you're kidding?" she screamed at him. "Half of us know who the others are and what they do, and those who don't could easily find out. At ten o'clock last Wednesday Bill wasn't at any Horton's Club or whatever it's called. He was in bed with me, had been all evening. Around eight I got up and made scrambled eggs, then we went back to bed."

"Is that true?" Hilary asked Simpkin, who shrugged and then nodded. "Two different stories. They can't both be right."

The round-faced young man called Pigling Bland said, "No, they can't. And I know who's telling the truth. A couple of days ago, I saw him—Peter Rabbit—walking along Piccadilly. He was with somebody who looked familiar, though I couldn't place him. But I knew who it was as soon as I heard his name today, because I've seen his picture in the papers often enough. It was this Scott, Llewellyn Scott."

"You're sure?"

"I can't prove it, can I? But yes, I'm sure."

"Does anybody else wish to speak? Very well. You have heard the evidence, and I don't think there's any need for a judicial summing up. Members of the jury, will those of you who find Simpkin guilty put up your hands." No hand was raised. "Simpkin, you are acquitted."

"That's not the end of it," Mrs. Tiggy-Winkle said. "He's the grass." She pointed at Peter Rabbit, who seemed suddenly as isolated as Simpkin had been.

"He was lying. He must be the grass—stands to reason." That was Samuel Whiskers.

"Do you wish to pass a verdict on Peter Rabbit?"

"I certainly do. Guilty." Mrs. Tiggy-Winkle's face was grim. The scar on it pulsed red.

"How many of you agree with her? Put up your hands." They all went up except Simpkin's. "Simpkin?"

"I just think he made a mistake. No need to suppose anything else."

"Then who do you think grassed on us?" Samuel Whiskers shouted. Simpkin gave one of his characteristic shrugs.

"Peter Rabbit, you have been found guilty without a single dissentient vote. Have you anything to say?"

The blond young man passed a hand through his hair in a gesture intolerably reminiscent of Charlie Ramsden, and cried out in bewilderment. "I don't know what's happening. This is all crazy, Hilary. You know me. You know it is."

"No names, Peter. You know the rules," Hilary said gently. He got up from his chair, walked over to the young man, held out his pack of Russian cigarettes. "Let's talk about it."

"I'll smoke my own." Peter Rabbit shook one from a pack, put it in his mouth.

"Here's a light." Flame shot up from the long, narrow lighter, and smoke came from the cigarette. Peter Rabbit looked at Hilary in total astonishment. He put a hand to his neck. The cigarette fell out of his mouth. He dropped to the floor.

Simpkin stood up. Somebody gave a cry, sharply cut off. Hilary giggled and held up the lighter.

"I got it from one of the NLG boys. An ordinary lighter; you've seen me using it. But if you press a button at the bottom a dart comes out." He pressed it and a tiny thing, hardly thicker than a needle, buried itself in Peter Rabbit's body in the wall poster. "Very effective."

"Nobody said kill him," Samuel Whiskers said.

"The verdict was yours. There was only one possible sentence."

"But he'd been in the group as long as me, as long as any of us."

"There are no medals for long service." Hilary gave his acid smile. "This door leads to a chute that will deposit Peter Rabbit in the Thames. If one of you will give me a hand, we can dispose of our grass. Then I suggest that we sit down and consider some new plans for raising the necessary cash to bring Mr. McGregor over here."

Simpkin helped him out with the body. They stood together while it slid down the chute and vanished. When they returned an obituary on Peter Rabbit was pronounced by Mrs. Tiggy-Winkle.

"Good riddance to bad rubbish," she said.

EPILOGUE

Just after three o'clock on the following afternoon, Simpkin, whose name was Bill Gray, entered an office block in Shaftesbury Avenue, took the lift up to the third floor and went through a frosted-glass door lettered *Inter-European Holidays, Travel Consultants*. He nodded to the girl in reception and walked down a corridor to a room at the end. There, in a small office with three telephones in it, including one with a direct line to Giles Ravelin, he found Jean Conybeare and Derek Johnson—alias Pigwig and Pigling Bland—waiting for him.

"My God, what a shambles," Derek said.

"Macabre." Jean shivered. "He enjoyed it, that Hilary Mannering. He's a real creep."

"It was a bad scene," Derek went on. "If it hadn't been for Jean here, I don't know what might have hap-

pened. 'He was in bed with me, had been all evening,' "
he said falsetto. "Wonderful."

"You provided the clincher, Derek, with that story
about meeting him in the street."

Derek Johnson shook his head. "Poor bloody Peter
Rabbit—it was a clincher for him, all right. It was just
his bad luck, Bill, that he saw you coming out of that
room with Ravelin and Scott."

Bill Gray was at his desk looking through papers
about Operation Wolfhunt. Now he looked up. "No
need for tears. He was just an upper-class twit who got
himself mixed up with a gang of thugs."

"Mannering isn't a thug, he's a psychopath," Jean
said. "The *pleasure* he took in using that lighter! I hate
to be in the same room with him." She asked curiously,
"Did you know he'd seen you at Horton's?"

"I was afraid he might have done."

"So what would you have done if I'd not come up
with that story?"

"Shot it out. But that would have wrecked the operation."

"Mannering should be in a padded cell."

"No argument. But let me remind you that if we take
in his crackpot Beatrix Potter Group, we lose a chance
of catching the Wolf. That's the object of the operation,
remember? Now, we couldn't let them get away with
kidnapping a duke's son, though I was able to make
sure everybody got clear. They still have to raise funds
to get the Wolf over here, and we've got to help."

They waited. Bill Gray's catlike features were intent;
he might have been about to pounce. "I think this is
going to come best from you, Derek. You've got a
friend who's a watchman in a bank in Cheapside. He'll
provide duplicate keys. There's wads of money in the
vaults; we knock out the watchman and pay him off,
collect the cash. The money will be slush, but they
won't need to use much of it until they pay out the
Wolf, and I'll put the word around so that in the meantime anything they use will be honoured. We'll talk
about the details, Derek, after I've set it up. Then you

can go to Mannering and talk about it. The Wolf's said to be in the Argentine at the moment, but he's in touch with an NLG man there and we have some contacts with him. When he knows that his fee's going to be paid, he'll come over."

"And until then?"

A smile touched Bill Gray's face and was gone like winter sunshine. "Until then we're waiting for Mr. McGregor."